aniel Shand was born in Kirkcaldy in 1989 and
:rently lives in Edinburgh, where he is a PhD candi-
:e at the University of Edinburgh and a Scottish
:rature tutor. His shorter work has been published
ᵐ a number of magazines and he has performed at
e Edinburgh International Book Festival. He won
e University of Edinburgh Sloan Prize for fiction
ɪd the University of Dundee Creative Writing Award.

ʳww.daniel-shand.com
ᵓdanshand

FALLOW

Daniel Shand

SANDSTONEPRESS
HIGHLAND | SCOTLAND

First published in Great Britain
Sandstone Press Ltd
Dochcarty Road
Dingwall
Ross-shire
IV15 9UG
Scotland

www.sandstonepress.com

Editor: Moira Forsyth

The publisher acknowledges support from Creative Scotland
towards publication of this volume.

ISBN: 978-1-910985-34-2
ISBNe: 978-1-910985-35-9

Jacket design by Jason Anscombe of Raw Shock
Typeset by Iolaire Typesetting Newtonmore
Printed and bound by CPI Group (UK) Ltd, Croydon, CR0 4YY.

For Ivy

1

Something had been in the night and rubbish was strewn all across the grass. I hadn't heard anything myself but there were crisp packets and beer cans and polystyrene trays scattered around the tent, our carrier bags torn open. We'd spotted some deer up in the hills a few days earlier but it could just as easily have been a fox or a badger or one of the other beasts that roamed around out there. I scanned the ground for human footprints and felt my blood go down when there were none to be found.

I pulled my head back inside the tent and wriggled into my jeans.

I must have disturbed Mikey. He mumbled something.

'What's that?' I asked.

He unzipped the door to the sleeping area and stuck his head out, a mess of greasy hair and beard.

'What's going on?' he asked.

'Nothing's going on. I'm just getting up.'

'You don't mind if I go back to bed?'

I told him to knock himself out and I crawled outside. The morning air nipped at my bare torso and I slid on dew as I skipped around, picking up the rubbish and stuffing it into a fresh bag. Once I'd tidied up I got the gas stove out from the tent and made myself some coffee. I sat on the groundsheet and rolled a fag while the coffee pot boiled.

A bird of prey swooped out from behind one of the mountains that flanked the meadow, flying in wide arcs, in perfect curves. I hoped it would spot some fluffy wee rodent down in the grass, maybe even whatever it was that ripped apart our rubbish bag. I wanted to see it dive towards the earth and snatch up its prey. It didn't though. I kept my eye trained on it until it went behind the mountain again, and then the coffee pot was whistling so I poured some coffee out into my tin mug and lit the fag.

I relished this quiet time in the morning, before Mikey woke. These were the only moments, apart from when I went to town for supplies, that I had for myself. I'd sit and have my coffee and my fag and listen to Mikey snoring and the mad gurgle of the burn down the hill. There was a road beyond the burn that cars rarely used and a house halfway between us and town. We'd selected the site for its remoteness.

Mikey yawned and began to move around inside the tent. Here we go, I thought. He squeezed past me carrying his boots. Same thing every morning. He'd hop around on the wet grass in his yellowing Y-fronts, trying to squeeze into his boots without untying them, before giving up and throwing them down beside the tent.

I watched his routine and sipped my coffee. It tasted horrible.

'Fuck it,' he said, chucking the boots away. He ran his fingers through his long hair and scratched at his beard. 'Morning then,' he said.

'How did you sleep?' I asked, knowing fine well that he slept like a log, because I was the one who had to listen to his snoring.

'Good,' he said, stretching and squatting. 'Well, not bad. Here, mind if I nick a cup?'

'Fine.'

2

He squeezed past me to get his mug out from the tent. He had no qualms about pressing his bare flesh against mine. Personal space was not part of his understanding. I poured him some coffee and he stood facing the mountains with his free hand on his hip. He drank a mouthful and I waited for his grimace.

'Paul,' he said. 'I don't really like coffee.'

'No,' I said. 'I know.'

'Do you mind if I...' he asked, miming pouring the cup away.

I shook my head. This was also part of his routine, trying my coffee and inevitably not enjoying it and being timid about throwing it out. That wasn't every day, like the boots. More like every other day.

After I'd finished the rest of the pot we collected our towels from the guy ropes and traipsed down to the burn for a wash.

'So,' said Mikey. 'What's the plan for today?'

'Same as always. I'll go into town for a bit of food and a paper once we've cleaned up.'

'Right,' he said, dropping his head.

'Don't sulk, Mikey.'

We faced away from each other once we'd taken off our boots and jeans and pants. It was difficult to wash in the burn, because of the cold and the shallowness. You had to scoop up handfuls of water to rinse your hair and squat down to let the water wash your arse and balls. I winced at the coldness that was also a kind of hotness.

Once we were dried off and back into our trousers we turned to face each other. 'Feels better,' I said.

'Yep.'

I spotted a car down on the road as we were walking back to the tent. It was one of those big four-wheel drives and it was parked in a passing place.

'Here,' I said, tapping Mikey's arm to make him stop. 'See that?'

He peered past me. 'It's a motor.'

I tried to make out who was inside, but it was too far off.

Mikey shook some of the wetness out his hair. 'Reckon they can see us?'

'I don't know,' I admitted. It was about half a mile down to the road, but there was a good chance they'd be able to make us out. Still, it would seem more suspicious if we stood there and watched it like that. 'Let's keep going,' I said.

Up at the tent I did my best to dry my hair before fetching a shirt from inside. All my clothes were getting foul and I knew Mikey's would be ten times worse than mine. At some point I'd have to make a special trip into town to use the laundrette.

'Right,' I told Mikey. 'I'm going to head down now. You going to be all right?'

'Aye,' he said. He was hunched in the tent's entrance, his head hidden beneath the towel. 'Like you said, same as always.'

'What do you say if someone comes?'

'That we're ramblers.'

'Good man.'

I walked down the hill towards the road and was relieved to see the car had moved on. It was only an hour or so into town, the road taking me past the wee house and then right down the valley. Again, this was time I tried to enjoy. There was the worry that some landowner or a group of hill walkers would chance upon Mikey and he'd panic and give them the wrong story, but I tried to ignore that.

What we called town was really just a village. There

4

was a Spar and a pub and a butcher shop and all the other things you'd expect from a place like that. I kept my head down as I walked, never wanting to become a familiar face to the people there.

The butcher was a rancid man. He looked up at me and gave me one of his red-lipped smirks as I entered. He was obese and ginger and had streaks of blood up his forearms.

'Hello,' I said.

He winked. 'Morning. What'll it be?'

'I'll just take four...'

He interrupted. 'Four sausages.'

'Aye,' I said. 'Four sausages.'

He winked again. 'Coming right up.' There was a big basin behind him that he washed his hands in. I could see through the door to the back room, where his acolyte was hacking at a hanging carcass.

'So,' said the butcher, turning to me and plucking a piece of cling-film from the dispenser. 'We've got Cumberland, we've got Lorne, we've got Lincolnshire, we've got ring.'

The back door creaked open and the boy emerged to gawk at me. His apron was soaked with blood.

I looked at all the sausages he'd named. 'Just norm...'

'Four normal sausages coming right up,' said the butcher, smirking.

He scooped my order up in his cling-filmed hand and put it into a plastic bag. I had my money ready, the change gripped in my hand inside the pocket of my jeans. I knew exactly how much four normal sausages cost. My grip was so tight that the coins hurt my bones.

The butcher paused as he was handing the sausages over the counter. 'Sorry,' he said. 'It's just... Andrew and I were wondering...'

'Yes?'

'Well. You come in here nearly every morning and ask for four normal sausages.'

I was starting to sweat under my collar. I gripped hold of my change. 'That's right.'

He leaned over the counter, smirking, glancing back at the boy he called Andrew. 'Only ever four sausages. For the past maybe two months.'

'Aye. That's true.'

He laughed. Andrew touched his bloodied apron. 'Well. I mean. Why only four?'

'I don't understand. I only need four.'

'What I mean is, what's to stop you coming in half as often and buying eight sausages or so on? Stock up?' He peered at me from under his orange eyebrows. 'They would keep.'

I swallowed. I looked at the obese butcher, I looked at Andrew's apron. 'My fridge is broken. I'm saving up for another one.'

The butcher's face fell. 'Oh.'

'Aye.'

'That does make sense I suppose.' He handed me the parcel of sausages and took the wet change from my hand and rung it up on the till. There was dried blood stuck to the cuticles of his fingers. 'Me and Andrew were curious is all. Cheerio then.'

'Right. Well. Cheerio.'

I kept walking until I was out of sight of the butcher shop, then I leaned again the wall of the Chinese and let my breath out. After a minute I ducked into the Spar to collect the rest of our supplies. Luckily they seemed to have a never-ending supply of teenage girls to employ; I never saw the same one twice.

I followed the road and then the burn out of town.

6

I passed the wee house and noticed the car parked in the driveway for the first time. It was only the bloody four-wheel drive from before! I thought about sneaking into the garden to try and have a look inside, but getting caught was too big a risk.

Mikey was messing about outside the tent. I could see him hopping around from all the way down at the base of the hill. He didn't notice me until I was right behind him. He was playing keepy-ups with a football.

'What're you doing?' I asked.

Mikey flinched and turned, missing the ball. 'Fuck Paul. You made me mess it up.'

'Where did you get that?'

He pointed to the thickets and undergrowth that marked the edge of the meadow, leading to the mountain's foot. 'It was in the bushes there.'

'Really?'

'Aye.'

'Did anyone come?'

He rolled the ball towards himself with his foot and kicked it into the air. 'Nope.'

I said, 'Good,' and put the bags down. I found our stove and the frying pan and set up the sausages to fry. 'When I was coming up, I went past the house further down the valley.'

'Oh aye?'

'Aye. The car from before was parked in the driveway. They must live there.'

'Right.'

'Doesn't that worry you?'

He caught the football on top of his boot and held it in the air. 'Why would it?' he grunted.

'Well, they seemed to be taking an awful interest, didn't they?'

7

'I suppose.'

'I hope we won't have to move on again,' I said, pushing the sausages around with a lolly stick. I kept forgetting to pick up some tongs or a spatula from town.

We'd been up in the valley for a month or two, as the butcher had said. Before that we'd camped out by a loch but fishermen started to show up when the season changed, forcing us to pack up and move on. Before the loch we'd been in fields behind the town where we lived, miles and miles from this little sanctuary under the mountain.

I dished out the sausages onto two cardboard plates. 'Leave the ball for now,' I told Mikey, handing him his.

He sat cross-legged on the grass, blowing on his sausages. 'Here, Paul,' he said. 'What's a sausage made out of anyway?'

'That'll be pig in that one, but you get all sorts.'

'Right. So it's like chops then. Pork chops.'

'Kind of. They put all the bits of the pig no one wants to eat in sausages.'

'Why're they so nice then?' He'd already wolfed down both of his and was huffing on the steaming morsels still in his mouth.

'I don't know. They just are.'

Mikey eyed my one remaining sausage. 'Are you going to finish yours?'

'We'll split it,' I said, cutting it in half with a plastic knife and giving Mikey the bigger half.

'Cheers Paul.'

I put the stove back in the tent once it was cool and threw away the plates. I dug the paper out from the Spar bag. 'I'm going to check this,' I told him. 'You wanting to look with me?'

He shook his head. 'Nah. It's too nasty. I'm going to stick at the football.'

I lay down in the tent's opening and leafed through the paper. I could hear Mikey kicking the ball from somewhere behind the pages. For the first few weeks after we'd left, Mikey had invariably been on the first page. He'd slowly descended through the paper over time and I was waiting for the day when he wasn't featured at all. Maybe then we could go back.

I was nearly at the sport section when I found him. 'Fuck,' I said. They'd printed a recent picture with the article. He had his long hair in this one, and his beard. For a long time it was the police mug shot they used, which wasn't so bad because the frog-eyed boy of thirteen didn't look much like the fully-grown Mikey. I didn't know if there'd been some court ruling that meant they could publish a new picture or perhaps they'd just stopped giving a shit.

I heard Mikey moan from behind my paper.

'Gone in the burn?' I called.

'Aye,' he said.

'Listen mate,' I said, laying the paper down on my chest. 'We're going to have to do it. They've got a new photo here. Your hair's all long in it.'

He put his hands on his head. 'We can't, Paul. It's the perfect length.'

'We'll have to, mate.'

His eyes started to redden. 'Maybe we could just wait and see what happens...'

'Fucken wait and see?' I said. 'How long you wanting to be stuck out here?'

'It's just...'

'Never mind *it's just*. Get your T-shirt off. Now.'

I found the scissors in my bag of supplies from the

9

shop. I made Mikey sit on the grass and I kneeled behind him. I cut his hair right down and he cried the whole time. I turned him around, wiped the loose hairs from his face and cut his beard down too. I gave him the cheap pair of sunglasses I'd picked up from the rack in Spar.

'Give them a try,' I said.

He put the glasses on and had a look in the superfluous shaving mirror we carried around. His face crumpled. 'I look like fucken… fucken Lou Reed.'

'Don't sulk. It had to be done.'

Mikey fished his ball out from the burn and I went back to the paper. We killed the afternoon like that. He practised his keepy-ups and I read every single article and completed every single puzzle. Once I was finished we played the football together. We used the gas stove and the frying pan as goalposts and I played goal. As Mikey was making shots past me he looked the happiest I'd seen him in some time, despite the haircut.

'There's this butcher in town,' I told him as I caught a lob he'd tried to put past my head.

'Oh aye?'

'Aye. Asking questions.' I threw the ball back.

Mikey caught it on his stomach. 'What sort of questions?'

'Asking questions like, how come I go in there so often and that.'

Mikey didn't answer me, just tried to send the ball low across the ground. It collided with the stove.

'Doesn't that worry you?' I asked.

'He's probably just taking an interest.'

'I think he knows. Might recognise me. Maybe the family resemblance or something.'

'How could he know?'

10

'He handles meat for a living Mikey. He knows who's lying.'

We got bored of the football soon enough. I tried to lie on the grass and have a sleep, but Mikey was too restless. He rolled around on the ground, pushing his head into the earth with frustration. 'I'm so bored,' he said. 'Bored.'

'I know. I am too.'

'But you don't get it. I'm *really* fucken bored.'

'You think I'm not bored?'

He shook me to make me open my eyes.

'But Paul,' he said. 'I'm really bored. Could we maybe, like, I don't know, go into town tonight?'

'Go into town for what?'

'Perhaps, like, the pub or something...'

I closed my eyes again. 'Forget it,' I told him. 'It's not happening.'

Mikey had been obsessed with the idea ever since we'd arrived. The bus had stopped in the village's main square and he'd spied this lassie, standing outside the pub, smoking, her heel up on the wall.

'Maybe we should stop in there,' he'd said. 'Get some directions and that.'

I'd told him to forget it then as well.

I panicked when I woke up and Mikey was gone. I checked in the tent for him, reasoning he'd maybe nodded off himself. Nothing though. He wasn't down at the burn either. I found him on the far side of the hill, facing the road. The four-wheel drive was back, parked up in its passing place.

'Look,' he said when he heard me approach.

I put my hand on his shoulder. 'Stop fucken pointing at it,' I hissed. 'Wave.'

'Eh?'

11

I tightened my hold on his shoulder. 'Wave,' I repeated.

The pair of us waved down at the motor until it pulled off and down the road. I turned on my heel and marched back up to the tent. Mikey was in hot pursuit.

'What's wrong?' he asked as I began to sort out the stuff for dinner. We were having rolls with cold meat.

'You know fine well what's wrong. Standing there gawking at the car like that. It's like you *want* us to have to move on again.'

'What's that you've got? That ham, is it?'

'Aye Mikey. It's ham.'

He nodded. 'It's always ham.'

Our routine for the evenings was that we would have our rolls or whatever we were having for tea and then when the sun went down behind the mountain we would put our jumpers on. Mikey would get to work, winding up the torch and the radio and once the sky was completely black, then we would allow ourselves to crack open the lagers I'd bought in the morning.

'Ah,' said Mikey as he took his first swig.

The beer was warm of course but it helped pass the days to have something to look forward to in the evening. Some nights we played cards, other times we had a go on the travel Monopoly board Mikey had brought along. It was important that I didn't always beat him at Monopoly, as otherwise he'd become fractious and sour.

Mikey rolled the tiny dice and moved his Scottie dog. He landed on one of the reds. 'Your turn,' he told me.

'Don't you want to buy that? It's a good property.'

'Nah. I'm saving up for the big tickets. Park Lane. Mayfair. Those are where the real money is.'

I felt myself want to explain that he would have to get a bit of cash in his pocket if he was to have any chance

12

of building on either of those properties, but I stopped myself. I would just end up upsetting him. He proceeded to go around the board five times without landing on either of the spaces he was waiting for.

I looked down at my pile of property cards. 'Shall we just pack this in?'

'Aye,' he said. 'OK then.'

'You're pissed,' Mikey told me.

It was late and he was right. You could hear the murmurs of night beyond us – the burn curdling, grasshoppers and swallows fizzing.

'I am pissed.'

'No, but you're really pissed.'

'I said I was, didn't I?'

Mikey was walking around in the darkness in front of the tent, kicking his legs out and squatting from drunkenness. I suppose he never got the opportunity to build up his tolerance during his teenage years.

He giggled. 'Whatever you say Paul. I know when you're pissed, and you're pissed. Here, how many cans have we got left?'

I check the bag. 'One each,' I said and threw his last one out to him.

'Cheers big ears. Did I ever tell you what we used to drink inside? At Polmont?'

'No, you didn't, but I don't want to hear about it.'

He wasn't listening. He was balancing the can on the back of his hand and attempting to drink it like that. 'The older lads used to put orange juice from the canteen in a bag and hide it in the cupboard.'

I put my fingers on the tent's zip. 'If you're going to talk about that then I'm going to sleep.' I couldn't bear it when Mikey talked about being on the inside. When

13

he first came home and used to talk to Mum about it I would have to slip upstairs.

'All right. Sorry. We can talk about something else instead.'

'Like what?'

He ran his hand over his fresh scalp. 'What do you reckon's on telly right now?'

'I don't know. What time's it? Back of eleven. Maybe a film or something?'

'I think it'll be a documentary that's on.'

'OK.'

'Something about Africa.'

'Right.'

We finished our final two cans and undressed inside the tent. Mikey wore an ancient Metallica T-shirt to bed. It was frayed to smithereens under the armpits. I just wore my pants. We crawled into our sleeping bags and I switched off the torch.

'What's the plan for tomorrow?' Mikey yawned.

'Same as always, mate.'

'Mm. Maybe we could try walking up the mountain again.'

The last time we'd tried climbing the mountain we had only walked for half an hour before Mikey started to complain about his feet hurting. 'Maybe,' I said.

I was somewhere between dreaming and awake when I heard the footsteps outside the tent. Footsteps and ragged breathing. Mikey sat up and I put my hand over his mouth. Whoever was outside was messing around with the rubbish bag. They were opening it up and rustling its contents.

'Shut it,' I whispered, directly into Mikey's ear.

The shadow of whoever was outside fell over the sleeping area. It poked something into the gauze.

14

'Hoi,' they said. A man's voice.

I felt my brother lick his lips beneath my hand and I tightened my grip on his muzzle. He would want to answer back, I could tell.

'I know you're in there. There's a pair of boots out here. I saw the two of you earlier on. Hello?'

Mikey closed his eyes. I had him right up against my chest, smelling the heat of his scalp.

'Fine. Well. This is my land. You can't stay here, it's not allowed. If you don't clear off I'll call the police.' A long pause, and then, 'It's not allowed.'

The voice trailed off and I let go of Mikey. Once I was sure the man had gone I slumped back onto my sleeping bag.

'Jesus,' said Mikey.

'I know.'

'What're we going to do?'

What were we going to do? I couldn't risk the man poking around again. What if he spotted Mikey? 'We'll maybe have to move on. Find a new spot.'

'Really? But I like it here. We've got the burn and those sausages are dead nice.'

'Well,' I said. 'I'll think about it.'

'Maybe since we're clearing off and you cut my hair and that, we could pop into the pub for a swift pint before we go?'

I didn't bother to answer him, just wound my neck up in the sleeping bag and forced myself to sleep.

We woke up to a barrage of rain on the tent. I could tell Mikey was sitting up, awake, without having to open my eyes.

I said, 'Have you left your boots outside again?'

'Aye,' he sighed.

15

We got dressed in silence and peered out of the tent's opening. The sky was bruise coloured and water ran over our noses and into our beards. Mikey's boots were lying in a puddle of caramel water, curled and wrinkled.

'Have we got enough cash for another pair?' he asked, streams of water distorting his features.

'Don't know,' I said, bringing my head back inside to look for my own pair. 'Maybe.'

The ditch that ran alongside the road to town had become waterlogged. So had the handful of potholes I had to step round on my way down. I stopped outside the butcher's shop, on the other side of the road. Rain fell on the hood of my anorak and through the swirling water that cascaded down the shop's windowpane I could make him out, behind the counter. He to-ed-and-fro-ed, busying himself with joints and racks and sides. The odd flicker of redness through the smears of rain - that was blood.

The butcher paused and looked through his window, right at me. Neither of us moved. He looked out for ten, fifteen seconds and then was away again, chopping and slicing.

So that was how he was going to play it, was it?

'All right,' I said to myself and headed for the square.

There was a shoe shop there. No one was on the till but they were open so I let myself in and made my way to the small display of men's boots near the back. Mikey would want something cool, something motorbikey, but that was outside of our price range and the shop only seemed to stock hiking boots. I selected a pair that looked comfortable with good ankle support and took them over to the till, ringing the brass bell on the counter.

It took the owner a long time to arrive. She was a wizened old thing, the sleeves of her cardigan stuffed with a lifetime of handkerchiefs. She looked me up and down.

'What?' she croaked.

'I was looking to buy some shoes.'

'We're not open yet. Didn't you read the sign?'

I looked over my shoulder. There was no sign on the door. Before I could comment she went on. 'But never mind. Never mind common courtesy. Pass them here.'

She rang the boots up on the till and asked for the money. My stomach dropped when I checked my wallet and saw how much we had left. Mikey's boots would eat up the lion's share of the cash I'd taken from our mother.

As I went out into the rain, pulling up my hood, the old woman muttered after me, 'Some people.'

What were we doing to do? The cash we had would barely last us another week. I would need to find some sort of work, that much was clear. Maybe I could get some part-time hours in one of the village shops. Maybe I could join the roster of teenage girls that the Spar seemed to work their way through so quickly.

There was no chance I was going back to the butcher shop, so I ducked into the Spar again. It was quiet and I selected my produce in record time. I bumped into an old friend beside the meat chiller though. I was examining a pack of bacon, wondering whether we could fry it in our tiny pan, when a chubby, red-haired hand crept across my eye line.

The butcher was loading himself up with pack after pack of sausages. It took him a moment to notice me.

He said, 'Oh.'

I looked from his face to the basket of sausages. 'Hello,' I smiled.

He looked at the sausages too. 'Right,' he said.

'It's all right…' I started to say, but he interrupted me. 'Had a bit of an issue with the fridges across the road.

You'll know about that better than most,' he laughed.

'Never mind,' I said and watched him scurry away. He glanced back at the end of the aisle to give me a dirty look.

I paid for the supplies and was getting ready to face the rain again when I spotted the classified adverts by the door. Handwritten postcards for people selling golf clubs and pedigree puppies and used wedding dresses. I scanned the board until one of them caught my eye.

Strong young men wanted for tedious labour. Must be physically able and moderately conscientious. Minimum wage, no benefits. Contact Duncan Weddle on...

I slipped the card into my pocket, not wanting every other fucker in the village with working legs applying and spoiling my chances. The rain eased up as I was coming out of town and I began to sweat buckets inside the anorak. The car was gone from outside the wee house so I took my chances and jumped the fence into the garden. From what I could make out through the back windows it was a nice enough place. A dog whined from somewhere inside and the garden had a view of the mountains. They were a patchwork of peat and stone, smears of moss and long steps of dead rock.

I would let the owner make the next move. If he was so keen to move us on he would have to do it himself. He didn't know who he was getting himself mixed up with.

2

When I made it back to the tent I showed Mikey the card. He nodded as he read it and I asked him what he thought.

'It says minimum wage. That means not very much eh?'

'It'll be about six quid an hour or so.'

'What are they wanting us to do? Like move rocks around and that?'

I laid out the supplies and threw the bag with Mikey's boots to him. 'First, there's no "us". I'll be the one working. And second, I doubt they'll be wanting rocks moved about. It'll just be gardening or something I'd say.'

'OK,' he said as he tried on his boots. 'Here Paul. These are dead fucken comfy. Look at this.' He squelched around the meadow like a soldier.

I put the bacon on to fry. 'That's good, mate.'

As I'd expected, the bacon didn't fare too well in the tiny pan. There wasn't enough space for it to crisp up, but we had it on floury morning rolls and Mikey seemed happy enough.

After breakfast he was keen to try out his new boots, so we tidied the site and headed up the mountains for a stroll. We had to jump over the burn to reach the path that snaked up the valley, flanked on either side by heathery cliffs. There were dragonflies skirting around the burn as the path climbed.

'Holy fuck,' said Mikey when he spotted them. 'Look at them fuckers.'

'Amazing, eh?'

'Are they like wasps or something?'

I always forgot how much he'd missed out on. He'd had his thirteenth birthday on the outside and then every other one until his twenty-fourth on the inside. He probably got lessons in Polmont but how would he ever have found out what a dragonfly was?

'Naw man,' I told him. 'They're just their own thing. Dragonflies.'

He shook his head and said he couldn't believe it.

The path took us right around the mountain in a helix until we were at the top. It wasn't that high, the mountain. I'd read in a guidebook in the tourist information in town that it was about a thousand feet or so. We were able to look down at the valley floor and see the village and then our camp further up. I could just make out the home of the man who'd been hassling us, the one I'd spied on earlier that morning. My blood kicked in, but I didn't mention it to Mikey.

'Look at that view,' he said.

'Aye.'

'You can see everything from here.' He pointed to a larger town on the horizon. It was pale and indistinct from its distance. 'Is that Glasgow,' he asked, 'or Edinburgh?'

I told him it was neither, that we weren't particularly close to either one and that, besides, it was too small.

'Amazing,' he said.

'How're the boots?' I asked.

'Fine.'

We bumped into a group of hikers on the way down and Mikey behaved impeccably. We nodded to each other and the hikers said, 'Morning,' and I said, 'Nice day,' to them and Mikey didn't say a word. I was happy with him.

So happy in fact that when he remade his case for going to the pub that evening – he'd had his hair cut, he would wear the sunglasses, etc. – I said, 'We'll see.' I felt like I could trust him. The pub would be dark and we could find a table in the corner and I could take him out for the pint I should've been able to buy him on his eighteenth.

He clicked his fingers and swaggered down the path, his gait made clumsy by the bulky hiking boots. He was so pleased with the news that he nearly fell into the deer that was lying in the path.

It might even have been a fawn. Its fur was pale and its face immature, though that might have been down to the tongue lolling from its snout. A dry gash was open on its side and a black-beaked bird was pecking at the bones. Mikey shooed it away. We looked at the deer for a few moments. I wondered if it had been the one to disturb our rubbish bag.

'Was this the way we came up?' Mikey asked, toeing one of the hooves.

I looked around to try and place us, but I couldn't be sure. The deer looked long dead, unlikely to have been killed in the short time we spent at the summit.

'I don't think so,' I said. 'Maybe.'

'What should we do? Are you supposed to do something?'

'I don't know.'

'Maybe call, like, the park ranger?'

'I don't think there's such a thing.'

There was nothing else to do but step around the deer's body and continue down the mountain. The hikers seemed like proper people. Proper countryside people. They'd know what to do if they came back down and

21

ran into the deer. They would know the right thing to do. Mikey kept glancing back up the path as we walked, no longer excited about that evening's entertainment.

I thought about the bird I'd seen the other morning, the eagle or kestrel or whatever it was. The hikers would probably have been able to tell me. I thought about it coasting along the clouds and letting its wild animal brain lock onto the sniffing, wandering fawn. I thought about its wings billowing out as it plummeted and its golden talons sinking into the fawn's plump side. I licked my lips.

Mikey walked with his hands in his pockets and we didn't speak until we were back at the tent. He'd always been sensitive, even when he was wee. I remembered how we would use a shovel to snip worms in two on the slabs of our mother's driveway and afterwards he would try and push the two wriggling segments back together.

We stayed at the camp for the rest of the day. I warmed us up some soup for lunch and then later we had cold meat rolls for tea. Once or twice in the afternoon I dug the classified card out of my pocket and read it over. I thought about the job, whatever it was. See, it was one thing taking Mikey to the pub, where I could... not control him, but make sure things didn't get out of hand. If I was going to be gone all day working, could he be trusted to look after camp himself, say the right thing if anyone came calling?

He started to get hyper at about five or six, chewing his nails, standing up for no reason and then sitting down on the grass again. At seven he crawled into the tent and emerged a good half hour later wearing a white shirt.

'What's this?' I asked.

'What's what?'

'The shirt.'

'This?' he said, pulling out the sleeve. 'Just a shirt. Nothing special.'

This was the first of me hearing about Mikey's white shirt. He must've been saving it someplace for special occasions. It was as wrinkled as an elbow.

'So are we heading off then?' he asked, clapping his hands once.

I checked my watch. 'It's only half seven.'

'Aye?'

'Well it's a wee bit early yet.'

His face fell. 'So when will we get going?'

'How about we say we head down when it gets dark?'

He agreed to that without looking happy about it, slumping on the ground. I thought about warning him that he would get grass stains on his back, but it wasn't the time. Perhaps I'd be able to nip inside the tent for an hour or two of shuteye, when... the paper! I'd forgotten to check that day's paper! I scrambled into the tent and flicked through the pages.

Again, he was right near the back. It was the same photo as the day before. I skimmed the article. They were calling him the 'Buchanan Beast'. That name had been all over the papers and telly when it first happened, but you didn't see it around so much anymore. Buchanan being our surname. This was a bad sign.

'That the paper?' he asked from outside. 'What's it saying?'

I swallowed. 'Nothing. Just the usual.'

'Right.'

Finishing the article, I was glad they had no new information. No new neighbour interviews, pieces of fluff that cast aspersions on the two Buchanan boys. There'd always been something *off* about them, even when they was young.

I did my best to sleep but I couldn't get the photograph out my mind. It was Mikey, emerging from the front door of our mother's house. Our house too, I suppose. I didn't remember the exact day it was taken but it would've been one of the first they all showed up. We hadn't told him they were out there, he didn't know the papers had his address. He'd stumbled out the door, going to the shops or something, and all the flashbulbs went off at once. The photo showed his mouth open, his hand halfway to his face to shield himself from the light.

I lay back in the sleeping area with the paper on my chest and closed my eyes, imagining how it would be when all this was over. We'd be able to go back to our mother, be able to sleep in normal beds again. The only real issues I could see were the subject of money, and then the butcher and the man with the four-wheel drive. Those nosy fuckers might prove to be something of a stumbling block. Mind you, the Buchanan boys had overcome worse obstacles in their time.

When I woke it was dark and Mikey's big face was looming through the sleeping area door. He was rummaging around me, trying to find something.

'What's up?' I croaked.

'The torch.'

I sat up. 'It'll be in the front. Did you check my bag?'

'No,' he said, but his face didn't leave the gap.

'What?'

'Well, if I'm needing the torch then it must be dark, eh?'

I couldn't help but laugh. 'Fine. Let me try and find a top that's not absolutely reeking.'

'Nice one,' he said and tried to stand up inside the tent, catching his head in the fly guard.

I located the least crumpled T-shirt in my pile of clothes. It was pretty rank in the tent by then. Mikey liked to ball his clothes up and stuff them down the side of his sleeping bag and everything had a faint scent of mustard, which couldn't be healthy. I was always very neat though, as far back as I could remember.

At night the darkness came alive with the creaking and ticking of insects, with the fluttering and swishing of birds. As we walked down the road to town I could hear toads bubble in the burn. We passed by the wee house and the car was parked in the drive. I could feel Mikey get excited.

'That's it Paul,' he hissed. 'That's the motor.'

'I know it is. Just keep walking. Don't look inside.'

I observed him from the corner of my eye. He couldn't help himself; his head turned ninety degrees to gawk into the house's glowing windows.

'Fucksakes,' I said, grabbing his arm and marching him down the road.

'What's the matter? I wasn't looking.'

'You were so looking. I seen you.'

I waited until we were out of sight of the house before I let him go. He rubbed his arm where I'd held it.

'Ouch,' he said

'Never mind *ouch*.' I pulled him in close to me and I could see myself reflected in his sunglasses. 'When I say to do something or not to do something, you do it. Or not.'

'Right,' he said. 'Sorry.'

'Good.'

We kept going and didn't talk until we were in town. The village was nice at night, it turned out. They had old-fashioned streetlamps and the light reflected on the cobblestones like glass bottles. It was difficult to appreciate all that because my blood had kicked in when Mikey had looked into the house and I was struggling to get it down again. That happened a lot with me, especially in tight situations. My blood would kick in and I would see red.

'Here we are,' said Mikey when we reached the pub. He looked inside and saw the crowd through sepia chunks of glass. 'Paul,' he said, shaking my arm. 'There are girls.'

We went inside and I scanned the room. It was one of those narrow pubs with the bar along the long side and a room at the back with pool tables and fruit machines. There was a good table near the door. Easy to nip out if things got odd. I pointed to it and Mikey sat down.

'Aye?' the barman said to me as I approached. He had a clutch of long but sparse hairs on his top lip.

I looked at the taps. 'Two pints of Dirty Monk please.'

'Dirty Monk's off. There's Carling there. Or Tennent's.'

'Two pints of Tennent's then.'

I put the drinks down on the table and sat beside Mikey. From our position in the corner we could see the whole bar, except the pool room. The outsides of the glasses were wet from the coldness of the drinks. Mikey sipped his lager and slapped his hands together. 'This is nice, isn't it?'

'Aye. It is a bit.'

We both took a sip.

'Aah,' said Mikey as he sat back in his chair and folded his arms. He smiled at me, smug. 'I told you it would be fine. I told you it would, and now look at us. In the pub, having a great old laugh.'

I said, 'Mm,' and sipped my pint.

'I'm enjoying this chair. No sitting on the ground for me tonight. Oh no. It's funny the things you miss, like sitting in a proper chair, eh Paul?'

Just as my blood was going down, it kicked in again. We'd had a whole conversation about this back at the camp. I put my hands on the table and breathed. I'd told him. I'd fucken told him. He was Alan, I was Rob. If we went in there swinging our proper names around like cats we'd soon come unstuck.

'That's not my name,' I whispered.

Mikey laughed. 'What?'

'What you said. That's not my name.'

He spluttered into his pint, mid-sip. 'What're you on about?' he asked, wiping his mouth on the sleeve of his shirt. I told him my name was Rob and he just kept smiling. He kept smiling until I gave him one of my looks. Then he thought about it. Then he remembered.

'Aye, that's right. Rob. I'm Alan,' he said, extending his hand for a shake.

I batted him off. 'Put that away.'

As we were draining the dregs of the first round, the posse of girls Mikey had spotted earlier came past us from the toilets. You could smell their perfume cutting through the dull odour of beer and carpets. Mikey gave me the eye and I nodded. He sat up sharper in his chair and smoothed down what little beard he had left.

'So,' he said. 'What about this job then? You fancying it or not?'

'Christ, I forgot,' I said. 'Meant to use the phone box on the way down.' I stood up. 'See you in a bit *Alan*.'

The barman was busy pouring himself a measure of Famous Grouse when I approached. 'Excuse me?' I said.

He flipped around. 'What? I'm the barman,' he said, holding up the whisky. 'It's allowed.'

'No. I'm sure it is. Have you got a phone I could use?'

He pointed me through the side door. It led to the toilets, where the girls had come from. There was a pay phone on the wall between the ladies and the gents. I fed it some change and dialled the number on the classified card. I hadn't allowed either of us a mobile. The government or the police could use those to find out where you were.

It took a while for my call to be answered.

'Aye,' said the voice on the line. 'Duncan.'

'All right? I, eh… I saw your card in the Spar.'

'Oh, right,' said Duncan. 'Aye, I put one there didn't I? So you're interested? It's not much money.'

'That's OK. I don't need much.'

'You're fit and that, aye? Can work all day? Heavy work.'

'Should be fine.'

'That's great news pal. Are you local? I can give you a run up if you like.'

I told him that would be grand and gave him the address of the wee house near camp. It would be easier than having him pick me up by the tent.

Mikey was gone by the time I got back. I'd been anxious that he'd have tried to talk to the girls in my absence and given away some crucial information, but he wasn't with them. They were in their circle, unpestered. I asked the barman for another round and brought the drinks over to our table. I leaned back in my chair and traced my fingers on the cold wet curve of the glass. I shifted the glass around on its beermat, tilting it each way. He was probably just in the toilet, I reasoned. No need to panic.

Wait though, I thought. Wouldn't I have noticed him going in?

I would give him five minutes.

The barman was pouring a slow pint for an old boy up at the bar but the crackle of conversation in the pub stopped me from hearing what they were saying to each other. The barman looked up from the tap and caught my eye.

I gripped my pint tighter and looked into it. I took a drink. When I stole another glance the barman was off doing something else. I really, really hoped he wouldn't end up being a problem for us. There was already enough people in the village trying to get in our way. I cast my eye around the rest of the pub. They seemed like a friendly enough bunch, the locals. All a bit bumpkinish and wrinkled but not nosy, which was the main thing I valued. There was another old boy at the top end of the bar balancing a fiddle on his knee, threatening to begin playing at any moment.

Mikey's empty glass went past my eyes and I snapped out of it. He swapped it for the full one I'd bought him and took a hearty swig.

I glared at him. 'Where've you been?'

'Just playing on the fruit machines,' he said, nodding behind himself up the length of the bar.

'Oh,' I said. 'All right.'

'This pub's OK. Nice beer, nice atmosphere.' He lowered his voice. 'Nice girls.'

'I phoned up about the job. I got it.'

He sat down beside me again. 'Congratulations. What is it?'

I thought about the job and realised I still had no clue. Telling Mikey as much, I emphasised just how desperate we were for money. I thought about how we'd have to scrimp and save until the first bit of cash came through from the job, whatever it was. I thought it might be gardening like I'd said before, maybe even be a building site of some sort. Perhaps farming.

And then I thought, where the fuck's this monkey getting money for the fruit machines?

'Eh?' he said.

'You heard me. How've you got cash for putting in the puggies?'

'I don't have any cash. This nice man up at the pool tables gave me some.'

I had a horrible feeling about that. I went up along the bar to check in the pool room and, sure enough, there was the butcher and his assistant in their jeans and polo shirts.

The butcher gave me a little twirly wave when he spotted me. 'All right Robbo? Just been talking to your brother. Great laugh that boy.'

'All right,' I nodded, backing away from them.

The butcher smiled and leaned himself over to reach the cue ball.

I got Mikey up by his collar and we both downed our pints. 'Come on,' I whispered to him. 'We're going.'

'But we've only had the two,' he whined. 'I thought we'd have at least one or two more. And besides...' He rolled his eyes towards the girls in the corner.

The road outside was fully dark by the time we fell from the pub's front door, cobblestones glistening like a reptile's back. I swallowed great big breaths of air to calm myself down. I bent forwards with my hands on my knees.

Mikey put his hand on my back. 'There, there,' he said.

'What did I fucken tell you about that man?'

I felt his hand leave me. 'What man?'

Standing, I let my face be close to Mikey's, close enough to make him cower. 'The fucken butcher, Michael.'

He sniffed and touched the back of his ear. 'The guy playing pool and that?'

'Aye the guy playing pool, and that.'

'I didn't...'

30

Then the pub door swung open and the man himself came swaggering out. He looked us both up and down.

'Evening gents,' he said, producing a pack of fags from his chest pocket. He helped himself to one and offered the pack to Mikey and me. It felt wrong, but I accepted. He said, 'Nice evening,' and fondled his lighter until a squat flame popped from its top.

'Aye,' I said, accepting his light. 'Nice in there too. In the pub I mean.'

'Aye. It's a grand place, the Shackle.'

The butcher rocked on his heels. He put his fag between his wet lips. Mikey observed the movement of his hand. I took a draw of mine and rocked on my own heels. The butcher smiled again and made a sound halfway between a chuckle and a sigh, winking at Mikey then at me.

'Adam and Rob was it?' he asked.

I nodded. 'That's right.'

'My best customer. Best sausage customer anyway.'

I laughed at that, but the chuckle escaped as a choke.

The butcher scowled. 'You all right?'

'Yep. Not used to the real thing,' I told him, holding up the fag, 'I'm usually a roller.'

'Excuse me?'

'A roller, as in rollies.'

'Oh,' he said. 'Right.'

The three of us stood in a triangle. Mikey put his hand on his neck and grimaced. He looked at his new boots and then looked at me. I couldn't think of a single thing to say.

Mikey scrunched his face up in panic and then rounded on the butcher. He opened his mouth wide and I thought to myself, you little –

'I was wondering.' he announced. 'What's your best meat?'

31

The butcher inhaled and the smoke made him close one eye. 'The best meat?'

'Aye.' Mikey looked at me. 'Your best one. Of meats.'

'I think what he's trying to say is, like, what your personal recommendation would be,' I explained.

The butcher scowled.

'Being in the trade and all,' I continued.

'Oh,' he said, mulling it over. 'The best meat. Um. Pork, I'd say.'

I nodded. 'Pork.'

'Why's that?' asked Mikey, looking genuinely fascinated.

The butcher winked at him. 'Versatility.'

Throwing my fag onto the cobblestones, I put my hand on Mikey's shoulder. 'I reckon we'd need to be getting back.'

'Aye,' said the butcher. 'Right enough. I'll see you tomorrow I'd imagine.'

'Maybe,' I said and guided Mikey down the road. 'See you.'

'Cheerio,' winked the butcher.

'Jesus fucken Christ,' I hissed, under my breath. 'The best meat. The best fucken meat.'

Mikey twisted himself free of my hand and stormed ahead. 'Well. It's not as if you were saying anything. It was weird. It was awkward.'

'Awkward.'

'Aye,' he huffed.

We went through the village like that, with Mikey a few steps ahead of me. This was how it had been when we were kids. We would be up the woods or at the swing park and it would all be fun and games until we fell out or I lost my temper or I suggested Mikey do something a wee bit too unusual and he'd storm off home. I'd be left to follow and try and get ahead of him so that I could speak to our mother before him. It was always important to me that I got my side of the story across first. I usually did all right.

My blood went down a touch as we left the village. I reasoned that it would do me no good to have Mikey in a mood with me. He was less likely to follow orders if he was pissed off. Not that I wanted to control him or anything, just make sure he was safe.

'Here,' I said. 'Mikey. How about them lassies eh?'

Even from behind I could tell he was smiling.

I went on. 'I think I saw a few of them giving you the glad eye, pal.'

He spun round. 'Aye?'

'I think so. I think I saw them giving you the... y'know.'

'See,' he said, thrusting his hands into his jean pockets. 'I thought so too. It's difficult to tell sometimes though eh?'

'It can be,' I said. 'It can be.'

Instead of taking the road out of the village our feet guided us up into the fields. It was faster that way but the country had a tendency to be muddy. While we'd been out drinking the night had turned cold and a frozen mist had descended from the mountains and hung in the valleys like wool. If I cast my eyes down I could see the water from the air collect in my beard like shining blisters.

'Not long now,' I told Mikey as we descended what I thought was the penultimate hill. 'Should be the next one over.'

'Grand,' he said. 'All that beer's made me sleepy.'

So we went through the mist in that final valley and everything above us was obscured. We were underwater in fog.

'Here,' laughed Mikey. 'This is like that film. What's it called? About the bad fog.'

'The Mist?'

'Maybe. We used to watch that one all the time in Polmont.'

I said, 'That's enough.'

The ground brought us upwards and the mist broke and we could see the tent silhouetted by the moon's light. I opened my mouth to say something about how the walk hadn't been so bad, but then I shut it again. There was a figure by the tent. It was poking at the canvas with a cane. I heard it say, 'Final warning. It's not allowed.'

We stopped and looked at each other. Mikey mouthed the words 'four-wheel drive' and I nodded. My blood was kicking in fierce then as we crouched down and hid ourselves in the valley and watched the man worry the tent. He kept at it for a long time before calling us bleeding gyppos and marching down the hill towards his car. Mikey made to skulk back up to the tent but I held onto his neck and made him follow me downwards. We watched the man start his motor and go off down the road.

'Let's just leave it,' Mikey whispered. 'Let's go home.'

I said, 'No,' and we wandered up and onto the road. We jogged along to the wee house and by the time we got there the man had already parked. I pulled Mikey into a copse of trees across the road from the house and we hid.

I knelt down behind a thick bush and Mikey squatted further back, among the roots of a yew tree. From my position I could see the three windows that made up the wee house's front. It was a bungalow with a small atticy-looking level above.

'What're we doing, Paul?' moaned Mikey.

I saw the man's head come through from the back of the house and go past one of the windows. All of them were burning light. Someone must have a few bob in his pocket, I thought.

34

I turned to face Mikey. He was huddled into himself, his lanky elbows and knees jutting out. 'You don't get it, do you?'

'What don't I get?'

'That they're not going to let us be. They're not going to leave us alone.'

Mikey looked at me. His eyes were like a little boy's.

'If we want to get left alone,' I said, 'if we want to get back home with Mum any time soon, we need to take matters into our own hands.'

'Paul…'

'It's true Mikey. I'm being honest with you cause I'm treating you like a grown up cause you *are* a grown up. Aren't you?'

'Paul,' he pleaded.

I made my mouth thin and turned back to the house. 'I expected more of you than this mate, I really did.'

There had been a dog barking, hadn't there? It hadn't sounded especially fierce. More like an excited lab or maybe a terrier. Nothing to lose sleep over. There had been a dog on our street growing up. I still had the scar on my calf from where it bit me as I tried to climb out of its garden. It went missing, that dog, not long after.

'Right Mikey, are you ready to listen?'

He made a noise behind me. A wet noise.

'Good boy. I'm going to tell you exactly what you need to do. As long as you do exactly what your big brother tells you then nothing bad will happen.'

That same wet noise again. I turned to face him.

'All right?'

3

I waited in the trees for Mikey to get the job done. He was a fast worker. I counted as I watched the two heads' shadows move between the lower windows of the house and I didn't get far. I watched the heads move apart and then towards each other. It was hard to tell which was which but once they fell to the ground and only one returned a minute or so later I knew it must be Mikey.

He flashed the lights three times when it was all over and I crept across the road and around the back. I knocked on the door and Mikey answered.

'Well?' I asked.

He wouldn't meet my eye. 'Like you said.'

'It's self-preservation, Mikey. You'll thank me one day.'

I needn't have worried about the dog. It was locked up in a run outside. Mikey followed me into the garden to check it out. When the beast saw us approach it lowered itself onto the breezeblocks and cringed. The floor of the run was dotted in dried turds.

'We'll need to get this seen to as well,' I said.

Mikey put his fingers through the wire and the dog ran its heavy pink tongue all over them. 'Hello,' he said.

'No one else inside?'

He shook his head.

We left the dog where it was and went into the house

to assess the damage. My brother had done a grand job. You went in through the kitchen, came to a hall with a living room joined onto it. A Ramsay ladder led to the upper floor, which I assumed was a bedroom. The man was on the floor of the living room. He'd been watching a porno film, the dirty old bastard. I couldn't help but laugh. The girls were still moaning and slavering, and here he was. Lying on the floor.

We carried the man out through the back garden and over the fence into the waste of nature beyond. The land was wilder there than up in the meadow. You could sense the mountains in the distance but it was so dark you couldn't make them out.

I got Mikey to run back to the house to fetch a shovel, leaving me alone with the man. I propped him up against a hump of earth.

'You thought you could get the better of me?' I said. 'You won't be making that mistake again, will you?'

I was chuckling and moving around him. I felt as though I took up the whole of the night. My mouth was the entire black sky.

I knelt down so we were face to face. 'This is what happens. Are you pleased with yourself? Are you? You just couldn't just let a couple of lads camp in peace, could you, you posh fuck?' I might have shouted that last part because when I was finished my throat was scratched.

Mikey came back with a pair of spades little bigger than trowels. Even in the dark I could tell his eyes were pink. He handed me a trowel.

'What do you call this?'

'It's all he had.'

'You're joking? These country folk, they've got all the fucken tools going.'

'They're all I could see.'

37

It took us quite some time to create a suitable hole. The earth was soft enough, it was just a matter of volume. We got him settled in the end but we were filthy when we made it back to the house. I sat in the kitchen and rolled myself a fag while Mikey heaved the sack of dog food out into the back garden. It was a nice place. The kitchen was done out all old fashioned, with one of them big ovens that's always switched on. I lit my fag and had a nose in the fridge. He was well stocked. Plenty meat, plenty beers.

I went through to have a look in the living room, tipping my ash on the carpet as I went. The porno film was drawing to a conclusion and I pulled the telly out at the plug, all that nonsense being of no interest to me. I heard Mikey close the back door and he came into the living room to join me. We took an armchair each. There was a tumbler of whisky on the carpet by my armchair that I dropped my singed filter into.

I looked around and said, 'How about this?'

Mikey was playing with his bottom lip. He nodded when I spoke.

'Aw,' I laughed. 'Come on now! You can't be serious.'

He shrugged, staring into the cream carpet.

'This I cannot believe. Mikey Buchanan, suddenly developing a conscience.'

'What's that supposed to mean?'

He said it in such a way that it made my blood kick in. 'You know fine well what that's supposed to mean.'

That shut him up right enough.

'Listen,' I went on. 'All right, agreed. Maybe, perhaps, this is some good fortune we've come into through less than ideal circumstances. I'll give you that, Michael. But come on mate. We'd be mad to pass it up. That'd be looking a gift horse right square in its gifty gob.'

'I suppose.'

'He supposes does he? Well very good. This is an opportunity. This is an opportunity to keep our heads down in relative comfort. Keep our heads down until it's all over back home. Until those hacks fuck off back to Glasgow or wherever.'

'I suppose.'

'I don't think I need to remind you of the reason why those fucken hacks are there in the first place, do I? I don't need to remind you whose fault it is we're even out here?'

Mikey gave me a look then. A look like he was going to say something to me. And I was ready. I had pure energy in my wrists, in my neck. I was waiting for him to say his piece. I wanted him to say his piece more than anything else.

But he didn't. He nodded and agreed with me, which was for the best.

I said, 'There we go.'

There was a bathroom across the hall from the living room, right beneath the Ramsay ladder. I even agreed that Mikey could go for a wash first. That was the kind of guy I was. We found him a good soft towel in an airing cupboard and we managed to get the shower to work. I sat in my armchair and listened to the water pour and rolled myself another fag.

We switched rooms when Mikey was finished. I brought my own towel and squeezed myself into the tiny bathroom. I got myself naked and looked in the mirror over the sink. What a sight. My own hair and beard had grown out considerably, although not as much as Mikey, pre-trim. My skin had taken on the sun – with that and sleeping outdoors it had become tough and dark.

I used the man's toothbrush on my teeth. I used his

floss too. I used his floss until my teeth were stained red from the blood and a clump of bloodied worms of floss lay in the sink. I conjured up some thoughts then and closed my eyes. They were good. Sometimes the thoughts I could conjure up when my eyes were closed would frighten even me. I finished myself off into a wad of toilet roll and climbed into the shower.

Ropes of brown water scurried off me instantly. Despite washing every other day in the burn and, before that, the loch, it seemed if you were living outdoors there were places the dirt got to that you just couldn't reach. I washed myself until my skin tingled and then I got out.

Mikey was in his towel in his armchair.

'What's up?' I asked, dripping onto the hall carpet.

'There's no clothes,' he said. 'It's all up at the tent.'

'Here, that's true. Never mind though.'

I climbed the Ramsay ladder and emerged into the bedroom. There was a huge bed up there and another telly and all the usual wardrobes and drawers and whatever else these folks have in their bedrooms. I found a couple of pants and a couple of T-shirts to get us through the night.

Mikey turned his nose up at them of course. Didn't like to wear a dead man's clothes apparently.

'Suit yourself,' I said, stepping into the kitchen to change.

Once I'd sorted myself out I decided to concentrate on my stomach. I opened the man's fridge again and had a more thorough nose through the contents. On the top shelf I found a parcel of quality looking steaks.

'Aha,' I said, taking them out and closing the door.

I set up a skillet on the hob and let it get good and steaming. The bottle of Glenmorangie had been left out, so I helped myself to a tumbler. I threw the steaks into the pan once it was hot enough and let them scream. After flipping them a few times I took my own steak out of the pan and gave Mikey's a few minutes more. He could be quite squeamish about things like that.

'There you go,' I said, handing him his plate and nodding for him to grab a can of beer from under my armpit. I noted that he'd got dressed in the end.

We ate our steaks and watched telly and it was strange after having not seen it in so long.

'This is mad,' I said, pointing a chunk of steak at the screen with my fork.

'How'd you mean?'

'Well, it's like you only get a wee minute of actual telly before they put the adverts back on again. It's as much adverts as it is telly.'

He chewed a mouthful of meat. 'And all the faces. They all look so big and orange. It's quite scary actually.'

Mikey took our plates through and we finished our beers. By that time it was really getting on. I'd nearly forgotten I had work in the morning.

We resolved to share the bed that first night with the proviso that we'd pick up an air mattress or something similar as soon as possible. The bed was more than large enough anyway. We settled ourselves in and pulled the duvet up to our chins and I switched off the bedside lamp. It was our first night in a proper bed for months. I sighed with pleasure.

'Paul?' said Mikey.

'What?'

'I don't feel good. About before.'

My blood had gone down by then so I knew he wasn't being difficult. 'Why's that?'

41

'I don't know. The old man.'

'We've been through this pal. We didn't have any other options left. That old man didn't give us any other options.'

'I know. It's still weird though, eh?'

'I know.'

He fell asleep first but I was pleased that he didn't start to snore. He wriggled in his sleep and made little yelping noises. I hadn't heard him do that before, but then, he'd been away from home for so many years that there was a lot of things he did I didn't know about. He'd been gone close to ten years and was only home for half of one before we'd had to run. I was glad he was being reintroduced to the world through me. It meant I'd be able to guide him. Make sure he saw things as they really were.

I closed my eyes and smiled to myself in the darkness. The mattress was soft and the duvet was soft and you couldn't hear any of the filth of animals and insects from the world outside the tiny window.

I woke to a car horn. I leapt from the bed and bounded across the room. There was an old camper van parked out on the road. It honked its horn again.

'Fuck!'

I dressed in a rush, pulling on whatever of the man's I could lay my hands on. Mikey got himself up too and dressed.

'You got time for breakfast?' he asked as I flew down the Ramsay ladder.

'You can hear him honking can't you? That's not just me?'

I pulled my boots on at the door and waved to the man in the van, showing him two fingers, meaning two minutes.

Mikey stood in the doorway to see me off. 'Good luck,' he said.

'Cheers. Listen. If anyone comes just you ignore it, OK?'

'Sure.'

'I'll see you tonight.'

The man, Duncan, I assumed, rolled down the window as I approached. 'Morning sleepy head.'

'Really sorry mate.'

The back windows of the camper were plastered in stickers giving the names of various countries and tourist attractions around the world. Climbing inside I noted that the theme carried over into the van's interior. Duncan was crowded by artefacts of international travel – strings of beads hanging from the rear view mirror, a boomerang jammed into the tape deck, some sort of African tribal mask resting on the dashboard.

'All right?' he said. 'Paul?'

'Aye. Paul. All right.'

I'd been anxious that he'd be annoyed about my having slept in but he seemed remarkably chipper. He shook my hand and smiled at me with the shiniest teeth I'd ever seen.

'Morning,' he said. 'Well met Paul. You feeling good? You in a working frame of mind?'

'I suppose I am.'

'That's what we like to hear.'

He started the engine, which whined and bubbled, and I put on my seatbelt.

'Nice place that,' he said as we drove off. 'Who's your mate?'

'That's my brother.'

'Sure, sure. He's not interested in a bit of work, no?'

'I don't know if he'd be suited to it.'

43

'Shame. We can always use an extra pair of hands.'

I told Duncan I'd have a word and he nodded with great enthusiasm. He wore his hair long and it sprung grey from his temples, turning black at the ends. There was a shark's tooth fitted into a necklace on his chest.

'So,' I said. 'What's the work?'

'Ha ha,' he said. 'Nice one Paul.'

I laughed too, thinking he was about to go on but no explanation was forthcoming. 'But seriously,' I said. 'What is it?'

He looked away from the oncoming road to meet my eye. 'You're serious? It wasn't on the card? We didn't go over it on the phone?'

'No. I don't think so.'

He yelled with laughter at that. 'That's hilarious,' he said. 'You're a brave man, Paul. Right. Well. It's archaeology essentially.'

'Archaeology.'

'Aye, that's it. Although what your doing's about as close to archaeology as growing wheat's to being a baker in fucking Paris.'

'Right.'

'Sorry. That wasn't nice. I'll show you what I mean when we get up there.'

He drove us up through the valley and away from the house and the village. The road was bright and clear and free of traffic. I was waiting for Duncan to ask me about myself, about Mikey.

I pointed to the paraphernalia littered around the front of the van. 'What's all...'

'In my line of work,' Duncan said, 'you do a lot of travelling. Too much actually. It makes it hard to lay down the old roots, y'know?'

'Right.'

'See, you've got your brother there. The pair of you are close, aye? Christmases, weddings, all that jazz. This dig's the first time I've been back in mother Scotland for I don't know how many years.'

'Right.'

We went by a long loch that stretched itself out beside the road. There was a white pebble beach between the tide and the tarmac. The mountains were low and dark on the far shore.

'So what's the story with you and your brother. He lives with you?'

'That's right.'

'OK.'

'He's a bit...' I held out my hand and tilted it this way and that and Duncan nodded to show he knew what I meant.

'I knew a guy like that, Jabbar I think, Lebanese, who we got to dig ditches, similar job to yours, Paul. He was a bit...' he tilted his hand side to side. 'He wore a shirt on his bottom half instead of trousers.'

'As in legs through the...'

'That's it. Legs through the armholes.'

'Wow.'

'That's what I said.'

'Mikey's not like that. He's just a bit... a bit sensitive.'

'Aye, some people are like that. We'll get him toughened up if he decides he needs a bit of work.'

I thought about the prospect of bringing Mikey along in future. There was the concern of exposing him to so many new people and the risk of him blabbing his mouth off. On the other hand, perhaps it was less risky to have him by my side than leave him alone in the wee house where anyone could come calling. At least if he was here I could give him one of my looks if I felt he was going down a dangerous road, conversation-wise. And besides, we could really do with the extra cash.

'I'll maybe say to him,' I told Duncan.

'Grand.'

The road started to descend and I realised we'd come through the hills and were going into the next valley over. After maybe half an hour we turned from the main road onto a dirt track and a huge sign, planted in the ground, read 'The Home of Your New *Mason Dew* Development'.

'Mason Dew,' I said. 'That's your company?'

Duncan shook his head. 'Not exactly. Mason Dew's the people that want to build but the council says they have to get a company like ours to survey the land before it's allowed. Make sure there's nothing, eh, significant underneath before the building starts.'

We went along the dirt track until we came to a cluster of cabins at the edge of an overturned field, a crowd of people gathered way out on it. Duncan parked up the van and we wandered over to the cabins.

'Rise and shine,' he shouted, throwing open the door of the first cabin.

'No fucking way,' said a voice from inside.

'I've got some more workforce for you here,' Duncan said, grinning at me.

A woman came to the door, wrapped up in a sleeping bag. Her hair was curly anyway but a night spent sleeping in the cabin had made it a riot. She rubbed her nose.

'It can't be morning,' she told us.

'This is Paul,' said Duncan. 'Our newest digger.'

The woman held the sleeping bag across her breasts with her forearm and extended her other hand. 'Sam,' she said. Her voice was syrupy, maybe Australian or even South African, I couldn't tell.

I shook her hand and she huffed. 'Right. Pleased to

46

meet you. Give me a minute to get my head together, eh Dunc?'

Duncan shut her inside and walked away, laughing. 'Best not to mention her staying in there, especially if any of the lads from Mason Dew show up.'

'She's not meant to be there?'

'Absolutely not. Nah, that's well against protocol. She got chucked out by her man.'

'How come?'

'She's a wild one is our Sam,' was all he said.

We went over to one of the other cabins and Duncan ducked inside, telling me to wait. I walked over to the edge of the field. I was just able to make out the crowd of people standing in the haze at the edge of the flat land. They didn't look like they were working yet. After weeks and weeks of being up within the hills and mountains it felt odd to be able to look around and have the land be unbroken between the horizon and me.

Duncan was crashing about inside the cabin and wasn't making any sign of returning, so I leaned on the field's fence and rolled myself a fag. I lit up and Sam emerged from her cabin. She'd managed to wrangle her hair into a scarf and looked surprisingly fresh for a person living in a large box.

She eyed my fag as she approached. 'Wouldn't do me one of those, would you?'

I let her have mine and rolled another.

'I'm supposed to have quit,' she said. 'But the smell.'

'It's bad for you, I suppose.'

'Yeah.'

She asked me what Duncan was up to in the cabin and I shrugged. She shook her head. 'Daft fucker,' she said. 'Did he tell you what you'll be doing?'

'Nope.'

She turned to face the field and I followed her. 'All that,' she said, 'needs to get ditches dug into it. The whole thing.'

'All right.'

'That's your job. Then we come along and see if there's anything of interest.'

I nodded.

'Good fun eh?'

I pointed at the crowd in the field. 'Are they all diggers too?'

'A mixture. We've got diggers in, we've got a few others like me and Dunc, people from the firm. We're not due a visit from Mason Dew for a while. That's who you want to avoid.'

'The company?'

'Well, no. But there's the supervisor. Mr Raymond.'

I was about to ask what was so bad about Mr Raymond when Duncan fell out the cabin.

'Are we not putting things away in their homes any more, Sam?'

'Honestly, Duncan?'

'What?'

'Fuck yourself.'

Duncan roared with laughter and got me to help him carry the equipment he'd managed to dig out. We went through the kissing gate and the three of us crossed the field. There were long lines of string running right along the length of it, spaced about six feet apart. I could see that some of the strings already had ditches dug beneath them.

'How did we get on yesterday?' Duncan asked Sam.

'Oh, fine. Another couple of ditches laid. I was up in the far corner because Pawel thought he might have found something important.'

'Oh aye?'

'Yep. It was roots.'

'Roots.'

'Like, a bunch of roots and the clay or whatever was caked around it in such a way that I suppose we can forgive him for mistaking it for a head.'

'He thought he'd dug up a head? That's hilarious.'

I thought about the man in the garden. I thought about his head, under the ground, and laughed at Sam's story. Both of them gave me funny looks. Perhaps I'd laughed a tiny bit too loud.

'You all right?' Sam asked.

'Yes,' I said. 'Fine.'

We came up to the people in the field. They were a mixture of brutish youths and wiry men and women. I guessed the brutes were my fellow diggers. They eyed me with suspicion and the wiry archaeologists looked right through me.

'Having your breaks before you've even started?' Duncan asked the group.

'What time do you call this, Duncan?' asked one of the archaeologists in a heavy South American accent. 'Did you sleep in?'

Duncan showed the South American a vigorous set of Vs and led me over to the far end of the field, to the first unworked string line. He told me to work it all the way down and showed me how I could measure it with my spade. The ditch would be as wide as my spade and half as deep. He said he would come and get me for morning break and that if I found anything I should put it to one side. I watched him stroll back to the cabin and caught the eye of the man working the string line to my left.

'Pawel,' he shouted over.

'Paul.'

49

'You're local?'

'Yeah.'

'Wow.'

The earth was baked dry by the heat. It took a good couple of heaves with the trowel to break the dusty crust. I scooped up a spadeful of earth and threw it onto the area between the string lines. Underneath the surface the soil was wet and dark as chocolate cake. Looking down the string as it stretched away from me I started to wonder if this was good work I'd got myself into.

Of all the jobs I'd had, working in the garden centre had been the best. You were supposed to make yourself available to customers at all times but the outdoor shopping area was so big you could hide behind fountains and sheds if you saw an old bag coming, wanting you to help her carry her solid concrete sun dial out to the car. She wouldn't even give you a tip either. It was boring, aye, behind the fountain or the shed, but it was better than having to deal with the customers. I worked there for a year and a half until someone made a complaint and they had to let me go.

We worked right through until eleven or so. Duncan stood at the cabins and yelled over to us. We put down our trowels and walked down our lines of string. There was warm squash and a plastic bag full of cereal bars waiting for us. Pawel had brought his own plastic tub of some sort of rice dish. I wolfed down my cereal bar and jealously eyed Pawel's tub.

Sam and Duncan and the rest of the archaeologists went into the cabin for their break and I was left outside with the rest of the lads.

'Here,' I said to Pawel, pointing my thumb to the cabin. 'One of them was saying to me about Mr Raymond?'

Pawel's face darkened. 'He's a terrible man.'

I pressed him for more details but they weren't forthcoming.

There were a few more breaks through the day with cereal bars and squash. I made good progress on my ditch. By the time Duncan came over to offer me a lift back I was nearly halfway down.

'You're a natural,' he said.

He stopped off at the cabin on the way back to give me my wages. Just over forty-five quid. I put the notes into my pocket.

Duncan tapped himself on the nose. 'And not a word to Mr Raymond or the good old HMRC.'

I slumped down in the passenger seat of Duncan's van, exhausted. My hands and arms and front were covered in a dry coating of dust and dirt. We drove down the track, past the sign for *Mason Dew* and onto the main road.

'How was it then?' asked Duncan. 'Your first day?'

I nodded. 'Fine.'

'Grand. I said it would be boring, didn't I?'

'I suppose.'

He went along past the long loch with the bone-coloured beach. The road began to climb and I knew we weren't far off. He dropped me outside the wee house and I climbed out.

'Same time tomorrow?' he asked.

'Aye.'

'Remember and say to your brother?'

'Aye.'

I found Mikey playing with the dog in the back garden. He was lying on the grass and letting it run and bounce near his head. It was licking his face all over when I came around the house.

'That's disgusting, Mikey.'

He pushed the dog away and it gave me a dirty look. I gave it one back and turned to Mikey. 'Do we know what it's called yet?'

'It says Doris on its collar,' he said, clambering up. 'How was the job then? What was it?'

'Digging ditches for these archaeologists. They're all a bunch of poncey bastards, like. I'm knackered. Have you done any tea?'

'I didn't know when you'd be back.'

'So you just decided to lie on the floor and play with the dog.'

'Sorry.'

I went in through the back door and sat at the kitchen table to roll myself a fag. I helped myself to another tumbler of whisky. The kitchen was soon full of blueish fag smoke, curling around itself in the light from the open door. The dog lay down in front of Mikey and put her head in his lap. Above them the mountain range stood, solid and dead.

I squeezed myself into the bathroom and undressed. My reflection in the mirror was rough. I was skinny and pale on the areas untouched by sun, my hair was unkempt and beard thick and scratchy. I got the shower going good and warm and went under the water. It was so hot that it stung. I lined my cock up with the plughole and pissed into it directly. I used the man's Head and Shoulders on my hair and I used his shower gel on my face. My skin was roasting from a day in the sun. I was thinking about the can of beer I'd open once I was dry and then the doorbell went.

The sound of the water pummelling on the bath's ceramic.

My breath in the wet heat.

I fumbled with the shower curtain and nearly fell over the side. My blood was kicking in something awful.

Wrapped up in a towel, I stumbled into the hall. Mikey was already there, watching the front door. Drops fell from me, water ran down my face.

'Who the fuck's that?' I hissed at him.

He gave a shrug.

I was imagining him, alone in the house all day. Picking up the phone, making a call to the police. Saying, My name's Mikey Buchanan and here's where I am.

If someone really had come for us...

Well, I wouldn't let that happen. I wouldn't let them take Mikey away. I couldn't have him talking to anyone like that. I'd worked so hard the first time the police came for him, I didn't know if I could pull it off again.

I turned to face the door. There was a shadow on the glass.

4

I touched the handle and looked at Mikey. I opened the door.

I said, 'Yes?'

The butcher nearly dropped his carrier bag with surprise. 'It's you pair!' he exclaimed, eyeing my bare chest and wet hair.

I felt Mikey settle beside me. 'Aye,' he said.

'What are... Where's...'

I could see a DVD case pressed against the side of the butcher's carrier bag. You could just make out the girl on its cover through the thin plastic. He saw me looking and swung it round behind his legs.

'Where's Jock?' he said.

'Off on holiday,' said Mikey.

'Or was it business?' I said.

'Could have been business,' agreed Mikey.

The butcher looked at us, dumbfounded.

'We're housesitting,' I explained. 'He employed us as house sitters.'

'House sitters,' said the butcher.

'That's right. Looking after the dog.'

'Doris,' interjected Mikey.

'Doris,' I repeated. 'Making sure the lights go on and off. That sort of thing.'

The butcher scrabbled at his scalp. He sucked his red

lips. 'I didn't know he was away. Jock never said. Where is it he's off to?'

'Spain, I think, was it?' Mikey said to me.

'I think he said the Costa del Sol. Maybe even del Brava. One of the Costas anyway.'

Mikey put his finger in the air. 'Did he say it was one of them special vouchers you get these days?'

'I think he might have done Alan,' I agreed, remembering Mikey's false name just in time.

'Not bad for some, Rob,' he said and we both turned to the butcher.

'I see,' he said. 'That's odd. Well...'

I pointed to his carrier bag. 'If you need to drop something off we can keep it safe till he gets back.'

'No, no,' he said, wrapping the carrier bag up to try and obscure the contents. 'That's fine. Tell him to give me a ring when he gets back.'

'Will do,' I said, closing the door. 'Cheerio.'

We scurried through to the living room and peered through gaps in the curtain to make sure he was leaving. When he was gone I turned to Mikey and found myself smiling.

'That was good,' I said.

'We did all right, eh?'

'We did.'

He was better than I gave him credit for, Mikey. Perhaps I could trust him with the job after all. I went up the Ramsay ladder to dry myself and get dressed. Afterwards, I threw a few chicken breasts in the oven for our tea and went outside to smoke. It was a fine evening. Mikey had put Doris back in her run. She was curled up in her bone-shaped bed.

'Hiya Doris,' I said to her and she didn't even look up. Ignorant beast, I thought, rattling the wire side of the run so the metal clanged. She jumped up in fright. 'That's better,' I said.

We had the chicken with mashed potatoes and gravy. I thought we should sit at the table in the kitchen – to celebrate our first proper night in our new house and my first day as a working man.

I told Mikey all about the people at the site, the archaeologists and the diggers. I described Duncan and Sam and how Sam was living in a cabin because she'd been sleeping around. He nodded and listening and chewed on huge mouthfuls of chicken and potato.

'They were talking about the boss or the supervisor of the company. He sounds like a bad egg. Someone to watch out for. '

Mikey nodded.

'So,' I said, putting my cutlery down. 'What do you reckon?'

'About what?'

'About making some money yourself.'

'How am I going to make any money?'

'Duncan was saying you could come along and do some digging.'

'For money like?' he beamed.

I laughed. 'Aye for money.'

That night I dreamed of a memory. It was the day it happened. Me and Mikey, fifteen and thirteen years old, ticking off the school. We were in the woods and something was after us. I didn't see it, in the dream, but I knew it was a monster and that it wanted to devour us. We found a ladder in the trees and climbed it to safety.

'What's happening?' Mikey asked me.

'Don't worry,' I said. 'I'll keep us safe.'

I woke and it was still dark. Mikey's snoring was at

full blast and I knew right away that I was up for good. I went down to the living room and rolled myself a fag, smoking in the dark. The clock on the mantelpiece said four. Duncan wouldn't show up until sevenish.

I went out through the back door into the garden and the huge sky. It was clear and the stars were fizzing. I climbed the fence by the dog's run and went out into the waste ground, pulling my jumper close around me. The land was covered in these twisting grooves, like miniature canyons. Like miniature ditches. They looked like a maze for rabbits.

I found the mound of overturned earth from the other night and I lay down on a cushion of moss beside it. I could see the wee house the way I'd come. I could hold out my hand and close it around the house and garden and it contained everything inside – Mikey, the dog, the house itself. Those were all mine.

I put my hand on the fresh soil the man lay beneath. It buzzed with life. There were atoms spinning in the earth, there were electrons moving through it like worms. I felt myself get hard in the pyjama bottoms.

I must have been tired because when I woke it was light. I got myself up and hurried back to the house. I had enough time to get myself ready and make sure Mikey did the same. We stood around in the front garden to wait for Duncan. It had been another misty night and all around us was heavy whiteness and the sun bled out into the sky and the entire sky was the sun and the mist was so thick you could look right at the sun like a white penny.

Mikey zipped his coat up to his chin. We'd tried to comb his hair back with some oil we'd found in the man's toiletry cabinet. It didn't make him look good exactly, but sufficiently different from the famous photographs of him.

He rocked from side to side. 'Where were you this morning?'

I looked away. 'Went out for a walk.'

'Really?' he asked.

'Aye,' I said.

A clatter of engine noise began to rise from the mist. We stood beside the road and waited until the ancient camper broke through, white clouds sprawling round its bumper, like a shark breaking through the water's surface. The engine sounded bad, much worse than yesterday. It chomped and stuttered at a ridiculous volume.

I got in front and Mikey climbed into the back, into the van's living area. Duncan drove us away and I craned over my shoulder to make sure Mikey was all right. He was sprawled on a couch, flung back by the van's acceleration.

'You'll be Paul's brother then?' Duncan shouted back, over the sound of the engine.

'Eh?'

I leaned over. 'He said you'll be my brother then.'

'Oh,' shouted Mikey. 'That's right.'

'What's he saying?' Duncan asked me.

'He was just saying aye, he is my brother.'

Duncan nodded, enthusiastic. 'I'm sure he *is* a good worker.'

'No. That he is my *brother*.'

Mikey leaned into the gap between the front seats. 'What's that?'

'I'm just saying to Duncan what you said.'

'Eh?'

I didn't bother to answer him, shaking my head instead and pointing to the van's dashboard as way of an explanation.

'Eh?' screamed Mikey.

'It doesn't matter,' I screamed back.

'What happened,' said Duncan, 'was that I ran over a goose last night, after I dropped you off.'

'A goose?' I said.

'All the feathers got sucked up in the air cooling system. It's like a duvet down there.'

'Did he say there's a goose in the engine?' shouted Mikey.

'A goose's feathers.'

'Eh?'

All three of us decided independently that conversation wasn't worth the bother. We sat in silence and watched the oncoming road throw itself under the van in a constant stream. We came out of the hills and left the mist behind. All around us were fields and the green and lilac lines of hedge between each one. The raw new sun ran waves through the leaves and branches and the shapes of the hedge lines morphed as we drove towards and then past them.

We skirted the long loch and the water made white-caps, creamy veins in the black water, like fat marbling in meat. We came to the *Mason Dew* sign and turned onto the dirt track. 'Nearly there,' shouted Duncan.

'Eh?' shouted Mikey.

Duncan parked the van by the cabins and stepped out and stretched. As I followed him out I thought to myself that the field looked quite empty. There had been a crowd of diggers there at this point yesterday. Duncan seemed to notice too. He scanned the field with his hand over his brow. 'No sign of the lazy fucks,' he said.

I rolled myself a fag and the three of us wandered over to the cabins to wake up Sam. Mikey and Duncan introduced themselves to each other, now free of the van's overwhelming noise.

Duncan slapped Mikey on the shoulder blade. 'Good to have you pal. Paul's told us all about you.'

Mikey and I shared a look.

We came up to the cabins but before Duncan could even knock Sam exploded out of her bunk.

'Have you heard, Duncan?' she said. 'Have you heard?'

'Have I heard what?'

She was holding onto too many objects. A small coffee cup and cigarette in one hand, a sheaf of documents in the other. I spied a newspaper rolled up beneath her oxter. 'Pawel and Karol and the rest. They've been deported.'

Duncan looked at Sam. He looked at me and Mikey. 'Deported?'

'They were illegals.'

'Pawel was illegal?'

Sam drank from the coffee cup and somehow managed to puff on her fag in the same motion. 'That's not all. The Toad's on his way up.'

Duncan put both hands on his head. 'The Toad.'

Mikey was behind me, his head close to my ear. 'Who's the Toad?' he whispered into it.

I shook my head.

'The Toad,' said Sam. She was moving side to side and back and forth with nervous energy. 'Duncan,' she said. 'The Toad's coming. Today. The same day the diggers have been shipped back to Fucksville, fucking Fucksylvania.'

Duncan put his hands on his hips and sighed. He looked at the sky. 'Well,' he said. 'Not all the diggers.'

'Who's the Toad?' I asked.

Sam turned, noticing Mikey and me for the first time. 'Mr Raymond. I told you about Mr Raymond? That's the Toad. He's coming today.'

Duncan clapped his hands together. 'Right. Lads. How do you feel about some hard labour?'

Mikey and I dug the ditches all morning. It was warm but between us we managed to finish my ditch from the day before and make a good start on a second. The sun stung our necks and Sam and Duncan and the rest of the archaeologists holed themselves up in the cabins. No one came out to tell us to have a break, so we took one for ourselves. I sat in the cool dirt of the ditch and rolled myself a fag.

Mikey crouched down in front of me and checked over his shoulder to the cabins. 'Paul,' he said, shiftily. 'This is terrible.'

'It's not that bad.'

'Aye it is that bad. Look,' he held up his hand, 'I've got all blisters on my fingers.'

'Tomorrow we'll bring some T-shirts or something from the house. You can wrap your hand up.'

'I hate working,' he moaned. 'It's the worst.'

My main concern that morning had been the tube of newspaper jammed into Sam's armpit. I wasn't able to make out the title but if it was a tabloid then Mikey was almost certainly somewhere inside. That wasn't to say she would come across the article or even recognise the photo. I looked along the ditch to my brother, his head slumped against the dirt we were yet to dig. He wore his sunglasses and his hair was stubbly and stuck up at the back, like a duckling.

We would be fine. Probably. I reasoned that Sam would be too preoccupied with losing her staff to give the paper a thorough browse.

'How come the rest of them aren't helping?' Mikey said, nodding backwards to the cabins.

I shrugged. 'Maybe they've got stuff needing done before this guy shows up. This Toad.'

Mikey said, 'Mm. Maybe we should just mess about until they come back up.'

'Like, just lie here?'

'Maybe.'

I thought about it. 'Aye,' I said. 'All right.'

I heard movement behind my closed eyes. It was so comfortable and warm in the ditch that it took me a few moments to summon the energy to open them. Sam and Duncan and the other two archaeologists were hammering across the field towards us, carrying bundles under their arms. I kicked Mikey awake and we both stood up in the ditch.

Sam careered past us, a set of tools in her arms, a lit fag swinging from her lips. 'Dig!' she told us. 'Dig!'

The four of them took a ditch each and spread out their tools and Duncan set up a worktable and me and Mikey went down on our knees to dig.

'Did they catch us?' Mikey whispered to me.

I shook my head. 'I don't know,' I said.

None of them was really working. They were kneeling by their ditch, watching the cabins and the dirt track.

I called over to Duncan. 'What's going on?'

He put the finger of one hand to his lips and pointed with the other. A silver car was coming up the track – a nice motor. It parked by the cabins and sat for a few minutes. They all held their breaths as Mikey and I scratched half-heartedly at the ditch walls. We all watched together as a figure manoeuvred itself out of the motor and trudged between the cabins, checking inside each one.

Duncan took a few steps forward and shouted, 'Hello.'

The figure turned. It observed us. I could see it touch its face before getting back inside.

'Watch this,' Duncan said to us.

The figure, the famous Toad, proceeded to clamber back into his nice silver motor. He performed a complicated turn beside the cabins and drove his motor right into the field, between the strings marking out the undug ditches.

'Always the same,' said Duncan. 'Can't bear to walk. Can't suffer it. Listen.' He looked at me and Mikey. 'You keep your heads down and whatever you do don't mention that you're cash in hand.'

The motor trundled over the earth until it came to a stop in front of Duncan's ditch. The window whirred as it lowered. Inside was the face of an ugly man. He was wearing a bulbous leather cap and had an ice cream cone in his hand.

'Get in,' he told Duncan and Duncan got in. They reversed all the way back to the cabins. Every metre or so the Toad would mess up his steering and get too close to the string. He'd have to go forward again to right himself. We all put down our tools to watch the car as it idled by the cabins. You could tell Duncan was getting a serious talking to, even from that distance.

'What's the problem?' I asked.

Sam coughed. 'Well,' she said. 'It's just… How to put it? It's just that we've been taking a long time to sign off on this site. It's been ongoing for a good couple of weeks now.'

One of the archaeologists I hadn't been introduced to piped up, saying, 'A good couple of months.'

'Yeah,' said Sam. 'Maybe. So obviously, for the Toad, for Mr Raymond, time is of the essence. He wants the field signed off ASAP so he can get the building started, get the cash rolling in.'

'ASAP as fucking possible,' agreed the unnamed archaeologist.

'But say perhaps we aren't signing off on the field as quickly as we technically – and it is a technicality – technically could. Perhaps we're finding certain items of significance and the Toad, and anyone else from Mason Dew, doesn't have the expertise to dispute these items' authenticity.'

Mikey scowled at her. He'd want this explaining later on.

'And say perhaps the longer the dig goes on the more pissed off the Toad gets and the more money we make and the, like, funnier the whole thing gets,' finished Sam with a smile.

Eventually Duncan was expelled and the Toad roared off in a cloud of aggravated dust. I could make out Duncan waving to the motor as it disappeared down the track and then turning to us and clasping his hands together and waving them over his head like a champion.

Mikey sat with his feet in the ditch and his arse in the field. He looked at each of us in turn and scowled.

After Duncan returned the archaeologists packed up their tools and hid in the cabins for the remainder of the afternoon, leaving Mikey and me to toil in the field. No squash. No cereal bars. I was famished and I knew Mikey would be worse, being typically very greedy. We finished our second ditch and broke the earth on the third in preparation for the following day.

It was around four when we decided we couldn't dig any more. I rolled myself a fag between filthy fingers and we strolled back to the cabins.

Mikey trudged in the dirt. 'Man,' he said. 'Hard day.'

'Aye,' I said. 'Hard.'

'What happens now?' Mikey asked when we reached Duncan's van.

'He gave me a run back yesterday,' I said. 'I'd better say to them. We'll need to be paid as well.'

I stepped up to Sam's cabin and opened the door. Duncan was lying on Sam's mat with Sam above him, the pair of them breathing and moving. They turned to me like deer in the woods at night. I thought about the fawn Mikey and I found on the mountainside. There was the paper, lying on the table by the door. I snatched it up and said, 'Sorry.'

Neither of them spoke but they scrabbled to cover themselves with what they had.

'Why did you say sorry?' Mikey asked as I closed the door.

'They were, eh...' I wondered how best to put it. We'd never spoken about anything like that. Never talked about the whole thing directly. 'Y'know.'

'What?'

'They were,' I nodded, 'you know.'

'Oh,' he said. 'Them two? Sarah and Dunc?'

'It's Sam, but aye. Them two.'

'Wow. What was it like?'

I told him to shut up and hurried over to the van. Behind the cabin was a copse of trees with a tiny shivering river running through it. I leafed through the paper and found Mikey's page, shredding it and casting it off into the water. The paper saturated and disappeared in the grit and stones. Mikey's face bled out and was gone.

Duncan was waiting by the van. 'Absolutely amazing,' he was saying. 'I'd thoroughly recommend it.'

'Right,' said Mikey.

'Just saying to your brother,' Duncan said, turning to

me, 'about Thailand. Bangkok. He was saying he'd never been.'

'No, I don't suppose he has.'

Duncan's hair was pulled back from his forehead as if he'd been given a shock. He was leaning against his van, cool as a cucumber. 'I'll give you a run home.'

We were well on the way before he remembered something and slipped an envelope out the pocket of his shorts. 'There you are,' he said. 'Another day's pay.'

I accepted it. 'Same time tomorrow?'

Duncan said, 'Same time tomorrow,' and the road pulled the van out of the fields and into the hills.

The first thing I did when we were back inside the wee house was check the envelope's contents. There was the cash for the pair of us and an extra fifty on top.

It was a quiet evening that followed. We washed and ate and Mikey took Doris out into the wilds behind the house for a walk. I stayed behind. I didn't care much for the dog, or dogs in general. They were too needy. Too keen.

I tried watching television but I couldn't settle. I would get involved with one channel and a moment later I'd be switching over, worried about what I might be missing. I got up and opened the curtains. There was the road and fields over the road and somewhere beyond that was our lonely tent. A car drove by. I didn't recognise it. If they were going to come for us, that was how they'd do it. A squad of them camouflaged in the wild grass and trees that edged the road. A single bullet flying through the air, breaking the glass, entering my throat. I would feel a blast as the metal burrowed into me at the speed of sound. I closed the curtains.

There was a telephone on the table by my armchair. I

66

picked up the receiver and dialled our mother's number. She answered within two rings.

'Hello?' she said.

'Hi Mum.'

Her breath caught. 'Mikey?' she said. 'Paul?'

We had similar voices and when we were younger people would often mistake us for the other on the phone. Sometimes, when Mikey was inside, I would talk to our mother when her back was turned and she would spin around and there would be light inside her. Then she would realise it was me and remember and the light would vanish. It made me hate her.

'It's Paul,' I said. 'I'm just phoning to...'

'Where are you son?' she said. 'You need to tell me where you've taken him.'

'Where I've taken him? What do you mean where I've taken him?'

She could sense the annoyance in my voice. 'I didn't mean it like that.' She paused. I heard her mind whirr. 'How are you getting on son? How *are* you?'

'I'm fine.'

'Good. Good.'

'How are you?'

'Oh,' she said. 'You know how it is.'

'Right. What's going on back there? Anything I should be aware of?'

'Nothing in particular.'

I didn't say anything then. I had imagined her being more grateful. I thought she would be on our side.

'So where are you then, if you don't mind me asking?'

'I'm hardly going to tell you, am I?' I scoffed. 'They might be tracing the call.'

She breathed through her nose and it distorted the line. 'Paul,' she said. 'Son. Who's *they*?'

'They. The police. The press.'

'You need to bring him back home. Please. If you bring him back, that'll be the end of it,' she said. 'This isn't the right way to go about things.'

My blood had been kicking in all through the call and now it was all the way up. How dare she dictate to me what the right way to do things was? 'I have to go,' I told her.

'Wait.'

'What?'

'Is he OK? Is he safe?'

'He's fine,' I said.

I hung up the phone just as the back door closed. I heard Mikey creep through the hallway and looked up to see him lurking by the living room door. I asked him what was going on and he shrugged.

'The dog caught a rabbit,' he said.

'Oh yeah?'

'Aye. It was running around in those tunnel things out the back. Doris threw it in the air and broke its neck.'

'What did you do with it?'

'Just left it.'

'All right. Did you see where she put it?'

'No. Why, like?'

'It doesn't matter.'

The man had some decent clothes but they were fairly baggy on us. We had to pull the belts down to the tightest notch and roll the sleeves on the shirts up. After we got dressed we lay on the bed and waited for it to get dark. We put our hands on our chests and watched the square of sky through the bedroom window go lilac. We watched the colour drain out of it to let the blackness in. Once it was dark enough we put our jackets on and climbed down the Ramsay ladder.

We took the man's car down into town. I was worried it would look suspicious but Mikey reasoned that people would assume he'd let us use it while he was away. I hadn't driven in some time but I soon got the hang of it. We were in the square in no time and I parked up across from the pub. *The Cask and Shackle* was painted in gold above the windows, the door and window frames bottle green.

Our table from the other night was taken by a huddled crowd of three heavily bearded men but we found another one closer to the pool room. Mikey's eyes were out on stalks when he noticed the same group of girls were sat in the far corner. I used some of the cash from Duncan's latest envelope to get a round in. There was a girl on the bar this time. She looked young. Too young to buy a drink herself even. Her hair was done up in a tiny bun that tottered on the top of her skull.

'Hello,' I said, glad the snotty barman from before wasn't around.

She looked me up and down. 'What d'you want?'

'Is the ale on?'

'The Dirty Monk?'

'Yeah.'

'Nah. There's Tennent's there. Or Carling.'

I asked for two Tennent's and as she was pouring them I sloped along to the end of the bar to peer up into the pool room. There was a pair of identical twins enjoying a game, chalking their cues after every shot, but no sign of the butcher. I would be able to relax.

The pub was busy for being so early in the evening. I had to fight through a crowd of patrons to collect our round. They were all around me, men in jumpers and suits, their chests and arms pressing against me. I felt a man's hair brush my neck as I squeezed through, holding the pints aloft, and I gagged. That was something I hated, crowds. It was a kind of claustrophobia I suppose, but more so. More of a disgust at the animalness of them, their chewing mouths and wet eyes.

We had an OK time, Mikey and I. We drank our first round and chatted about the people up at the site. I explained the scam to him, how they were dragging their heels to rinse more money out of the Toad and his company. He nodded as I told him.

'That's clever,' he said.

'I suppose.'

'You know,' he went on, holding his pint to his chest, 'I never knew that was a real thing.'

'Archaeologist?'

'Aye. I thought it was pretend. Like a wizard or something.'

I sipped my pint. 'Huh.'

The pub was alive with lights and chatter. The fruit machines gabbled and pinged, their garish lights racing. You could hear snatches of conversation, the odd 'I know eh?' and 'Aye fucking right'. As long as I wasn't in the crowd I didn't mind it. Perhaps this would be a good place for the pair of us to settle down in after all, I thought. Who said we had to rush back to our mother as soon as things died down at home? It looked as though with this new information we had on Sam and Duncan we were well placed to make a nice earning.

'But I suppose they are real,' Mikey shrugged.

'Oh no, they are real. Definitely.'

'It's funny, eh?'

'What is?'

'Just the stuff you get confused about. It can be funny.'

I nodded. 'I suppose it can be.'

70

We finished our pints at the same time. Mikey raised his eyebrows to me. 'Another one?' he asked.

I nodded. 'Aye,' I said. 'Why not?'

The circles of men around the bar parted reluctantly to let me through and I managed to get my hand on the wood. The barmaid was chatting to one of the identical twins, ignoring the rest of us crammed against each other, waiting.

A hand grasped me on the shoulder and I leaned in to let whoever it was past. The hand didn't budge.

'Here,' said a voice. 'I know you, don't I?'

I held my teeth together and gripped the edge of the bar.

5

Here it comes.

Here's the hand on the shoulder, the knee in the small of the back. Faces turning to look, to truly see us for the first time. Recognition. Revulsion. They'll fall upon us, drag us out into the flickering streetlights, into the square. I'll be held back while they tear at my brother, at my flesh and blood. The Buchanan Beast, the Beast of Buchanan. There'll be chanting and the piercing lights from mobile phones as they film him writhe or choke as they pull the rope around his neck.

All for something he did when he was thirteen years old. All for that.

I turned to see a squat face looking up at me from underneath a leather cap. 'Don't I?' it said. 'Know you?'

I stopped myself from saying his name. His nickname. 'Maybe,' I said. 'From the site over the hill.'

'Thought so,' the Toad muttered. 'So are you one of that lot then? One of them fucken PhDs or whatever they are?'

'I'm just there to dig. Just labour.'

He glared up at me, no taller than five feet. The cap he wore was bizarre. It didn't have the rigidity to be a fedora or trilby but was too round to be a baseball cap. 'Well,' he said. 'You can't tell with you lot, can you? Your mates, Sue and Derek or whatever they're called. They look like a pair of clowns, but they're PhDs or MCDs or NWAs, I don't know what the letters are.'

'Right.'

'Or so they tell us anyway. I don't know. So how's it going up there? I can't get a straight answer out of the hippy one for love nor money.'

'Like I said, I'm just digging.'

'Good man,' he said, being shunted towards me as the identical twin left the bar. His skin was silvery up close. 'Pass the buck. There's no shame in passing the buck. None at all. Some people say you should accept responsibility for things.'

'I suppose.'

'Fucken bollocks that. Listen to me pal. Never get into business, never put your hand up if someone asks you to, cause there'll always be someone waiting to shaft you if you do. Like that lot up at the site.'

I nodded. 'OK.'

He looked around the pub in a fury, perhaps hoping to spot Sam or Duncan to give them a piece of his mind. 'So what are you then? You do that full time, digging?'

'No, not really.'

'Well?'

'Do odd jobs on the side. Housesitting just now.'

'Housesitting?' he demanded, reacting to the word with barely contained rage. 'Housesitting?'

'Aye.'

'Like with babies, but a house?'

'Kind of.'

He shook his head from side to side so fast his cap came away from the skull. 'Who with? On your own?'

I said, 'No,' and nodded towards Mikey, leaning against the wall, fiddling with a beer mat. He waved at the Toad.

'Who's he? He your boyfriend is he?'

'No.'

'Well. You can't tell these days, can you? I don't know whether I'm coming or going most of the time, these days. Can't say poofter, can't say chinky. Can't get anyone to sign off on your fucken site fast enough that you're not losing money hand over fist,' he poked me in the chest, 'daily.'

'Aye,' I said. 'All right.'

'Is anyone serving up there,' he said, standing on tip toe to crane over my shoulder. 'I'm spitting feathers.'

He had this way of talking, the Toad, where he spoke at you without stopping to look for a reaction. He scratched his brow with the brim on his cap.

'Listen,' he said, eyeing the optics. 'I don't suppose you'd be interested in making a wee bit extra cash would you?'

'What d'you mean?'

'A wee bit extra cash in your pocket at the end of the month?'

'How?'

He fished inside his jacket and pulled out a business card. It read *Angus Raymond, Site Supervisor, Mason Dew* and was followed by a landline number.

'You keep that,' he said, 'and if you can give me any information that would, y'know, grease the wheels and so on, it would be greatly appreciated.'

As I looked the card over he pushed in front of me and gave the barmaid his order. 'You snooze, you lose,' he told me with a wink.

Mikey was eager to find out what the Toad had been talking about. He inspected the business card as he drank his pint. 'So he's Duncan's boss, is he?'

'Not really. He's the boss of the company who employs Duncan's company.'

74

He smiled and turned the card over in his hand. He shook his head. 'I don't understand.'

'That's all right.'

We stayed for another couple of rounds and as we drank I was aware of the Toad watching us from his position at the end of the bar. 'Think about it,' he shouted as we made our way to the door.

The next day at the site, we dug all morning. The summer was in full swing by then and we worked with the sun in our hair. We'd brought along T-shirts from the house to wrap our hands up in and pillows to kneel on. We'd frozen a couple of water bottles so that the ice melted throughout the day and provided us with trickles of cold water.

Down at the cabins there was a Portaloo but once you were up in the ditches it was easier to nip over into the trees that flanked the field. At around noon I told Mikey to take a break and I wandered over to the coverage the woods provided. I kicked a groove into the earth with the toe of my boot and took my trousers down to shit into it. From my position I was able to peer through the bushes to see my brother. He was sitting on the edge of our newest ditch, squeezing the ice bottle into his gob. I watched as Sam came into view, wandering up the space between two ditches.

She stopped by Mikey and they began to talk together. Their bodies morphed and shimmered in the waves of heat that hung in the air between me and them. She was probably asking him how he was getting on, if he was settling in all right. He would say he was settling in fine and she would smile down at him. All friendly on the surface, but trying to worm information out of him. Maybe even laying out small hints that maybe he shouldn't always listen to his big brother, that maybe he should think for himself now and then. That was the sort she seemed. One of those woman that thinks they can do whatever they want and just because they're a woman no one's going to say anything to them. Clearly she'd never met me before.

There was plenty leaves on the ground that I could use for my arse and I stood and belted up the man's trousers.

Sam turned as I crossed the field towards them. 'Hi Paul,' she said.

I made it over and looked at them both. 'Hiya.'

'I was just telling your brother that you're both doing a great job out here. I know it's shit work but we really appreciate it.'

'Oh,' I said. 'All right.'

'I was saying we've put up a couple of ads in town for more hands. Need to replace Pawel and his lot.'

'I see.'

Mikey squinted as he looked up at me and the sun behind my head. 'There's a night out planned,' he told me.

Sam clapped her hands and pointed them in my direction. 'That's right! A team night out tonight. We're all going to pile into Dunc's van and sniff out a club, if you two are interested?'

Mikey was smiling anyway, from the sun in his eyes, but his grin widened at her question.

'We'll think about it,' I nodded.

'Super,' said Sam.

I watched her as she walked away. She was slim on top but her legs bulged at the thighs and calves.

'A club,' said Mikey. 'A night club.'

I stepped down into the ditch to get back to work. I said, 'Mm,' and picked up my spade.

'That's interesting,' he said. 'A proper night out.'

I scooped up the displaced soil and tipped it up into the field. There were only another few metres to go on this ditch. We'd be able to finish it off and make a good start on another before the day was over.

Mikey sighed.

I asked him what was wrong and he sighed again. That's when I realised. He'd never been on a night out before. He'd been to the pub a few times in the months he'd been out but had never gone to a bar or a club late into the morning. I asked him if he wanted to go and he nodded furiously.

'Well,' I said. 'Let's see how we get on with this work and we can have a chat about it later.'

The Toad showed up again as we were readying ourselves to leave, late in the afternoon. We were helping Duncan to load the tools back into the cabin when he drove his motor up along the dirt track and parked it up.

'Here we go,' Duncan said, leaning a shovel against the side of the cabin. Sam and the others were still out on the far side of the field but I could tell they were standing to get a better look.

The window came down. He was holding another ice cream cone in his pudgy fist. 'All right?' he asked the three of us.

'Afternoon Mr Raymond,' said Duncan, strolling over to the motor. 'What's up?'

With his free hand the Toad ejected a clipboard through the open window into Duncan's waiting hand. 'Need to get your autograph on that.'

Duncan took the clipboard and leaned on the motor to read the paperwork.

'Watch the paint,' said the Toad. 'That's the metallic option. You pay extra for that.'

His gaze fell on Mikey and me, watching the exchange. 'This what you're paying them to do?' he asked Duncan. 'Just stand around with their thumbs up their arses.' He took a heavy lick from the cone.

Duncan peered at us over the clipboard. 'They're just packing up. It's finishing time.'

'Huh,' coughed the Toad. 'Finishing time.'

Duncan signed the paperwork and handed it back to the Toad, who snatched it away and tossed it onto the passenger seat. 'Any progress?' he asked, jerking his head towards the field.

'I'm afraid not. We've just come across an interesting patch of ridge and furrow.'

'Ridge and furrow?'

'That's right, see there.' Duncan pointed over the cars bonnet to the far end of the field where the other archaeologists were staring back. The earth there was gently rippled.

'The fuck's rig and furrow?'

'*Ridge* and furrow. It's too early to say. Going to need a bit more investigation. Could be quite significant.'

The Toad looked at the far end of the field and tapped on the steering wheel. He let out one sharp breath and closed his eyes. 'Ridge and fucken furlow,' he seethed, before the window zoomed up and he was gone.

Duncan began to laugh as the motor pulled out of sight.

The road took us once again alongside the narrow loch. Something about the light that day made the water dark as whale skin. There was no wind so only light ripples of movement disturbed its surface. I imagined the inside of it thick with weeds and bloated wood and hurrying cold animals. There would be an eel in there somewhere, I decided. Fat and long and smiling. The king of the water. It was the object the other water beasts hid from, in crevices and holes in the silt. The eel stalked the blue and green and black water, curving its fatness and its wetness around the branches of driftwood, in among trailing sea grasses. Its eyes never closed. Its smile never faltered. It was quick when it needed to be. It...

Duncan chapped on the dashboard. 'Hello?'

I turned away from the window and the water. 'What?'

'Did you get any of that?'

'No. I... I don't know. I was miles away.'

'I was just saying, what about if we picked you up at about nine or so. If you're interested?'

The night out. Of course. I looked around to see Mikey's hopeful face peering back at me from the gap between the seats. 'Aye,' I said. 'OK.'

'Grand,' smiled Duncan. 'Should be fun.'

As we were climbing out of the van he stopped us and cracked open the glove compartment. There was fat manila folder and a wrap of brown envelopes inside. He counted out our pay from a stack of notes inside the folder and slipped them into the envelope. I noted that he was giving us more than we were due.

'Thanks,' I said as he handed me the envelope.

Duncan nodded.

There was an odd noise coming from inside the house. Mikey opened the front door, cocked his head and frowned at me. It was a scuttling sound.

'What's that?' I said.

'Don't know.'

We creeped inside and I left the door resting on the snib. As we went through the hall I peered into the living room but there was nothing there. We looked into the kitchen and there was Doris. The fridge was open and the tiles were littered with pieces of shredded food. A packet of bacon reduced to smatterings of red jelly, a cheese rind rocking. The dog was jumping between items, excited about her feast. That was the scuttling sound – nails on tile.

I marched forward and got the dog by the collar. She began to buck as soon as I put my hand on her but I quickly got her under control. I made her lie on her side and I pressed on her neck.

'Stop,' said Mikey, pulling on my shoulder.

'I'm teaching it,' I spat, 'a lesson.'

The dog flinched and opened its mouth and looked up at me, its eyes' whiteness bulging. I held its neck against the tiles. 'See what happens?' I said to it. 'See what happens?'

Eventually Mikey managed to pull me off and the dog launched herself up and bounded into the back garden. Mikey went after her and I sat down on the kitchen floor, against the wall. There were chunks of gnawed carrot between my feet. My breath was going like a pump, filling me with warmth and anger. I closed my eyes and imagined gliding along in cool water, my long slick belly brushing sand, the pure ice of the water flowing into my open, smiling mouth.

Mikey came back inside, having calmed the beast down and locked her in the run. We cleaned up the remains of the dog's dinner and after that we washed and ate. Mikey washed his good white shirt in the kitchen sink and left it on a radiator to dry. I managed to pull together something vaguely appropriate from the man's collection.

Once we were dressed we sat in the living room together to wait. It had been a long time since I'd been on a proper night out. There had been the odd one here and there with the various workmates I'd had over the years. It was difficult to keep those friendships though. Something would always come between us.

At about half eight Mikey started to get antsy. He would get up from the armchair, put his can of lager on the table, and peer out the window. He would go through to the bathroom to check himself in the mirror and then pace around in the hall for a bit.

'Sit down,' I said. 'You'll make yourself ill.'

'What do you mean?' he said, poking his head through the doorway. 'What sort of ill?'

'Not *ill* ill, just you're not going to enjoy yourself if you're so wound up about it all.'

Duncan honked for us when he was outside. We locked up and climbed into the van with Sam and the others, whose names we learned were Jose and Fia. They both had toffee coloured skin and dark shining hair. Fia was up in front with Duncan but Jose was in back with us. They gave off the air of being a couple but showed no outward signs of affection to each other. There was a bottle of foul European spirit being passed around. It stung your tongue and filled your nostrils with spice.

Duncan called through to the front, 'Everyone belted up?' and they all laughed because there were no real seats in the back of the van, never mind seatbelts.

And then off we went.

Duncan struggled to find a parking spot, the van was so large. We'd driven straight through the village and then onto a B road that joined the motorway. As we came into Glasgow you could see all its yellow lights and the misty fire they caused in the clouds above. Drunk men knocked on the van's side when we were stopped at traffic lights and taxis swerved in front of us constantly.

He managed to squeeze the van down an alleyway and we all piled out. There was a heated discussion about where to go but in the end they settled on a place called Quick William's. You went down a set of stairs once you were past the bouncers, then you paid your money and then you were in. Because of the time we'd taken driving and finding a parking space the place was already packed. They were playing David Bowie's Changes and everyone was singing along out of tune and forgetting the words.

I was dizzy from the syrupy spirit so I didn't mind squeezing my way through the crowd. People rubbed against me as they danced and it didn't make me ill in the same way. Duncan bought a round for himself and Mikey and me. He bought us sour whisky and Cokes and put his arms around us.

'You're some of the good guys,' he shouted in our ears. 'That other lot. Pawel and that. They never came out.'

'All right,' I said and Mikey looked up at him with eyes of adoration as he struggled to get his arm up to sip his drink.

Duncan threw his whisky back and asked for another. The girl who served him had the back of her head shaved, leaving just the fringe and sides hanging, dyed pink. I'd never seen that before and didn't care for it.

Duncan threw his second whisky back and let out a shout.

We had to leave the bar to let others through and we found Sam and the rest by the dancefloor. The music was louder there and I couldn't hear what she said to us, even though she screamed it. The music changed to something I didn't recognise and Sam pulled us through the bodies to dance. I gave it a go for as long as I could but it got too much for me and I had to leave to linger by the edge.

I watched the people moving and jumping and their bodies were pink and green from the lights and occasionally bright flashing white, each of them visible for only a moment before they were gone. I could feel the music in my arm hairs, it made growling sounds inside my chest. People were moving around me and I felt shoulders in my chest, tits against my flank. Mikey was holding his hands in the air and stomping his feet and the others were clapping for him. All the bald spots, all the hands.

I finished my drink and put it down. The Hungarian stuff was wearing off. I managed to find the toilets nearby and locked myself in a cubicle. I sat on the toilet lid and put my feet up against the door and closed my eyes. Girls screamed through the walls and men laughed.

Some lads were chatting at the urinal. 'Nah,' one of them said. 'No fucken way.'

'Aye,' said the other. 'You wait and see.'

I sat like that for some time, until I'd calmed down. I washed my hands before I went back out again, to make it seem proper. It took a while to find the group. They were deep in the crowd over the dancefloor. They'd all paired up, Duncan with Sam, Jose with Fia. Their faces were smashed together and they were still dancing and had their hands everywhere.

I touched Duncan on the back and he turned.

He laughed at me. 'Here he is,' he shouted. 'Here's misery guts.'

'What?'

'Never mind,' he slurred. 'Just dance, man. Enjoy yourself.'

'Where's Mikey?' I said.

'Who?'

83

Sam leaned over. 'What're you saying?'

'You don't know where Mikey is?'

They both shrugged and went back to each other. I fought my way through the dancers. Misery guts, he'd said. My blood was all over the shop – I pushed past people and drinks went onto me, onto my front. Climbing the stairs at the far end of the dancefloor, I managed to get a good look around. Mikey was tall, it shouldn't be too hard, and I knew he wasn't in the toilets. I scanned the bobbing heads, trying to pick him out.

Nothing.

He wasn't at the bar either when I checked. I was swearing over and over beneath my breath. The man at the desk gave me a stamp on my hand and I went outside for a smoke, to calm down. Quick William's was on a corner and I skulked around the side to roll my fag. I paced as I smoked it, going down the block and then walking back up. On my third go around I happened to glance down an alleyway.

There he was, pressed up against a wall. A girl was on her knees in front of him and I stood and watched. She was really going at him. I flicked my ash and the movement must have caught his eye. He pushed her off and pulled up his jeans and she wiped her mouth and looked at me.

I said, 'Hello.'

'Paul,' said Mikey.

'Who the fuck's Paul?' said the girl.

I told her that I was and I took a drag on my fag. I beckoned Mikey towards me and he waddled down the alley, zipping his jeans and casting a mournful look back at the girl. I got him by his arm and walked him along the pavement.

'What're you playing at?' I hissed at him.

'Nothing,' he hissed back.

We went by the door of Quick William's and Mikey's head turned. I told him not to even think about mentioning it, my voice shaking. We walked the streets instead, dodging drunks and stepping over splatters of vomit, until we came to the van. I let go of Mikey's arm and leaned against the bonnet.

'This is the plan? We just wait?'

I nodded. 'That's it.'

He flung himself against the bonnet too and crossed his arms.

We waited like that for some time. Static hummed between us but we didn't speak until the rest of them showed up. Duncan let out a shriek when he saw us, running down the alleyway and wrapping us up in his big hairy arms.

'Look Sam,' he shouted into our necks. 'I found them.'

'I know, I know,' said Sam as she stumbled along. She was smiling at first but I saw a flicker of something else when she met my eye. Probably thought I was a misery guts too. They probably all did.

Fia had stopped drinking earlier and was all right to drive. Jose sat in front with her and was asleep within moments of the journey home. Mikey and I sat on the sofa in the back and Sam and Duncan leaned against the units in the kitchen area.

'So,' said Sam, playing with Duncan's hair. 'What happened to you two?'

'Just got bored, needed some air,' I said.

'Both of you?'

'Yeah. Both of us. Eh Mikey?'

'That's right,' nodded Mikey.

'I see,' said Sam. 'You missed yourself. It was a great laugh.'

I smiled at her. Right at her. 'I bet it was.'

She laughed, cruelly. 'All right,' she said.

Once we were off the motorway you could see nothing of the world outside as Fia hurtled us along. I sat stiff in my seat and Sam and Duncan kissed on the floor and I didn't even look at Mikey. I had to direct Fia for the rest of the way. She knew how to get to the village but had never gone to the site via our house.

'Cheers for the lift,' I told her as we climbed out.

She told me it was no problem. Everyone else was asleep by then.

Mikey followed me up the garden path and we went inside. I said he should probably see to the dog before we went to sleep. I waited for him in the kitchen and rolled a fag. I could hear that fucken dog bound around on the grass. There was a mug on the table that I used for ash.

He came in behind me and walked around the table, heading for the hall. I tapped my fag on the mug's edge. 'Where you going?'

'Bed,' he said. 'We're up early.'

'Come here,' I said, nodding at the chair across from me.

'Why?'

'I want to talk to you.'

He looked up into the hallway and then came back across. The chair squeaked on the tiles as he sat down.

'What you did tonight.' I let the silence hang in the air. 'What you did.'

'It was nothing.'

'Nothing?'

He kind of screwed up his mouth. 'Well,' he said.

I had been very still as I sat there, but that 'Well' made something happen to me. My legs jerked upwards and made the table rock. Mikey's mouth opened. I said, 'Well?'

'It doesn't seem like that big a deal. If she hadn't recognised me already then I don't see what...'

Mikey didn't finish that sentence. As he was talking I reached over and held onto his wrist. I pulled his hand towards me over the wood-effect table top. I turned his hand over and I put my fag into his palm. The fingers closed automatically from the shock and I held them there, tight.

'You don't see?' I said.

He was gasping too much to answer me, tugging his arm and breathing and blinking. I thought of the fawn we'd come across in the mountains. I thought of another animal I'd come across once before. A mole that turned up in the fields behind our mother's old house. I didn't know what had happened to it but it was on its way out. When I found it there wasn't much time left. Its whole front was wide open, purple mole guts this way and that. If you put your finger into the gap the mole shivered and flicked its legs. It made the tip of your finger as warm as fire.

I repeated myself. 'You don't see?'

He couldn't speak to me.

'In future try your very fucken hardest to see. Do you hear me?'

I let him go and he stood up and the fag butt went flying. He rinsed his hand under the sink and wouldn't look me in the eye.

'You should get some peas from the freezer,' I said. 'It helps with the burn.'

I found him some frozen sweetcorn and he pressed it into his hand, taking it off every few seconds to inspect his palm.

'Good job the dog didn't get into the freezer too,' I laughed.

'Yeah,' he said. 'I suppose.'

My mind was crafting itself a nice little plan. I had the Toad on my mind. I had Sam and Duncan on my mind. I had Duncan turning to me and calling me misery guts on my mind.

Misery guts? I thought. We'll see about that.

6

Up at the site the following day the mood was poor. Duncan had been silent as he drove us along, a sheen of sweat on his cheeks and the tiny hairs at his temple clinging to the skin. He kept opening his mouth to speak before deciding against it. The van trundled along at a snail's pace and Duncan gripped the steering wheel like a life-ring.

The archaeologists kept to the cabins while we dug the field. I myself was in fine spirits. There'd been a touch of hangover in my eyes when I woke but I took an ice-cold glass of water in one go and I was right as rain. We worked through the morning without discussing the night before and it wasn't until we are taking our morning break that Mikey brought it up. He unwrapped the T-shirt to inspect his palm. He poked the burn and winced.

'It hurts,' he said.

I took his hand to check it over. I gave it back to him. 'It's fine.'

'Mm.'

I looked up at the cabins and saw Jose move from one to the other, carrying a plastic tray of objects found in the field. He waved at us and I stared back.

'Nice guy that,' said Mikey, holding up his good arm.

'You think so?'

'Aye,' he said. 'Why not?'

I shook my head, as in: I'd better not say.

'What?' he demanded. 'Go on.'

'It's just… Aw, I don't like to say this, but they were really laying into you last night when you pulled your wee disappearing act. It was ugly.'

He blew air from his mouth, dismissively. 'No they weren't.'

'It's true,' I said. 'I had to walk away. I couldn't listen to it.'

'Fuck off.'

I sat down in the ditch with my legs crossed. I leant against the wall. 'Don't believe me if you don't want. No skin off my nose.'

'No,' he said. 'Tell me.'

I shook my head. 'Just calling you a mungo, calling you a spastic, calling you thick as shit.'

Mikey turned away from me and put his hands on his hips. Then he turned back. 'No way.'

'Why would I make that up? I felt sick.'

He kicked some dirt down into the ditch and made a watery sound in his throat. 'Man,' he said.

I let him have his little tantrum and we got back to work. We went straight through until finishing time and then Fia gave us a run down the road. She told us Duncan was too sick to drive – he'd been throwing up in the cabin all day.

'Just hope Mr Raymond doesn't show up,' I laughed.

Fia made a cross with her fingers over her breast and laughed. 'Heaven forbid.'

I found myself to be exhausted by the time we were home. I lay across the armchair with my head on the arm and slept. It nourished me and I woke up stronger than ever. Mikey was sat up at the kitchen table, looking at an atlas he'd dug up somewhere.

'Fancy the pub?' I said.

'Aye,' he said. 'Go on then.'

I could barely make him out over the noise the pub was making. Putting my finger in my other ear, I hunched over the phone.

'Say that again?' I said.

The Toad huffed. 'I said that what you said was very interesting. So all that nonsense, all that ribs and fallow, that was all bollocks?'

'Aye.'

'How do I prove it?'

'How should I know? Get someone to check it out.'

I could hear the Toad's mouth moving at the other end of the line. His lips smacking, his teeth touching. The air leaving his nose. 'I was hoping for something more concrete.'

'Look,' I said, checking over my shoulder. 'Just get someone to check it out. You'll see.'

'Hm.'

'So. What about my pocket?'

'What about your pocket?'

'You said that...'

'I know what I said,' laughed the Toad. 'I'm only messing around. I'll see you at the site, OK?'

I said, 'OK,' and replaced the receiver. I went into the toilet there for the first time. It was empty and had one of those old fashioned ceramic urinals where the piss runs along a gutter at the edge of the floor. I spat into it then pissed into it. I washed my hands in the sink and watched my face as it moved around inside the greenish mirror. There I was. I smiled at myself and myself smiled back. That was a winner's face.

I hated it, so so much.

I scowled at it and then pinched myself on the cheek.

Mikey had already finished his first pint and was itching for a second. The Dirty Monk was still off so I asked for the usual.

The barmaid screwed up her face. 'The usual?'

'Two of what we usually ask for.'

'I've never seen you before,' she said, her bun wobbling.

'Two pints of Tennent's,' I said.

As I brought the pints over the pleasure must have shown on my face because Mikey eyed me. 'What's up?' he said.

'Oh,' I told him. 'Nothing.'

'You were a while. Were you on the phone?'

'On the phone?' I smiled. 'No.'

I ended up roaring drunk that night. Maybe I was making up for going so softly the night before but I kept getting rounds in and I lapped Mikey once or twice. We were remembering a story our uncle used to tell. It was about when he was young and had moved to London for work with a group of pals. They'd all roomed in a boarding house in Crystal Palace. One of them, not our uncle, had got himself mixed up with some gangsters, meaning a lot of late night door bashings and threats made against the whole group. They'd got the train back up together with their tails between their legs. We forgot some parts of the story but between us we managed to piece it together.

I killed myself laughing thinking about our uncle, huddled in a grotty London boarding house. A couple of people looked round.

'You all right?' Mikey asked.

'I'm fine,' I said. 'Fucken marvellous. We've got some good times ahead of us, you and me.'

'Why's that?'

I tried to tap myself on the nose but ended up touching my mouth. I turned it into a shushing motion. 'Never you mind. Never you mind.'

I was far too gone to drive so we left the car in town and walked back up the road. I walked with my arm around my brother's shoulders and he stopped me from swaying out into the grassy ditch that ran beside the road. When cars came by we jumped across the ditch onto the field to let them pass. They threw cones of light onto the black countryside and you could see them flash on-and-off, on-and-off, as they made their way into the hills.

I was lying on top of the duvet, drifting in and out of consciousness. I could hear the Ramsay ladder rattle and then Mikey's head came up through the floor. He got down to his pants and vest and slipped into the covers. The lights were off but the window provided a thin moonlight.

'What do you think Mum's doing now?' he said.

I thought about it. 'I don't know.'

'I don't know either. She used to visit all the time at Polmont, but I never knew what she was like.'

'How d'you mean?'

'Like, I don't know what she's interested in. Does she have any hobbies?'

I thought about that too. 'Not sure. Maybe. Maybe bingo?'

He nodded. 'Maybe bingo.'

'She's probably just glad that someone's here, keeping you safe. That's probably her main concern. Other than bingo.'

'Hm,' he said.

'I think she's probably sat in her chair, looking out the window, and thanking her lucky stars that you're safe and that we'll be home soon.'

'Will we though? Be home soon?'

'Aye,' I nodded. 'Soon.'

'When's soon?'

I told him to go to sleep and then I turned away from him.

Duncan was in better spirits the next day but I was not. I'd woken with a head full of hot wool and my tongue was coated in filth. I'd showered for nearly half an hour to try and wash away the hangover but it hadn't done much good. I sat in the front of the van, slumped against the window.

'Sorry about my performance the other night lads,' Duncan said. 'It was that awful Hungarian pish. It knackered me, that.'

'Never mind,' I wheezed.

'You enjoy yourselves?'

Mikey called through from the back. 'Aye, it was grand.'

'Mikey,' said Duncan. 'What happened with you and that lassie? She was nice.'

I didn't turn to look at Mikey but I could feel his discomfort. 'Nothing,' he said.

'Ah, that's a shame,' said Duncan. 'Can't win them all.'

When we were at the site he remembered our pay. He took that fat envelope out from the glove box and counted the notes for the day before.

'Can we have today's as well?' I asked.

'Aye, don't see why not,' he said, shuffling the cash. 'And a little something extra for being so agreeable.'

I said, 'Thanks,' and stuck the envelope in the pocket of my jeans.

The morning that followed was much like the others.

Mikey and I dug together and the archaeologists were either holed up in their cabins, doing whatever it was they did in there, or moping at the far end of the field. On lunch break I wandered over to fill up our water bottles. I found Sam and Jose inside the cabin with the tank. They stopped talking when I entered.

'Everything all right?' I said.

Jose stood up and left, leaving me alone with Sam. She said, 'Everything's fine Paul.'

'Good,' I said and I bent to fill my bottle. Bubbles of air gurgled up the tank as I used it. I knew that Sam was watching me.

'Paul,' she said. 'What sort of person are you?'

I turned round to face her. 'What do you mean?'

'I mean what are you like? It's hard to get a handle on you.'

The cabin was small. It was dirty and cluttered. I screwed the lid back on my water bottle. 'Just normal. Just a normal guy.'

'Hm,' she said. 'I look at you and... nothing. Most people there's something.'

'What are you trying to suggest?' I said, then, added for emphasis, 'Sam.'

She laughed, enjoying the challenge. 'I'm not *suggesting* anything. I find you interesting, if anything. What I do disapprove of is how you treat your brother.'

There were no windows in the cabins. Whatever happened in there was between you and the metal walls. I held onto my bottle. 'My brother?' I asked.

'That whole thing the other night, not letting him back in the club because he went off with some girl. He's, what, twenty-four or twenty-five?'

'And?'

'I'm just saying.'

I put my water bottle down on the floor and I approached Sam. She was sat right back in an office chair, a bundle of papers on her lap. I leant over her and she started to protest. I leant over her and put my hands on the wall behind her head. Our faces were inches apart.

'Get off me,' she said.

I smiled. 'I'm not on you.'

I loomed over her like that and she cringed and looked away. There was a smell of rubber in there from the pile of boots in the corner. A single bulb hung from the ceiling. Up close I noticed that Sam had a tiny stud in her nose. It was like the sparkle of ice.

'Can I ask you to do something for me?' I breathed.

She screwed her face up. 'What?'

'I don't want you to talk to me about my brother ever again. I don't want you to think about my brother. I don't want to see you look at him or talk to him or seem as though you're thinking about him.'

Sam sniffed.

'How does that sound?'

She nodded and I stood up. Her legs were tucked up beneath her and she had her arms crossed over her tits. I turned away to fill up Mikey's water bottle. The tank spluttered as it dispensed.

'See you,' I said and I hopped through the cabin door. I marched up the field and I was powerful. The hangover was gone and I was free.

I had won. I had won and these fucken so-called geniuses and experts didn't even know.

It was late in the afternoon when the cars came.

The pair of us were out in the field, adding the finishing touches to yet another ditch. We stood with our backs to the trees to admire our work. Row after row of ditches ran along in front of us, leading towards the cabins half a mile away.

'Not bad,' I said.

'Aye,' said Mikey. 'Not bad. We should ask for a bonus.'

'Maybe.'

Mikey looked at the ditches for a while and then he squinted over to me. 'What are they for?' he asked.

I shook my head. 'Who knows?'

Mikey scratched his head. He said, 'Still though, absolutely top notch ditches.'

I was nodding and appraising them when I noticed the red dust clouds rising from the direction of the track. I blocked my eyes from the sun and saw a small hive of nice, expensive motors rumbling across the dirt in the direction of the cabins, Mr Raymond's motor at the lead.

'Here,' I said, gesturing to Mikey. 'See that?'

Mikey mirrored me, holding his hand above his brow. 'Who's that?'

'Looks as though the game's up,' I said. 'Looks as though their chickens are coming home to roost.'

Mikey flashed excitement. 'Eh? Chickens?'

'It's just an expression.'

We watched the cars pulled up outside the cabins and all at once a squad of men the same size and shape as the Toad lowered themselves from their nice motors. They scurried around and banged on the doors of the cabins. They were like a pack of terrier dogs, circling the cabins, knocking on the doors, approaching and moving away from each other.

'What's going on?' said Mikey.

I laughed. 'Wait and see.'

One by one the four archaeologists emerged from the cabins. It was too far off to see the expression on anyone's face, but I knew they would be delicious. I had a notion of walking by them as their bosses laid into them and smiling at Duncan's sombre face.

Cheer up misery guts, I would say.

And then there was a final car, bringing up the rear. It was white and had fluorescent marking on its side.

My mouth opened up.

It was a fucken police car! That bastard Toad had called in the fucken police. What was he doing calling the police over a fucken misdemeanour?

All at once I saw how it would play out. Regardless of whether or not they took the complaint seriously, the police would want to speak to us all. They'd want to know our names, see our IDs. If Mikey gave another name that Sam bitch wouldn't let it slide. If he used his real name, there would be a flicker of recognition on the officer's face. We'd been safe among these people who were from other countries or had been abroad so long that they had forgotten Mikey's story. But, oh no. This officer would know. He'd roll the name round on his gums, testing its familiarity.

Mikey, he'd say. Mikey... Buchanan, was it?

I saw how it would happen. I saw the officer's eyes moving across all of us in turn. I saw him reaching for something on his belt. I saw Mikey's sternum crashing into the bonnet of the car, hands behind his back, the officer calling it in. The Buchanan Beast, he'd say. The one who's been missing every single one of the pre-arranged meetings with his social worker? The one who absconded? Sit down Young Michael, you fucking nonce. Tell us Young Michael, what really happened all those years ago? What's the real story?

Fuck.

The police car pulled up beside the other motors and

the officer climbed out, putting on his hat. He joined the scrum of people over by the cabins.

'Come with me,' I said, walking backwards, towards the trees. 'Come on.'

Well, well, well. If it isn't Michael Buchanan. The Buchanan Beast. Why don't you get into the car Mr Buchanan? We want to speak to you. Find out your side of the story.

Mikey followed me, hunched himself over slightly.

'Come on,' I said, reaching the tree line and slipping between two trunks. 'Keep going.'

He did as he was told, ducking into the woods after me, where we kneeled down and watched as the action played out at the far side of the field. The figures were moving against each other, possibly squaring up, possibly pushing, it was hard to say. I saw one of them leave the group and move towards us. I saw them scan the field and then call back to the rest.

A muscle moved in my eyelid.

'Get up,' I hissed, pulling Mikey to his feet with me.

We sprinted through the trees, away from the ditches, tumbling between trunks and branches. Mikey was following close behind me. I looked over my shoulder but already our field was out of sight. We were deep in the woods and running, running, running.

Until.

Until the ground was gone.

I fell forwards, my legs still running and my arms helicoptering. I landed in the soft soil of another field, freshly ploughed. Mikey was in the dirt beside me. The woods behind had come to an abrupt stop, the trees giving way to a sudden steep slope. We got ourselves up and kept on going. The sun was low over the land we were chasing, the field was golden and the sky was cream. We ran and ran and when we reached the far end we met a dry stone wall. I leaned against it, coughing from the exertion.

'What happened there?' said Mikey.

'Didn't you see?'

'See what?'

'They called the fucken police Mikey.'

'Did they?'

'Aye. Did you not see the police motor?'

'I didn't notice. I just saw Mr Raymond and that.'

'Well they were there. I'm sure they were there.'

We jumped the wall and sat down on the dirt behind, leaning against it. Even if they had followed us through the woods and into the field, they wouldn't be able to see us here. We were facing into the sun as it bloated and bled down near the horizon, spilling out over the new, identical field we'd come to.

'Were they there...' began Mikey, stopping and rubbing his legs. 'Were they there for me?'

'Probably. That Sam or that Duncan probably worked it all out and made the call. That'll be why Mr Raymond showed up. He wouldn't want one of your lot associated with his firm.'

Mikey nodded, swallowing the lie. 'OK,' he said.

After a short rest we set off again, following my vague memory of the way home. I knew that the road was somewhere far on our right and that if we kept going we would meet the long loch and once we were there we could risk walking the road back to the house. We kept running. We jumped dikes and hedges and we kept running. My lungs ached and my spit burned metallic.

The running made me remember the afternoon all those years ago. Me fifteen, Mikey thirteen. We were meant to be at school. We were ticking it. Went in for registration and first period and had arranged to slip out between first and second, meet under the railway bridge. No firm plans. We killed time hanging around beneath the bridge, having a fag, throwing rocks against bottles. Then Mr Pin, the jannie, showed up and found us. That was why we were running, why I remembered then.

It was Mikey who gave up first. He came to a gradual stop as we were crossing a field of fiery yellow rape. He leaned forward, pressing his hands against his thighs, shaking his head. 'Can't,' he said.

I walked back towards him. 'It's not much further,' I said. 'If I can manage it so can you.'

He shook his head again. 'It's my legs,' he said.

'What about your legs?'

'They're fucken agony,' he told me, pointing at his gusset, still breathing deep from the run.

'Show me.'

'I'm not going to show you that.'

'Show me,' I said, 'or else how can I help?'

He faced the sky and sighed and proceeded to unzip and pull down his jeans. His thighs were a mess. The area where they met was rubbed lobster raw, tiny droplets of blood poking through where the skin had broken.

'Jesus,' I said. 'Why'd you keep going if it was so bad?'

He shrugged, wincing from the pain. 'Don't know.'

I looked around the field of rippling yellow flowers. I was fucked if I knew how to treat chafed thighs. 'Take your jeans off,' I said. 'Just keep going.'

'Just run through the field in my pants and boots?'

'What else?' I said.

Mikey swore at the top of his lungs and threw himself back into the crop behind him. He pulled his boots off and slid the jeans down his legs. He forced his feet into the still-tied boots and stood up. His pants were white.

'Let's go,' I said.

'Honestly Paul,' said Mikey, testing his legs. 'I can't. It's too sore.'

'Yes you can,' I told him and I gripped his arm tight and pulled him along.

The land we were running across began to change. It sloped upwards beneath our pounding feet and the neat, well-tended fields gave way to harsher terrain. The ploughed earth and tall crops turned to rocky bluffs and heathery embankment. We were coming up into the hills and mountains and the long loch couldn't be far off.

Mikey was struggling. He was running ahead of me and I could see tiny trickles of blood wiped back and forth between his scissoring legs. The crest of a large mound rose above us and we jogged to the summit and looked over.

The land released itself beneath us and there was the loch, snaking along beside the road. The sun was lower still and richer bluer clouds were moving in. Wrinkles of dark reflection interrupted the swathes of orangeness that were the loch's surface.

'Here you are,' I said. 'Not long now.'

We trundled down the hill and followed the natural pathways of grit that wormed through the heather and the gorse. We crossed the tiny burn that fed the loch at its tip and worked our way along the beach with the road coming ever closer on our right.

'I need to stop,' said Mikey. 'I'm needing a break.'

'Fine,' I said, watching the sky, thinking that we had some time.

He sat himself down on a big white boulder with his legs akimbo, fanning air onto his swollen thighs.

There were rowan trees hanging over the loch from the embankment behind him. I stood on the beach, facing out. The water made sound. A constant swelling and gargling and birdsong from somewhere. Layers of chittering and tiny fast wheezes. I remembered about the eel, out there somewhere. It was a nice thought.

'Right,' I said, after I felt he'd rested enough. 'How're you doing?'

He stood up and attempted to walk, screwing up his face. 'It's bad Paul. It stings.'

I checked the sky. Still some time left. 'Why not get into the water for a bit? Maybe that'll cool them down. Or something.'

Before I could stop him or tell him to take his boots off he'd lunged across the beach and was splashing into the loch. He sent out massive ripples of sunset as he went. When he was up to his waist he turned back.

'Good?'

He nodded. 'Aye. Much better.'

I took his place on the boulder and thought about our plans. We'd have to collect the man's car from town – it was still parked outside the pub from the other night. And what then? We wouldn't be able to stick around. Duncan would put two and two together and come looking for us. Might even do a bit of research for himself – that was the last thing I needed. We'd have to hit the road again, find a new place to hide out. Maybe head further north, someplace really remote. Maybe even the islands they had up there, islands with strange short names.

I watched Mikey move around in the water. Already his jacket was sodden, a dark line of moisture rising to his oxters. He seemed happy though, glad to have his thighs soothed.

'Had enough yet?' I shouted.

'Just a wee minute more,' he shouted back. 'Here Paul, there's a load of fish in here.'

103

'Aye?'

'Aye. We should come fishing or something. Save some money.'

'Maybe.'

A light breeze rustled the rowan tree and shook one of the branches over the water. When I looked closely I could see minnows and their shadows darting in the loch's shallows, coming up to worry the fallen leaves. A car passed along the road behind me.

I was thinking about that afternoon. About running away from Mr Pin. He'd shouted after us by name, so we knew we were caught. Might as well take the whole day off. Be as well getting hung for a sheep as a lamb. We'd run from the jannie until we were in the huge park a mile or so from the school. I remembered it was a good park. A big duck pond in the middle you could take pedalos onto in the summer, a community centre and a swing park too. That was the first thing we'd done, was have a shot on the swings. It was full of bairns but we pushed our way onto the swings and swung them too hard so that the mums came over and told us to piss off.

I hadn't liked that, the mums telling us off.

'Paul,' said Mikey. He was coming out of the loch and I could see his legs, pink with watery blood. He was nodding to the road.

I twisted around on my boulder to see Duncan's van pull into the passing place beside us. Mikey was smiling up at him and waving. Launching myself up from my seat, I crossed the beach and plunged into the water myself. I waded towards Mikey and held him by the arms.

'He's coming for you,' I told him.

'He's not,' he said. 'He's just driving home.'

'You saw them all up at the field. You saw that, didn't

104

you? The Toad, the police car? Duncan knows about you.'

I could hear the van's door opening and closing behind me. Mikey's eyes were moving between me and Duncan.

'Do you understand?' I said. 'He knows. They all know. They all know what you did and they fucken hate you for it.'

Mikey shook his head. He rubbed at his nose.

'Hey,' shouted Duncan.

I ignored him.

'Tell him there's something wrong with your legs,' I said. 'Ask him to help.'

Mikey looked at the sky.

I got so close to him I could smell the sweat on his face. 'They fucken hate you Mikey. Do you understand? They want to take you away and put you inside and this time you'll be away for even longer. Do you understand?'

He said something so quiet I couldn't hear.

'What?' I hissed.

'I didn't even do anything,' he whispered.

'Aye,' I said. 'Aye you fucken did.'

Duncan was at the shore, twenty feet away. 'What's going on lads? Did you see what happened up at the site? The Toad called the cops! Can you believe that?'

'Mikey's hurt,' I shouted. 'I think something bit him.'

'Bit him?' shouted Duncan. 'Seriously?'

'Aye, I think so,' I said. 'See the blood? Can you give us a hand, mate?'

'Jesus. I mean, aye, of course.' He began to wade into the water, coming towards us.

'All right?' I whispered to Mikey.

'All right,' he said.

Duncan was near. 'Ach,' he said. 'That's not too bad. Looks like you've scraped them or something.'

105

'Come and give us a hand to get him back in,' I said.

He came towards us and looked at us both and put his hands on Mikey, smiling.

Mikey reached over and got him by the head and neck and I pulled his legs out from beneath him and we held his body and pushed and carried him out into the deeper water. He was thrashing and spluttering and saying, 'What? You fucken...'

We held onto the body and helped it down into the loch, the dark green loch. We held onto the neck and head and arms and made it be under the water. The body's fingertips broke the surface and I could feel the kicking legs disturb the water on my shin hairs. The body looked surprised. Its eyes were open and full of whites and the mouth was moaning, bubbles of air breaking free like floating pearls.

We held the body until the water held it by itself.

Out in the middle of the loch the king eel awoke. It opened its eyes and uncoiled.

7

We drove home in our wet clothes. Mikey had lost his jeans in the confusion of getting back to the van and getting away, so he sat beside me in the front, slumped right down in his seat, legs bare and knocking. Already it was dusk. Duncan had made the van look like an easy drive but it wasn't. I struggled to move it around even the shallowest bend in the road.

I was on fire though. Nervous energy powered me and it felt superb. I chewed, despite having nothing in my mouth. I played high-tempo beats on the dashboard with my fingertips. I drove into the oncoming dimness and all I knew was the magic of possibility. The only thing spoiling the mood was my brother.

'I know what you're thinking,' I said, fiddling with the van's controls to make the lights come on.

'Aye?'

'Aye, I do. You're thinking about what just happened. You're sulking about it.'

I was focused on the road, but I could tell he was scowling.

'I've said it before pal but it was a matter of survival. That fucker knew. He worked it out. Maybe he didn't work it out himself, maybe his bitch pal told him, but he knew. Why else would he be coming looking for us like that? It was self-defence.'

'Hm.'

'And now look at us! We've got freedom. We can go wherever we like. Anywhere. Find a new place every single fucken day if we feel like it.'

'What about the house?'

'The house is a goner. We head back and sort some stuff out and then we fuck off. They knew we stayed there, that Fia dropped us off remember? They'll come looking for us there next.'

I looked away from the road for a moment. Mikey was staring at me and he wasn't sulking anymore. He was thinking.

'It's really the best possible outcome as far as me and you are concerned,' I added.

'But what about going home? What about Mum?'

'Listen pal. That's our primary aim. That's aim numero uno. And believe me, I'm monitoring the situation. That's at the – what's it? – at the forefront of my mind. I'm monitoring it constantly. But until then,' I said, sweeping a hand over the dashboard, 'absolute freedom.'

We crested a hump in the road and the wee house was below us, glowing in the dark valley.

'All right,' said Mikey. 'If you say so.'

I smiled. 'That's a boy.'

We'd done our best to push Duncan out into the water. He'd floated though, so I'd scooped up some of the larger rocks from the loch's floor and stuffed them into his pockets and down his jeans. It wasn't ideal. The nice thing about having the man buried out the back was that you knew where he was. You could even go out and visit him, if you wanted to. I was concerned about Duncan washing up on shore in the future, but we'd be long gone by then.

I sent Mikey into the house, telling him to pack us some clothes and whatever food was left in the fridge. Once he was inside I checked the glove box. The cash was there. I thanked my lucky stars and did a hasty count. There was more than I had thought. A fair bit more.

I crossed the road and leaped into the fields. I paced through the darkness in the direction of our old camp. A foul reek escaped from the inside of the tent as I opened it. All of our dirty clothes, stewing in the sun for days. I thought about the best way to get what I needed back down. 'Fuck it,' I said, and set to work pulling the poles out. I threw them away and gathered the tent up by its door, slinging it over my back like a sack.

I came down the hill towards the house, checking up and down the road for anyone coming. We were safe. I threw the tent-sack into the back of the van and then went to find Mikey.

For some reason the television was on. It was the only source of light in the whole place. He wasn't in the kitchen, so I ascended the Ramsay ladder. No sign of him up there either. An open suitcase on the bed though.

I tracked him down in the garden. He was sat on the slabs with the dog between his legs. It was burrowing into his oxters and elbows and opening its mouth to beg for affection.

'What are you doing?'

'Saying hello to Doris.'

'You think you have time for that?'

'It'll just take a minute.'

I stood in the doorway and watched him, sitting like a teddy bear, holding the dog by the snout and running his hands along her twisting spine. She was enjoying it, even I could see that. She took a look at me. I looked into her eyes and all I could see was black, wet circles.

'Right,' I said, coming down the step and across the slabs. 'That's enough. Put it in the run.'

Mikey looked up at me. 'Aren't we taking her?'

'Eh? No, we're not *taking* it. We're not carting around a fucken mutt. That's the last thing we need.'

'Well we can't just leave her. She'll starve.'

'Stick the dog food in with it. That'll keep it going till someone comes.'

'What if no one comes? What if she starves?'

I growled in frustration. Every time I worked things out for us this idiot would put obstacles in my way. He didn't appreciate the work that went into looking after him and his daft head.

'Put it in the run,' I said.

'No.'

I asked again and he didn't respond, so I crossed the slabs and ripped the dog from Mikey's grasping hands, jerking it up by the collar. Holding it aloft, I marched across the garden to the back fence. The dog's tongue was extended, its eyes were rolling. Mikey shouted. I held it up by the collar and its body dangled and swung. Its front legs were going up and down, as if it was climbing an invisible ladder or grovelling for scraps.

'See what happens?' I said to the dog.

'Let her go,' shouted Mikey.

I launched it over the fence into the wild. It hit the earth with a sharp yelp and rolled to its feet. It looked back at us. Mikey was at the fence by then, holding onto the wood.

'Fuck off,' I shouted, making a cone of my hands. 'Get lost.'

The dog yelped again, thumping its front paws on the grass. Please, it was saying.

'Get away Doris,' said Mikey, reluctantly.

He pointed out into the wilderness, into the mountains. The dog put its ears back and cocked its head. I kicked the fence as hard as I could and the impact reverberated along it, twanging and shuddering. The dog took off into the night, its black and white coat flickering like a cartoon as it merged into the dark, bit by bit. I saw it plunge into the mazeish network of burrows that covered the land.

'There,' I said. 'That's another thing off our minds. Let's get a move on.'

Mikey climbed up onto the fence and bellowed across the great expanse between the house and the mountain, 'Goodbye Doris!'

We went inside and locked the back door for a final time. I stuffed as much of the man's clothes as I could into the suitcase and Mikey swept everything the fridge and freezer held into black bin bags. It all went into the back of the camper with our balled up tent.

'Right,' I said. 'That's us then.'

Mikey leant against the van's side. 'Are we off?'

I nodded and then looked back at the house. I thought about the nights we'd spent there. I imagined the place swarming with our germs, surfaces thick and clotted with our hairs and smudgy fingerprints. I thought about my DNA clogging up the drainpipe.

'Give me a second,' I said.

I jogged up the path and back into the wee house. I found the turps in the cupboard beneath the kitchen sink. Room by room I squirted the bottle over everything. It stank. A foul oily odour. At the front door I made a ball of cigarette papers and used my lighter on it, throwing it onto the hall carpet once it was alight. A sheet of fire sprung up, covering the floor and descending into the kitchen and through into the living room. I closed the front door and ran to the van.

Mikey was waiting for me in the front. We sat and watched as the house caught, a crazy orangey brightness

111

ascending through the windows. Cruel chemical smoke came billowing from the chimney and the doors and we took that as our cue to leave. I started the van's engine and pulled it out into the road.

We left the dying house behind and drove down into the village. We passed the pub and the butcher shop. I thought about putting the butcher's windows in but I didn't have anything heavy to hand. We passed them by.

You escaped by my good grace, I told the butcher. The only thing that saved you was my benevolence.

I saw him in my mind, prostrate before me.

Once we were free of the village limits I glanced at Mikey.

'Where to then?' I asked.

'Where is there?' he said.

I thought about it. Where could we go? There was a whole country at our fingertips – the cities, the highlands too. We could drive to the far north, see the wild tropical looking beaches they had there. We could drive to one of the towns and spend a bit of Duncan's cash. We could take the tiny capillary roads up into the raw mountains, I guessed about a hundred miles north of us. See the true heartless centre of the country.

'All sorts,' I said. 'What kind of thing do you fancy?'

'Maybe someplace fun?' he ventured. 'Have a bit of a laugh?'

I nodded. 'Hm. Maybe.'

I checked the clock on the dashboard. One in the morning. One in the morning and I wasn't a bit tired. Even after the running through fields all evening, even after struggling with Duncan in the water. I felt satisfied, full, like I'd just finished a rich, nourishing meal that my body was using to produce good, clean energy.

Mikey was less sprightly. His eyelids were heavy and

shiny and his head was nodding. Eventually he gave up and slept where he sat, leaning forward, suspended by his seat belt. The van's movement rocked him left and right.

'Lazy bastard,' I muttered, with no contempt.

We drove through a series of villages, all of them similar to the first one. The same cobblestoned squares, the same pubs, the same shops. At perhaps the third or fourth I parked up, spying a phone box across the road. I darted across that village's central square, past the dry copper fountain that was the centrepiece.

I fed the phone the rest of the change from my pocket and dialled. The lower windows of the phone box were warped and toffee-coloured from historic arson attempts. A low buzzing was coming from the light above me. The phone took a long time to be answered.

'Hello?' she said.

I gripped the receiver. 'It's me.'

'Paul,' she whispered. 'It's Mum.' Her voice was rich and heavy, full of sleep and yawns. Even those three words put an ache in my head.

'I know,' I said.

'Are you coming back yet son?'

'No.'

She sighed. 'Why are you doing this to me?'

'I'm saving this family,' I told her. 'It'll all be over soon.'

'Is there anything I can tell you to make you change your mind?'

I shook my head, closing my eyes. 'It's not about my mind,' I hissed. 'It's about Mikey.'

With my eyes closed I could see her, sitting on the arm of the sofa in her dressing gown, her fist opening and closing on her thigh. I saw her hand, loose-skinned and veiny.

'Why are you phoning?' she asked.

113

'I wanted to tell you we're moving on. You won't find us in the old place.'

'But I didn't know where you were before.'

I thought about it. She was right. 'Well,' I said. 'Never mind that then.'

I went to replace the receiver but she began to protest. Bringing it back to my ear, I heard her say, 'Wait. Wait.'

'What?'

'When are you going to phone next?' she said.

I looked around. 'Hard to say.'

'If you wanted, I could arrange to have someone here when you call back. A professional you can speak to?'

'A professional?'

'If you want.'

I replaced the receiver and stormed from the box. I slammed the van's door shut behind me. A professional! Here I was, in a car with one of the most infamous child killers in the country and my own mother was wanting to get *me* a professional. Meaning a shrink, a quack, a fucken brain doctor. They'd want to make me remember all the things I could from being a bairn and tell them about it.

And how did you feel, Paul, they'd say, when you fell off the climbing frame at nursery school and got concussed so bad you were off school for weeks? How did that make you feel Paul, that brain fucken injury? Were you pleased or annoyed about how your blood started kicking in so that you couldn't control yourself? That when Scott Soutar told you your brother was a mungo it made you hold onto Scott Soutar's hair and make his face smash against the tarmac again and again?

I tried to close my eyes, as I sat in the front of the van. Tried to relax and calm myself down, get the blood

114

flowing normal again. It felt as if I was in a rollercoaster, creeping upwards towards the apex, the excitement and the dread churning my stomach. Breathed deep through my nose. I said, 'Ah,' out loud.

Mikey woke up with a sniff. 'Where are we?'

I said, 'Nowhere.'

'How come we've stopped?'

'I needed a rest.'

'Right.'

Mikey asked for permission and then slid down an alleyway for a piss. I was calm by the time he came back. We looked at each other and nodded with grim smiles.

'So,' he said.

'Aye,' I said.

We drove on.

We kept going out of the village and the lightless country swallowed us up.

The ghost rattled on the window and Mikey snored. Through bleary, sleep-thick eyes I saw it press its pale features against the glass, its palms too, with fingers splayed. I was dreaming. I was dreaming of a ghost. More amused than scared I watched it move between the van's small windows, gawking into each one and running its knuckles down the pane.

I snorted and shook my head. The ghost noticed the movement and scuttled around to the window nearest me. It was waggling its ghost head and drumming those knuckles and I sat up on the sofa bed, my elbows behind me. It wasn't a ghost. It was a man with a mop of white blonde hair and the palest skin I'd ever seen.

'Christ,' I said, hauling myself up.

The man slapped on the glass, excited, nodding. I did my best to stand up in the van's back. The man made a let-me-in gesture with his hand.

I shook my head.

He nodded his.

'Piss off,' I muttered, squeezing through and parking myself in the driver's seat. I watched as the pale man hurried round to the front of the van. See how you like this, I thought, starting the engine as he planted his hands on the van's bonnet. The whole vehicle rattled from the effort the engine made and the pale man laughed, a wet smile breaking his stubbled face. He was enjoying this.

I leaned forward and mouthed for him to fuck off and he laughed again, shaking his head. The night before we'd parked against a wall down a country lane. Trees hung over the top of us and I had nowhere to go.

You couldn't run a man down like that in cold blood. It wouldn't be right.

I tried honking the horn to scare him off and Mikey shouted. I heard him say 'Eh?' from behind me.

'Look at this clown,' I said, feeling him stumble across towards me.

'Who's that?'

'Fucked if I know.'

The pale man was waving at Mikey, his other hand firm on the van's bonnet.

'What does he want?' Mikey asked.

'He wants in.'

Mikey reached over my shoulder and chapped on the driver's window, motioning for the man to come round. I cracked the window an inch. The pale man worked his way around the corner of the van, keeping his palms against the bonnet and then door. He pressed his mouth against the opening.

'All right?' he said.

'All right?' said Mikey.

'What do you want?' I asked.

He had his lips inside the van. His pupils were flying between me and Mikey and his wild grin was still wide. 'Where yous going?'

'Never you mind,' I said. 'What d'you want?'

'I'm looking for a lift.'

I shook my head. 'Nah. It's not happening mate.'

He held up a finger but kept his mouth close to the opening. 'Ah ah ah,' he said. 'I can pay. I can pay for the lift.'

'We're not interested.'

I released the handbrake and let the van roll forward down the embankment.

'Woah, woah, woah,' he said, rushing around to the front again so that I had to brake. He pushed against the bonnet, laughing and shaking his head. 'What's it going to take lads? You wouldn't leave a fellow pilgrim out in the sticks, would you?'

We looked at each other, Mikey and I. I sighed. 'Get in then,' I said and Mikey ducked into the back to unlock the door.

The pale man whooped and jumped and sprang to the side door, rubbing his hands. He pulled himself up into the back of the van and vigorously shook both our hands.

'You've no idea how much this means to a weary traveller,' he said. 'An absolute belter of a favour lads.'

He gave his name as Isaac and proceeded to collapse onto our recently vacated sofa bed. After a minute I realised he was asleep, lying on his front, his face bundled up in our sleeping bags.

'I don't understand,' said Mikey. 'He's just gone to our bed. Is he allowed to do that?'

'I suppose he must be,' I said.

Mikey came up front to sit with me, scandalised by

117

the man's rudeness. I'd given him a fresh hair and beard trim after we'd pulled up the night before, even shorter than the first time. As I looked at him I realised I'd gone a bit too bald in places – the bony bits of his skull and jaw where the skin shone through. The pale man garbled in his sleep and I revved the engine.

We drove on.

It was a bright morning but I had something like a hangover from the excitement of the evening before. My head was slow and my vision was slow. Still, I drove down the country lane and back onto the road with no trouble.

'I'm starving,' said Mikey. 'I could eat two horses.'

'I am too actually. Let's find someplace for breakfast.'

Mikey eyed Duncan's envelope. 'Do you think we could go for fry ups?'

I nodded. 'Aye, why not?'

He pumped his fists and flipped on his sunglasses. We played the only tape Duncan had, which was an old American singing low and sad. He sang to us and I drove into the morning sun and the nutter in the back muttered.

We found a gigantic Tesco at the edge of someplace that had a banner saying HOT FOOD SEVEN TO SEVEN. I parked and shook Isaac awake. His lids shot open, revealing his eyes, as light and as blue as glaciers.

He scrambled for the sleeping bag, pulling it to his breast. 'What the fuck's going on?' he shouted, his pupils swivelling.

'Here,' I said. 'Calm yourself down. You asked us for a lift, remember? You crashed out on our sofa bed.'

He sat up and looked about himself. 'Aye,' he said. 'Course I did. Aye.'

'We're going for breakfast. You wanting to come?'

'Breakfast? Oh, aye. Breakfast. Aye, please.'

They worked out the price of your Tesco breakfast by how many breakfast items you ordered. All three of us choose as many items as you were allowed. We found ourselves a table and Mikey brought over the cutlery, napkins and sauce sachets. The breakfasts steamed.

Isaac attacked his plate. 'So,' he said, chewing a rasher. 'What's your guys' story then?'

'What's *our* story?' I said. 'What's *your* story?'

Isaac chortled. 'It's a fucken epic not a story mate,' he said, waggling his knife as me. 'It involves intrigue.'

'Is that right?'

'It is right. I just realised, I don't know your names.'

We gave our names and he nodded. 'Fine names. Michael and Paul. Good Bible names there. Have you had your conversion yet Paul?'

'What d'you mean?'

'Your own personal road to Damascus moment?'

'I don't know what you're on about.'

'Never mind,' he said, scooping up half a fried egg with his fork. It bled a string of daisy yolk. 'You're brothers.'

'No,' I said. 'Just mates.'

'You are brothers, I can tell. There's a strong family resemblance. Although it would be stronger if you,' he said, pointing the knife at Mikey, 'had your hair long, like his. Or vice versa.'

'I used to have it longer,' said Mikey.

'Oh aye?'

'I cut it off though.'

'I can see that,' nodded Isaac. 'Look at mine. See that? See how bright that is?'

'Aye,' I said, sawing a sausage. 'That's bleached isn't it?'

Isaac shook his head and smiled as he shovelled beans

119

around his plate. 'Oh ho ho,' he said. 'A very reasonable mistake to make, Saint Paul. Very understandable.' He leant over his breakfast, displaying his crown, his manic grin returning. 'All natural that.'

He was bullshitting. His hair was dyed. It was dried out at the ends, white as snow, and darker and greasy at the roots. I'd seen a hundred lassies with hair just like it.

'Au natural,' he said, smirking, desperate for us to ask more.

'It doesn't look natural,' said Mikey, who'd already finished his massive plate of food. 'It looks like you've dyed it.'

Isaac laughed. 'See, it wasn't always this colour. Not when I was a bairn. Oh no. Brown or something back then.'

'What happened?' Mikey asked.

'I'll tell you later,' he said. 'It's a good one. But no. I asked, didn't I? What your guys' story was?'

I scraped up the scraps on my plate. 'We're just on holiday. Just enjoying ourselves.'

He ignored me and leant towards Mikey instead. 'Did we go to the school together? I'm sure I know you. Absolutely positive.'

'Nah,' said Mikey. 'I think I'd remember.'

'Where do I know your face from then?'

'He's just got one of those faces,' I said, bristling. 'One of those familiar faces.'

Isaac collected in the plates and stacked them up, ignoring me. 'Would anyone else like a pastry? My treat.'

When Isaac's back was turned I leaned into Mikey. 'After breakfast we need to lose him. We'll distract him in the shop and once he's lost we'll drive off.'

Mikey nodded. 'He's weird, eh? What's wrong with him?'

120

'One of them religious folk,' I said. 'Too many pills as well by the look of him.'

Isaac slid a plateful of dry croissants and Danishes in front of us.

'There we are,' he said. 'Something a wee bit more cultured for pudding.'

'Cheers,' we said, diving in. He was maybe mental but you don't say no to a free pastry. We ate those in silence, enjoying the luxury of it.

I brushed the stray flakes from my beard. 'Well,' I said. 'That was good.'

'Wasn't it just?' said Isaac. 'Shall we get a move on then?'

'Aye,' I said. 'Where is it you're needing a lift to anyway?'

'Just as far as you're going. Any direction.'

'All right.' I brought the van keys out my pocket and bounced them off my palm. 'Let's go.'

We wandered back through the Tesco, dodging trolleys and squeezing by packs of manky bairns. I asked Isaac if he wouldn't mind picking up a couple of cans of juice for the journey. He nodded and said it would be his pleasure. We loitered in the foyer until he was out of sight and then we bolted.

We raced through the car park, towards the van, right at the back. I looked over my shoulder and saw a white haired head through the foyer's glass.

'C'mon,' I said, pulling Mikey along. 'Hurry.'

I tried to start the van but all the engine did was cough. I jerked the key in the ignition again and all I got back was a dull burr.

'Start it,' moaned Mikey. 'Get it going.'

'I'm trying, amen't I?'

A chap on the glass. 'I got us all Tango, that all right?'

121

asked Isaac, holding up three cans. His face fell when he heard the engine's dry wheeze. 'That doesn't sound good,' he shouted through the glass. 'Open her up, let me have a look.'

I pulled the handle by my knee and released the van's bonnet.

'What's he doing?' I asked Mikey as I tried to peer round the upturned bonnet. 'Can you see?'

'Nope. Well, not properly. He's fiddling with something in the engine.'

'Do you think… do you reckon it was him that broke it?' I whispered.

'Nah,' breathed Mikey. 'Couldn't be. Didn't have the time.'

'I suppose.'

The bonnet slammed down and Isaac dusted off his oily fingers. 'Try it now,' he said and I turned the key. The engine choked into life.

'It's working,' I admitted.

We set off, each of us sipping from a Tango can. I decided, without telling anyone, that we would make our way to the city. I'd had enough of fields and mountains. I'd had enough of endless sky. You could hide in nature but conversely you could make yourself anonymous in a crowd. I was driving towards the motorway, the same one Duncan drove on the way to the club.

Isaac and Mikey were sat together in the back, enjoying their drinks. We'd be able to lose him soon enough now that the van was running. Maybe stop off at a services and gun it away when he was using the bogs. Maybe even open the sliding door and have Mikey shove him out as we raced along. I didn't want it to come to that but I was prepared for it.

I checked the clock. Still only ten in the morning. The

whole day was ahead of us. What day though? I realised then that I had no idea what the date was. I didn't even know what day of the week we were on. I'd been keeping up by checking the newspaper each morning but it had been a while since I'd bought one. I didn't even know if Mikey was still featured. What did it matter though? The decision of when we went home was my call. It wasn't based solely on the paper. My word was final and I had to listen to my intuition.

I zoned out from my thoughts and let my ear wander around the rattling, shuddering van until it fell upon my brother and our new companion, chatting in the back.

'Aye,' Mikey was saying. 'It was all right. We were digging these like long holes. Like open tunnels.'

'Ditches?' asked Isaac. 'Were you laying pipes or something?'

'I don't think so. We were working with these people. They were... *somethings*. One of them jobs you're not sure if they're real or not.'

'Like a wizard?' said Isaac.

'Aye,' said Mikey, excited. 'Like wizards.'

'You should stay well away from that sort. The Bible says not to go messing about with mediums and necromancers.'

'No,' said Mikey. 'It wasn't anything like that. It was science. Science of the ground.'

'Sounds well dodgy mate. It was a good idea getting shot of that lot, I'd say. All these scientists. It's just theories they come out with. Nothing concrete. Did you know that?'

Mikey said that no, he didn't. Isaac started to drone on about how evolution was only a theory and that there were some scientists, scientists who didn't get the *approval* of the mainstream media, who said that it was

123

very likely that life on earth had been seeded by aliens. That there were various clues, dotted around the globe, that the discerning mind could connect to illuminate a more rewarding theory of how life began.

'And those aliens. Do you know what the Egyptians called the glowing lights in the skies above Cairo?'

'No,' said Mikey.

'Ahmon-Ras. *God flashes*. Can you believe that?'

'No,' said Mikey.

Isaac started laughing then and Mikey asked him what was funny.

'I've just realised,' he said. 'I do recognise you. I fucken knew it.' I heard him clap his hands. 'You're Mikey Buchanan. You're the one that's been all over the news. I said I recognised you. Didn't I? Did I or did I not?'

8

There was a lay-by a few miles up the road. I kept calm and kept driving and trained an eye on the pair of them in the rear view mirror.

'It is you, isn't it?' Isaac was saying. 'Off of the telly?'

'I don't know what you're on about,' Mikey said.

'Aw, come on mate. Just tell me if I'm right or not.'

I pulled into the lay-by and parked the van. Duncan's beads rattled from the force of the manoeuvre. In one fluid swerve I jerked the handbrake up and used it to swivel myself around and into the back of the van.

'Close the curtains,' I told Mikey, nodding to the sleeping area's windows.

Isaac was on the sofa. His eyes followed mine as I moved towards him and grabbed his jacket and moved him over the sofa's back and onto the floor of the kitchenette.

'Christ almighty,' he said as he hit the floor.

I was on top of him. I got his shoulders beneath my knees to control his arms, but he wasn't resisting. His gob was open with wonder and he was gazing at Mikey and me. There was nothing heavy to hand. I leant over and checked in the wee cupboard beneath the sink.

'You're looking after your brother,' said Isaac. 'It's beautiful.'

I put my hand on our gas burner, stuck between a plastic basin and a pack of toilet rolls. Isaac's face

125

changed when he saw me swing the canister up.

'Woah,' he said. 'Hold your horses, hold your horses. You don't need to do this.'

I weighed up the canister in my hand. I could bring the bottom down, hard. 'It doesn't matter,' I told Isaac.

'It *does* matter. It does. You don't have to do this. I'm not going to fucken tell anybody, am I?' Isaac nodded at Mikey, stood behind me. 'He's done his time. He's reborn as far as I'm concerned.'

I held the edge of the canister against Isaac's forehead, causing him to wince. He began to pray, under his breath. It was too fast and too quiet to make it out but as far as I could tell it was gibberish.

The canister pinged as it rolled across the floor of the van and connected with the sink unit. I got myself up and squeezed past Mikey, back into the front.

'You deal with him,' I said, restarting the engine. I let my foot rest against the accelerator for a minute, listening to Mikey heaving Isaac up and onto the sofa bed.

'All set?' I asked, checking them in the mirror.

'Aye,' said Mikey, hopping into the front. 'Let's go.'

'Mind and put your seatbelt on,' I said.

We came to the city deep in the afternoon. The motorway curved around its northwest quarter and it all seemed mechanical to me, having spent so long in the wild. I wasn't used to the stone and the brick and the metal crash barrier. People too. So many people.

Isaac woke up with a sneeze, falling from the sofa bed. He moaned. 'My fucken head!'

'Just be glad you still have it.'

'I'm trying. Christ. Where are we?'

'Glasgow.'

'Since when?'

126

'We just arrived.'

'Sweet fuck. I can't believe you knocked me fucken out. I said I wasn't going to say anything.'

I said, 'Well,' and kept driving. He wasn't a threat, this lunatic, and I had no appetite to clean bloodstains from the van's carpeted floor.

I was looking for a place to stay. We had the van but I didn't fancy the prospect of kipping inside it in the middle of town. That was sure to raise a few eyebrows. I pulled up outside a likely looking establishment called the Groveview.

'You two stay here,' I said. 'I'm going inside for a scope around.'

The hotel was done up like an old wifey's front room. Chintz and doilies covered the reception, which was staffed by a broad woman. She gave me a sickly sweet smile as I entered.

'Welcome to the Groveview,' she simpered. 'Do you have a booking?'

'No,' I said. 'I was wondering if you had any rooms.'

'I'll see,' she said gravely. 'It's a busy weekend.'

She heaved open the massive ledger before her on the desk and began to scan through the miniscule entries with the nib of her biro. I put my palms out on the desk and leaned. There was a ceramic frog playing the banjo an inch from my pinkie nail. I picked it up and inspected it.

Her biro paused. 'Don't touch that,' she told me. 'It's a collectable.'

She went back to scanning the ledger once I'd replaced the frog. I paced around reception, glancing into the lounge. There was no TV, no computer, no sign of the daily papers. These were all goods signs.

'As I was saying,' she told the ledger, 'it's a very busy

weekend. We've got a convention in. Some of our most loyal customers.'

'It's all right,' I told her. 'If you haven't got room then you haven't got room.'

She looked up at me. 'I think we can squeeze you in. How many?'

I told her three and she nodded. 'There's a few beds going in the bunkroom. How does that sound?'

The bunkroom, it turned out, was a series of bunk beds crammed into a garret at the top of the Groveview. The woman on the desk had described it as an economic option, meaning it was for teenagers and backpackers. Mikey, Isaac and I stood in the doorway. Nearly every bed was filled either by a sleeping youth or their rucksack. I found our three empty units and we put a piece of clothing on each one, just in case a Manuel or a Margueritte decided to branch out into our space.

'So,' I said. 'This is us.'

'It's very… eh…' said Isaac.

Mikey loved it. He claimed the top bunk and climbed up. 'Bagsy this,' he said. 'This is mine.'

'That's fine,' I told him. 'Top bunk's the worst.'

'No it's not. Bottom bunk's worst.'

Isaac intervened before things could get too heated and we headed outside. The woman ignored us as we passed through reception. We stood on the pavement with our hands in our pockets. A bus's gears crunched as it sped past and a constant stream of pedestrians waddled by.

'What now?' said Mikey.

'I don't know,' I admitted, then turning to Isaac, I said, 'What about you?'

'What about me?'

'Well,' I said. 'No offence or anything, but we don't know you. What's your plan?'

'I'm heading north, but I'm in no rush.'

'What's going on up north?'

Isaac shook his head. He had a penny sized bruise above his right temple where I'd dinged him with the canister. 'Couldn't be telling you that, Saint Paul. Top secret. Top secret operation.'

'Right,' I said, not wanting to get drawn into his nonsense. 'Let's get some food.'

We caught one of the buses going the other way into town. Mikey and Isaac sat together and I had to park myself beside a smelly man in fluorescent work gear.

'See the thing about this,' said Isaac, nodding to the world lurching by the windows, 'is that it's all an illusion. It's a trick the mind plays on itself. To cope.'

'Aye?' said Mikey, checking the sandstone tenements and flat roofed pubs.

'Aye. It's been researched. The mind can't cope with how fucken...' Isaac shook his hands by his temples, 'with how fucken weird the world is. So we see a *version* of reality. Like this, for example.' He held the front of his jacket closed over his shirt. 'What colour's my top?'

Mikey shook his head. 'Can't remember.'

'See?' He opened his jacket up again. 'It was white. But you didn't know that because your brain hid it from you. It's all a fucken mirage.'

I watched as Mikey pulled his own T-shirt out from his stomach. He looked down at it and nodded. I was sure he was telling himself the colour in his head, in case he forgot.

'I found that out the hard way,' said Isaac.

I leaned forward, onto the backs of their seats. 'Found out what?'

'About it all being an illusion. That's what turned my

hair white. When I found out it was such a shock that it went white and never turned back.'

'What happened like?'

'So, it must have been… I want to say five or six years ago. I was in a bad place. A bad old place. I was very, very alone. Lived alone, slept alone, so on. I was doing a lot of late night reading.'

'Right.'

'I was staying, for some reason, up in Dundee. In this horrible place… I don't even want to describe. But I got a call from my cousin. My cousin's a good person. You two'd like him. A very gentle person. He says to me, he says, Grant, there's a party this weekend. You need to come to this party.'

Mikey's head flicked round. 'Grant?'

'Aw. Aye. Grant's my real name like. My civilian title. Anyway, my cousin comes and picks me up and we drive down. Only thing is, is this is no normal party. It's one of those whole weekend things in a field. Big fucken generator slap bang in the middle of it all. Girls man. Girls all over the shop. And all the way down I've had this worm in my ear. This little worm talking to me. Telling me I'm this, that, and the next thing. Saying, Aw Grant, aw Isaac, you're no good. You're a piece of shit, no one's going to want to talk to you. That sort of stuff…'

He trailed off and scratched at the skin behind his earlobe and I sneered at the back of his head. This nonsense, I thought. This bullshit.

'Mate,' he said. 'That worm. I had that worm for a long time. A good long time. But as soon as I got myself in amongst that party, it was gone. Gone for good it turned out. I had what you'd call a dead good time that weekend, I'm sure. I woke up in the mud, Monday morning. My cousin was gone and I felt like a railway had been like installed over the top of me. I reached out, through the filth, and my hand touched upon this.'

He reached down and fiddled inside his boot. He pulled out a torn pamphlet. On the front I could make out the words 'Let HIM understand you.'

Isaac slapped the front of the pamphlet. 'The Church of the Real Presence of the Divine Christ. That was how I found them. A fucken book, buried in the dirt at a rave. Tell me, Mikey. What're the chances of that?'

Mikey shrugged.

'I'll tell you what the chances are. They're so low as to be impossible. Something that I very firmly believe is the concept that there are absolutely no coincidences in this life. Something meant for me to be there, to reach my hand out and grasp this fucken book.'

He twisted in his seat and held the pamphlet over his shoulder to give me a look. Beneath the dry crust of muck on the front cover was a Chicano gentleman holding a bowl of bananas.

'I've been a fully paid up member ever since. Never been so happy. Never been so whole.'

Mike and I sat in silence, digesting the story.

'Wait,' said Mikey. 'What about the hair thing then?'

Isaac laughed. 'Oh aye. The hair thing. Well, I managed to cadge a lift back up the road with some truckers and they were giving me funny looks the whole way. When I got back home I was supremely surprised to check myself out in the mirror and see this,' he held out a strand of his hair, 'staring back at me.'

'So is that where you're off to?' I asked. 'That church? The real thingy of the special Christ?'

'The Real Presence of the Divine Christ,' corrected Isaac. He thought about my question. 'Sort of,' he said.

The bus dropped us off in town and we found ourselves

a pub that did food. A table near the back with no one around. We put in our orders for burgers and pints up at the bar and settled down to wait.

'Never mind about me,' said Isaac, leaning into the table, checking for eavesdroppers. 'What about this one,' he nodded at Mikey. 'What's your story then pal?'

Mikey took his pint away from his mouth. 'What story?'

'All the intrigue, all the drama. You got the fucken *jail* man.'

I put my hand down on the table. 'I don't know if this is a good thing to talk about.'

'It's fine,' said Isaac. 'There's nobody about. Let him talk.'

Mikey shrugged. 'It was all right.'

'No,' laughed Isaac. 'Come on. This is a safe place, me and your brother. You can talk about it. In the eyes of the Christ you're forgiven.'

Mikey moved his pint around in a circle, cycloning the liquid. 'I mean, it was boring, aye. Really boring. You could go to the gym or do some work, do some cleaning and maintenance and that.'

'Right.'

'But everyone there was…'

'What?'

'They were so horrible man. Just, like, so fucken rude and nasty. You'd go to the gym and try and have a go on the machines and then someone would come along and make you get off them cause they wanted a shot. So you'd just go back to the cell and then you'd have to sit with Ricky.'

I frowned. I'd never heard that name before. 'Who's Ricky?'

'He was the guy in my cell for most of the time. He

never told me what he did. I didn't say to him about mine either, but he knew. Everyone knew. Fuck...' he said, breaking off and holding his fingertips against his eyes.

'Here,' said Isaac, but then the barman was bringing the food over, so we all stopped talking and sat their quietly as the burgers were distributed. On our best behaviour for the barman.

We ate our meals and drank our pints and went looking for another pub. There was a lot of wanky-looking places in that bit of town. A load of guys with their hair shaved funny at the sides, hanging round outside having their fags. I rolled myself one and we went past those places and found somewhere more suitable. I let them head inside to get the round and I stood by the door to finish my fag.

I would need to watch that Isaac character. He was too mad to be a threat to us, but I didn't like the way he made Mikey talk. That sort of thing could be dangerous. Luckily if he ever did mention it to anyone there was no chance they'd believe him. Plus, there was something amusing about his deranged stories. It made me feel good to listen to them and notice all the lies and misunderstandings.

I remembered the day Mikey came back, on the bus in the afternoon. I stood at my bedroom window and watched him come up the path, carrying everything he had in one clear plastic bag. Our mother was pleased to see him and I suppose I was too. He came inside and I went down to say hello. I'd been along the road to visit him over the years. I'd seen him age in fits and bursts.

He was quiet. He stood in the kitchen, leaning on the counter, as our mother made cups of tea and he looked at something on the floor.

'How's it going?' I'd asked.

'All right,' he told the something on the floor.

This pack of social workers and police had come round within a week. Three of them in total. They wanted to speak to Mikey alone. I stood behind the living room door, listening. They were telling about all the expectations society had of him now he was on parole. All the things he couldn't do, like leave the country or even spend a night away from home. He'd be able to do those things in future if he proved to them he could be trusted. They wanted him to speak to *someone*, because they'd heard from his social worker in the jail how beneficial it had been for him.

What did he think of that?

He thought it might be all right.

Just before the end they'd asked him whether or not he was concerned about whether or not anything in his home environment would put him at risk of reoffending. He'd been quiet for a long time. Someone had gone, 'Well? Is there? You need to tell us if there is, Michael.'

I had my ear pressed tight against the wood, seething, fuming alone in the hallway. We'd already had to move house in anticipation of him coming out. The social workers had visited us and explained that we were too close to a school or a park or something. What else did he want? What else did the little shit fucken expect?

'No,' he'd said. 'It'll be fine. I'll try my best.'

'That's a good attitude,' one of the others had said. 'Good for you, Michael.'

They'd come every week and demand the living room. Our mother usually went out but I'd pretend to head up to my bedroom. I'd always sneak downstairs and listen in. They were sorting him out an ongoing appointment with a local shrink. Someone the wee lamb could talk to, discuss his offending in a safe place.

It wasn't long after that the press showed up in the

street. I had to take things into my own hands. There was no other option, as far as I could see.

I ground my fag against the wall of the pub and went inside to find Mikey and Isaac.

We drank into the night and once the pubs were closed we began the long walk back along Sauchiehall Street to the hotel. Isaac was mad with the drink. He was stumbling and whirling about, falling into the gutter. Mikey and I had to carry him between us. When we got to the Groveview I made him stand up by himself.

'Pull yourself together,' I said, 'or they won't let us in.'

'You pull yourself together,' he laughed.

'Right,' I said, holding him by the shoulders, seeing how well he could stand.

The same woman as before was sat up at the desk. She gave us a brief glance as we passed. 'Evening,' I said.

She said, 'Hm,' and went back to her ledger.

'Is it evening?' shouted Isaac, falling into the door to the lounge. It swung open, revealing what was inside.

'No,' said the woman, standing up.

All the furniture had been pushed against the walls and a huge plastic sheet was spread over the carpet, swathed in some kind of oil or jelly. A gaggle of shining middle-aged people looked up at us from the sheet, all of them naked, most of them in various stages of intercourse. The loyal customers.

'What...' said Mikey.

'Close that door,' the woman said, barrelling past us and slamming it herself.

Isaac leaned on the wall. He hadn't seen inside the lounge. Too pissed.

'Upstairs,' said the woman, furiously. 'Now. This is your last evening at the Groveview.'

We waited until we were at the top landing before we burst into laughter. We wiped our eyes and howled outside of the bunkroom. Mikey put his hand on my shoulder to steady himself.

'Christ,' he said. 'Did you see...'

'I know,' I said. 'I know.'

'Wassit?' asked Isaac. 'What's all the? Y'know?'

He was out like a light when he hit his bunk. Mikey and I sat on the corner of mine as our laughter fizzled out. Our shoulders were touching and we looked at each and the look we gave was: everything's going to be all right, eh?

'Oh hell no,' said a voice from across the bunkroom. 'Oh no you don't.'

I went creeping round the bunk beds to see what was going on. I found a boy and a girl, lying on their fronts between two bunks. There was a battleships board and a bottle of vodka between them.

They looked up at me. 'Hey,' said the boy. 'Sorry. Did we wake you? I just got my frigate sunk.'

'No,' I said. 'It's fine.'

'G5,' the boy said to the girl.

'Nothing,' she said. 'Nada.'

The boy took a deep swallow from the bottle of vodka.

'G5,' the girl said too and the boy shook his head.

'You motherfucker,' he said, removing a peg and taking another drink from the bottle. He offered it up to me and I accepted.

'What's your name?' asked the girl. They were both dark – dark haired and eyed. I told her my name and she smiled. 'You're local. That's good. You never get to meet locals in places like this.' She rotated her head around to mean the bunkroom.

I handed the bottle back to the boy and he told me

his name was Brett. 'And this is my sister, Lou.'

'Hello,' I said.

'A7,' said Brett.

Lou shook her head and Brett drank some vodka.

'Have you seen what's going on downstairs?' I asked.

'There was a whole bunch of people waiting when we came up,' said Brett. 'A very excited bunch of people. They asked Lou and me if we wanted to hang out.'

'They're swingers,' I said. 'There's a big swingers party going on in the lounge.'

Lou laughed. 'We dodged a bullet there.'

I realised then how drunk I was. It wasn't like me to talk to strangers like that. My mouth was running away from my brain.

'We've been kicked out,' I said. 'The woman on reception.' I couldn't get the idea out of me in a way that made sense.

The pair of them laughed. 'So what'll you do?' asked Brett. He twisted around on the floor to look up at me and I saw the muscles beneath his T-shirt move.

'Dunno. Just find somewhere else.'

'We're heading off tomorrow too. We're going to get the train down to Ardrossan. You can catch a ferry, I think, from there?' He looked to his sister.

'That's right,' she said. 'To Arran. The Isle of Arran.'

'You could come with,' said Brett. 'On the train.'

When I got back to our bunks Mikey was asleep too. I stood on my bed and pulled myself up to the top bunk so I could see him. He was curled up in a ball with the duvet wrapped in his arms. I freed it from his grasp and laid it out over him so he wouldn't get cold in the night.

Isaac was laid flat on his back, his arms at his sides. I didn't bother fixing his duvet for him. I slipped into my own bunk. It was the first night I'd slept without Mikey by my side for some time. We'd been in the tent, then the man's bed and then the van the night before. I spread out my arms and legs.

'What's your angle?' said a voice behind me. I shot up. It was Isaac. He was on his side in the bunk at right angles to mine. His face was a mess from the drink.

'Eh?'

'You heard me. What's your angle?'

'You're pissed,' I said.

'Maybe,' said Isaac. 'Maybe.'

'You just keep yourself to yourself, all right? Be glad you've only got a bruise on your head.'

Isaac laughed. 'If you strike me down I'll come back more powerful and... eh... something.'

We weren't even given the luxury of a long lie the next morning. The receptionist burst into the bunkroom to rouse us.

'Check out's in quarter of an hour,' she said, leaning into my bunk.

I glowered at her through my hangover. 'Fine,' I said.

She turned to go but her fury stopped her. 'Do you know,' she hissed over her shoulder, 'the work I had to do last night? All because of you and your drunkard pal?'

'I don't.'

She started to explain but evidently was too annoyed. She stormed from the bunkroom, her dress trailing behind her. I got Mikey and Isaac up and then went to the toilets for a wash. I took a detour past Lou and Brett's bunks, hoping to catch a glimpse of them, still asleep. Despite the rank cloud in my mind I could still remember Brett turning on the floor to look up at me, his back all twisting vines and ropes.

They were gone though. My stomach sank. Beds empty

138

and hastily made. I shuffled into the bathroom and ran myself a shower. Once the water was as hot as it would go I stepped inside. My chest and thighs and cock screamed from the pain. It was good though. My skin went pink as peaches and my eyes and brain cleared.

Mikey gave me a funny look as I sat down on my bunk, a towel round my waist.

'You all right?' he said.

'Aye,' I said. 'I got some water in my eye.'

Isaac and Mikey didn't bother with full showers, deciding to wash themselves in the sink. We dressed and went downstairs and handed the keys over to the receptionist. She snatched them out my hands, sucking on her own mouth with anger.

As we passed by the lounge I glanced inside. The same crowd was in there, only now the sheet had been taken away and the furniture pushed back. They were all sat around having frothy coffees and chatting away. The receptionist coughed from behind me, so I followed Isaac and Mikey out into the street. We piled into the van and I started the engine. They were in the back, quarrelling over who would be allowed to lie down on the sofa bed. Isaac was convinced he should have it, due to being the oldest.

'But the van's half mine,' whined Mikey.

'Let him lie down,' I said. 'Don't be rude.'

I drove down the road with an idea of where to go half forming in my mind. If either of the clowns in the back questioned me, I'd tell them to mind their own businesses. I was driving and it was up to me where we went. The roads were quiet – it was a Sunday and still early. I made my way to the city's heart, following road signs for what I was looking for.

I pulled the van up outside Central Station, behind a line of black cabs.

'What's going on?' asked Mikey.

I looked behind and saw he was pressing his nose and hands up against the glass, staring at the station's atrium.

'Hold on,' I said, rolling down the window, scanning the crowd on the pavement opposite.

'Are we getting a train?'

'No.'

I saw women and men and boys and girls but I couldn't see the faces I was looking for. It was a long shot anyway. It was a daft idea. I restarted the engine and put it in gear.

'Right,' I said, turning the steering wheel.

And then I stopped. A pair of dark-haired figures emerged from the newsagents on our side of the road and crossed over towards the station, only a few taxis in front of us. I honked the horn and they stopped, turning to us.

I rolled the window down and leaned out, waving.

They waved back.

'Yous wanting a lift?' I shouted.

The two faces broke and scurried across the road to meet us. Lou got into the back with the boys but Brett stood by my window, his hand gripping the pane. His knuckles were sharp and had veins running over them.

'This is amazing,' he said. The wind moved his hair around.

'You should get in,' I told him.

Isaac had woken up by then and Brett got inside and I drove us away. Introductions were exchanged and everyone settled in to the journey. Lou told the boys we were going to a place called Arran and we were going to have the best time ever.

I drove us south across the bridge and the Clyde was slimy and dark. I imagined Duncan beneath the surface, looking up at me as I sped over the bridge. I beat you, I told him. You, with your education and your travelling and everything you had, you couldn't beat me. I beat everyone in the end.

He blinked and swam away, down river, towards the open sea. I smiled to myself as I watched him go.

'What's so funny?' asked Brett, sat beside me.

'Nothing,' I said.

We drove through the city's Southside and out into the country again. We were headed for the ocean. This vehicle was my hand and everyone inside was mine. I was in charge of where we went and when we went and I held all of them in my smooth palm. If I wanted to, at any second, I could close the fingers, and that would be it. That would be it. I could turn the steering wheel and plunge all five of us into a wall, if I wanted to, or out into open water. I could do anything I wanted to.

I wasn't going to though.

I had other, better plans.

9

There was confusion at the ferry terminal. First, it was Isaac.

Ardrossan was only an hour or so from the city and we'd spent the journey in friendly conversation. Lou and Brett told us about their travels so far, how they'd flown in to Belgrade and worked their way west. How they'd slept on the beach in Croatia, ridden funicular railways in the Alps, eaten warm oily pasta in Florence.

'And now we're here,' said Lou, casting her hand at the flat land moving by the van's window.

'And now we're here,' repeated Brett.

'How've you found it?' asked Isaac. 'It's shite, eh?'

'No,' said Lou, offended. 'It's a beautiful place. We went all the way up last week, didn't we Brett? We were in Mull. Oban and Mull.'

'Aye,' said Isaac. 'Bet it was shite though, wasn't it?'

By the time we made it to the harbour the boat was already waiting. It towered above the cars, its great black hull dull and massive.

'Em,' piped up Isaac. 'What's the fucken story here then?'

I ignored him, paying the man at the stand and joining the queue of traffic waiting to embark.

'What do you mean?' I heard Mikey ask and I twisted round in my seat to look into the back. Isaac was on his knees, crouching down to take in the ferry's height through the window.

'I mean, what's the fucken story with this great big fuck-off boat? Nobody said we were getting on a boat.'

'We told you,' I said. 'We told we were going to the *Isle* of Arran.'

'Aye, I know, but I thought that was just an expression. A turn of phrase.' He looked terrified. 'I'm afraid my good people that this is where we part ways. Nice to meet you all.'

Mikey frowned and looked at me. 'Are you joking?' he asked Isaac.

'No pal, no jokes. Me and the water, we don't mix. Like, eh, oil and water. Well,' he said, looking at each of us and then clapping, 'cheerio.'

He shook Mikey by the hand, opened the van door and hopped out. He slid it closed and blew us a kiss. We all watched in bemusement as he weaved away among the queuing traffic, his hair as bright as a halo.

'What did he give you?' I asked Mikey.

Mikey unfolded the item Isaac had slipped him and studied it. 'It's a map,' he said. 'I think.'

'Pass it here,' I said.

It was a napkin from the pub the night before on which Isaac has drawn a crude map of the West Coast, all the islands and sounds and peninsulas scribbled in chunky crayon. 'Fucken hell,' I said. Up at the top he'd drawn a star and written, in a childish scrawl, *Very Heaven*.

I held it up so that Lou and Brett could see.

Brett took it from me. 'I mean...'

'What an odd person,' said Lou and we all laughed, even Mikey.

'Very Heaven,' I muttered. 'Do you know what that means?'

Mikey shook his head. 'No. Well, maybe. He said he was heading north didn't he?'

'I suppose.'

Brett handed the map back to Mikey. 'Where did you dig him up from?'

I explained that he had tagged along with us, how we'd been camping and he'd just shown up one morning. I neglected to include where the van had come from or the reason we were camping out in the countryside in the first place.

I parked the van deep inside the belly of the boat and we went up on deck to watch the island approaching. It was a shadowy mass out on the horizon, mountainous in the northern regions, hulking stacks of grey hills rising from the Clyde Firth. It wasn't a particularly choppy crossing but Lou ended up going green. I told her she could go downstairs and sit in the van.

'I'll come down with you,' said Brett, taking the keys from me.

'You don't have to,' I said. 'She'll be fine, it's a comfortable van.'

But he went anyway.

Mikey and I got sick of watching the island so we went down to the bar. I had a shandy and Mikey had a proper pint. It was our first time alone together for a day.

'That was funny,' I said, 'about the map.'

'Oh aye,' laughed Mikey. 'He's some boy.'

'Did he say anything to you?'

'Say anything about what?'

I drank a mouthful of the sweetened beer. 'You know what I mean. About the whole situation. I mean, what's he doing giving you a map like that? Just you.'

144

Mikey stared into the bottom of his beer. 'He didn't say anything in particular.'

I said, 'Mikey,' in one of my voices.

'Right. OK. All he said was that maybe running away from my problems wasn't the best solution. That was it.'

'And what did you say?'

'Can't remember.'

I sighed and drank some more. There was a strong smell of grease and fish coming from the ferry's canteen next door. 'When are you going to learn to trust me?'

'I do trust you. It's just that...'

'It's just what?'

'I know you said about all the newspapers and that outside, but I never saw them. You just told me.'

I leaned over our drinks so that my whisper would carry. 'You're calling me a liar, is that it? You think that I wanted to go trailing over the whole fucken country? Like, that's my idea of fun or something?'

'No,' he said. 'Course not.'

'Good. I'm glad that's not what you think because otherwise I'd be left feeling like I'm wasting my time.'

'Fine,' he said. 'I'm sorry.'

'Forget it,' I said.

'He also said I'd be in trouble.'

'Why's that then?'

'For missing all them parole meetings. Mind, it was meant to be every week that I saw the social worker and police. And I never went to any of the psycho... psychom...'

'The psychologist.'

'I never went to any of the psychologist meetings they set up.'

I shook my head. 'They'll understand. When we get back and I explain it all to them, about the press, about the harassment.'

'You're sure?'

'I'm sure.'

We finished the drinks and went upstairs to stand at the prow and watch as the ferry inched closer to land. The island was something else. The land looked alive and real. Solid and green and purple and brown with plump clouds full of delicious water. We watched as the ferry came alongside the jetty and some men threw ropes to each other. When that happened we knew we'd better get downstairs sharpish.

Lou and Brett had found a photo album.

'Hey,' they said, looking up as I slid the door open, 'who's this?'

I took it from them. It was a series of pictures of a small, blonde boy. The small, blonde boy standing beside a snowman, full of pride. Riding a tricycle down a brown-carpeted hallway. Using a fork and knife on a comically large pizza. I flicked through it, confused, trying not to show it. I came to the final photo and there was Duncan, kneeling on the grass beside the small, blonde boy. On the back cover someone, an adult, had written *To Daddy, with love, from Carl.*

I held up the final photo to show the Americans. 'There's the chap we bought the van off,' I told them. 'He must've forgot it was in here.'

The opening to the parking hangar was beginning to crack open, letting in a chink of sunlight, so I ducked into the front to start the van up.

'Oh my god,' said Lou. 'That is so sad. You have to make sure you give it back to him. It's his little boy!'

I kept the photo album on my lap and Mikey slid the door behind him. 'Aye,' I said. 'Maybe.'

We followed the slow crawl of traffic out of the ferry

and onto the harbour. As soon as we hit the tarmac the ocean smells started to seep into the van. There was a petrol station immediately outside the ferry terminal. I parked there and waited for the Americans to run to the tourist information office to find someplace to crash.

I flicked through the album and scoffed. 'What a fanny that guy was,' I said. 'Duncan.'

'He wasn't a fanny,' said Mikey. 'He was just a bit… y'know.'

'No, he was a total fanny,' I said and I peeled the final photograph from the album. 'There,' I said, crumpling it between my hands and tossing it from the open window. Mikey watched it fly, blinking back some kind of displeasure.

'What?' I said.

He shook his head. 'Nothing.'

Brett and Lou wandered back from the tourist information. 'There's a nice sounding spot up in the north of the island,' said Brett, parking himself in the passenger seat and closing the door.

'Whatever yous say,' I said, and off we went.

The road clung to the beach for most of the journey. We went out of the main village and around the coast, heading north. A family of seals were sitting out in the bay, their heads and tails extended to heaven, their fat bellies resting on underwater stone. They watched the van pass with complete lack of interest, with dull dogs' eyes. Above the road as we came out of the village was a grand castle or country home, red as raw bricks and empty.

'The girl in the place said we'd pass that,' said Brett. 'I think she said it was an old… maybe a hunting lodge? I don't remember. Lou?'

147

'Oh yeah,' piped up Lou. 'I think it was a hunting lodge.'

'It looks scary,' said Mikey.

'Don't be silly, sweetie,' said Lou. 'It's just old.'

We drove past the castle or house or lodge and the land above the road grew wilder. We passed through a handful of tiny villages, with their milk-white pubs and decorative fishing boats in the harbours. Eventually the road went inwards, away from the coast and into the higher land. The mountains were piles of boulders and scree up close, bare rock held together by moss and heather and damp. Much harsher than the mountains we'd had by our camp.

'Woosht,' said Mikey, gazing at the ragged molars of rock. 'Look at those.'

The road began to descend again and a road sign told us we were entering Lochranza, which Lou explained was the very place in question. The village was built around a wide bay with a narrow mouth. A decrepit castle was perched on a slip of land by the opening. We passed a distillery and a campsite and a string of tooth-coloured houses, built back from the road, mangy fields between us and them.

'Right,' I said. 'Where am I going?'

'Shit,' said Brett. 'I don't know. The girl just said it was here, the hostel.'

I drove the village's length once to try and locate the hostel but I saw no sign of it. There was another, smaller ferry terminal at the far end where the coast turned back in on itself. On the way back I parked up outside the village shop, *Marigold's*, to ask for directions.

There was a young girl seated at the counter, her head buried in a book.

'Sorry?' I said.

She looked up, smiling, fresh faced. 'Hello,' she squeaked.

'Hiya. Do you know where the hostel is here?'

'It's a half-mile or so down the road. There's a big sign.'

'Oh,' I said.

'Remember Marigold's for your messages, eh? Sorry, I'm supposed to say that.'

I said, 'That's all right,' and I went back to the van.

I told the others that we were a pack of clowns. There was a sign for the hostel facing the other way down the road. A gravel path led up the hill to a bright pink building.

'Is this it?' asked Mikey. 'Is this the place?'

'I suppose.'

I parked the van and ushered the rest of them inside. I wasn't worried about them spying on Mikey – the hicks in these parts wouldn't know a newspaper article if it bit them on the arse. Lou and Brett hiked their rucksacks up their backs and I carried Mikey's and my bag. There was a vast woman seated behind the reception of the hostel. Her hair was shorn short and she wore an African-style dress. She wore a name badge that read *Mother Senga*.

She said, 'What?'

'We're looking for some beds,' said Lou, looking back and counting us. 'Do you have room for four? Four people?'

'Aye,' said Mother Senga. 'Yous go up and find yourself a spot. If the bed's made it means it's free.'

The four of us climbed the stairs and opened the first door we came to. Lou and Brett unpacked their bags onto a set of bunks. Brett's bag fell open and a bag of grey powder flapped onto the sheets. I asked what it was and he slipped it back inside.

'Don't worry about it,' he said. 'It's not a big deal.'

After we unpacked it was decided we would drive down the western coast. It was flatter and less wild than the east. We came across an abandoned graveyard. The stones were covered in moss and standing at acute angles. Lou begged me to park, so I did. We nipped over the road to inspect them, reading the names and dates.

'See,' said Lou. 'Part of the point of coming here was that in a roundabout way Brett and I are from here.'

'Eh?' asked Mikey. 'I thought yous two were Americans?'

Lou stroked the upper curve of a weathered stone. 'No, we are. But our ancestors came from here. They got a boat over some time in the nineteenth century.'

'I'm sorry,' said Brett. 'Is that offensive? With the clearances and so on?'

'I don't feel offended,' said Mikey. 'Do you Paul?'

'No,' I laughed. 'It's fine.'

Brett said, 'Phew.'

Mikey and I stood by the fence, watching as Lou and Brett examined each gravestone, comparing it to a list of ancestors they had with them. When they were far enough away Mikey sidled over to me.

'They're funny, them two.'

I watched Brett squat before a stone turned green from lichen. 'What d'you mean?'

'I mean, like, they're just funny. They look really similar. It creeps me out a bit.'

'But they're a good asset,' I explained. 'They're foreigners so they won't recognise you. Say we need messages or something and I'm busy. We just send them two in for us.'

He said, 'Hm,' and jammed his hands into the pockets of his jeans.

After they'd checked every stone they came back towards us, Lou ahead of Brett, upset.

'I know,' she was saying. 'You don't have to be an asshole about it.'

'An asshole?' said Brett, following his sister past us, out the graveyard. 'An asshole? I'm being a realist, Louise. All I'm saying is what are the chances of finding one or two names in a whole island of dead fucking bodies?'

'So it's the ritual or nothing?' she shouted, slamming the van door closed behind her.

Brett stopped in the road when his sister used the word 'ritual'. He turned to us, slowly. 'Girls,' he smiled.

I felt Mikey gear himself up to ask the question we were both thinking, but I got in there first. 'I think we need some food.'

Further down the coast there was a van selling ice creams and hot dogs. It had stopped by the beach in one of the villages we went through. I sent Brett over with some cash to pick us up hot dogs and we ate them on the beach. Lou stood a few feet away from us. I watched as the man from the food van began to close his van up. He looked over to us from the harbour. He stared and then began walking over.

Mikey was pushing the last of his mustard-soaked bun into his gob, oblivious to the man's approach.

'Let's head back to the van,' I said, calmly. 'We'll need to get going.'

'I thought we could maybe take a walk,' said Lou. 'It's a nice beach.

'There's no graves on the beach, Lou,' said Brett.

'Oh Jesus,' she said.

'Mikey,' I said. 'Do you want to get into the van for me?'

He looked over at me, puzzled, then he spotted the oncoming man behind my head. 'Aye,' he nodded. 'All right.'

The two of us headed away from the man and towards the van, pulling the Americans along. They were so angry with each other that they didn't seem to care and didn't even notice the man until we were driving off. He was standing on the beach, watching us drive away.

'Hey,' said Brett. 'That's weird. There's the hot dog guy. Was he following us?'

'No,' I said. 'I don't think so.'

'Huh,' said Brett.

I stopped in at Marigold's on the way back to the hostel and I bought a paper from the fresh-faced girl there. I'd dropped the van off with the rest of them at the hostel, so I walked back from the shop flicking through the paper.

I found something bad.

On page eight there was a sizeable spread on Duncan. I folded the paper over to display the half page he was featured on, skimming the article. The headline ran:

COLLEAGUE MAKES EMOTIONAL APPEAL FOR INFO ON MISSING ARCHAEOLOGIST.

The gist of it was that Sam, who the paper called Samantha Swart, that sour bitch, had done a big look-at-me press conference asking for any information about her pal.

My blood was kicking in big time and it was only going to get worse.

I read the article's final line. 'Reports that recently released and wanted-for-parole-violations Michael 'The

152

Beast' Buchanan was casually employed by the same company as Duncan Weddle are, as yet, unconfirmed.'

I could read between the lines. Who else but Sam could have given the papers and the police and whoever else the info that Mikey was even involved? That fucken cunt, I thought, crumpling up the paper. The article mentioned that she'd said she would 'stop at nothing to make sure those responsible would be met with justice'. The cunt.

The hostel put on an evening meal for its guests. It was a bowl each of pink, quivering stovies. The four of us and most of the hostel piled into the dining room and paid our two pounds to the woman and wolfed down our food. I was still in a black mood from reading the paper. Mikey was the only one of us whose spirits remained high and he scraped his bowl clean.

Lou and Brett excused themselves early, leaving most of their food behind.

I told Mikey, in a whisper, about what I'd read. He nodded as I spoke. I waited for him to react. He didn't.

'Am I going mental?' I asked. 'Does that not worry you?'

'Nah,' he said.

'How not? It's there in black and white. We're associated with him, in the paper. It's there.'

'I mean, aye, it's bad. But what can we do about it? You shouldn't worry about the shite you can't change.'

'Where did you hear that? On a fucken beer mat?'

'I think someone told me that once,' he said. 'Inside.'

'It's bollocks,' I said. 'You can always change the shite.'

The van was the main thing. Perhaps I couldn't fix the exterior but I could certainly do a job on the inside. I stole a bin bag from the hostel's kitchen and went to work, stripping off the remnants of Duncan's travels. I tore off Estonian bumper stickers and decorative plates from Jordan. I untangled the beads from the rear view mirror and I threw the photo album down on top of all that tat inside the bin bag.

Checking that no one at the hostel was observing, I stole down the gravel path to the road with the bag in my fist. Sam would not beat me. I would not allow it. She could try her very best but in the end she would find, like everyone did, that I would always come out on top. I stuffed the bag down deep inside the bin at the end of the path. I stood and rolled a fag. Try and calm down, I told myself. If you're stressed and angry then that's where the mistakes slip in.

I held my nail of a fag between shaking fingers and looked across the bay, at the castle, at the mull and the black sloping hills beyond, falling forever into red water. There was a family of deer in the bay. They too were black against the sinking sun like ideas of animals, black shapes, like cave drawings. The old mind's knowledge of what the deer looked like, black legs and black bodies and black antlers.

I thought about the day where it all went wrong. I had let a mistake slip in then too. After Mr Pin had chased us from the bridge, after the mums had chased us from the swing park, we'd wandered. We'd been aimless. Full of the anger that you have at those ages – frustrated, aimless anger. Deep in the woods we'd found a pile of decaying bricks, arranged as if they'd once been a building. We took turns hurtling chunks of pink brick at the trunk of a vast tree. Our missiles had flown through the air, stinging the tree's sides, nipping off a sliver of bark here, a chunk of fibrous wood there. We'd thrown bricks until we were exhausted, until it looked as if an animal had attacked the tree in a frenzy.

Out in the bay one of the smaller deer approached the biggest one, the one with the largest antlers. It butted its side or perhaps just licked or smelled the old male. Something harmless. The old bastard put his head down low and used his antlers on the youngster, sending him packing with a wave of the gnarled head-bones. I threw the wizened butt of my fag into the trickle of water than ran down beside the gravel path.

That day we ran ourselves out. We rampaged through the trees, yelling and screaming. More animal than child.

Why were we so angry?

The evening before, Mikey had come home in a strop. He wouldn't tell our mother what the problem was but I got it out of him. I'd always had ways of getting things out of him. I'd pushed him up against the wall of our bedroom and threatened to spit in his face if he didn't tell me what the problem was.

I was a very curious teenager.

He'd admitted he'd had a problem at school. He'd been in his English class at the end of the day. Mr MacPherson was one of the ones who took English. I'd never had him myself but there were myths of his brutality. You heard that he once denied a boy access to his asthma inhaler. You heard that he positioned short skirted-girls in the very front row of his classroom.

They'd been studying some book or another and Mikey had given a less than satisfactory answer. Mr MacPherson had demanded he stand at the front of the class. He'd told the room that this boy, this Michael Buchanan, was an example of a young person who would never amount to anything. The reason? Because people like this boy were too lazy, too bone idle to ever really *try* at anything.

He told me all of that, then I let him go from our bedroom wall. He wouldn't meet my eye. I said that we

155

would take the next day off, that we'd just tick it. That would show them. That would show them all.

The deer herd out in the bay had vanished while I'd been lost in my memories. The sky was warm and filled with misty fingers of cloud. I strolled up to the hostel, feeling better. I'd purged Duncan from the van and, in addition to that, I always felt better when I thought about that fateful day. It reminded me that, in the end, I always won.

I found the Americans sitting on Brett's bunk. The packet of grey powder rested on the duvet. They stopped talking mid-word and Brett's hand covered the packet.

'Hey Paul,' said Lou. 'Could you give us a moment?'

'What's going on?' I asked.

Brett smiled at me. 'I'm not supposed to say.'

'Oh my God,' moaned Lou. 'Why are you constantly so full of shit?'

'In what way am I full of shit?'

'All this, oh no, I can't tell, my bitch sister won't let me. You're not a fucking martyr Brett.'

Brett shrugged at me and said, in a nasty, sharp voice, 'She says all that but ask her if I'm allowed to talk about it?'

I rubbed my face. They were so young. I had little experience of the way people that age, twenty, twenty-one, could be. I'd missed Mikey's late teenage years of course.

'Listen,' I said. 'Tell me, don't tell me. I could not give a shit.'

'OK,' she said. 'Look. So. Brett's got this batshit crazy idea in his head. About this powder. About a ritual.'

'See Paul, that's the best thing about my sister,' he said, pointing to his temple. 'She is so fucking open minded.'

'Let me explain OK? So Brett here's got it into his head he can use this mushroom stuff,' she prodded the packet, 'to get in touch or whatever, to communicate I suppose, with our ancestors.'

'She's talking as if I've done, like, zero research.'

'You've gone on-fucking-line. Anybody can go online and find out whatever they like.'

'Places have an energy, you'd agree with that Paul?'

'I suppose,' I said.

'But where does that energy come from. Why does location A have energy X and location B have energy Y? What's the reasoning? See? You can't tell me.'

'I suppose I can't,' I said, realising I would agree with whatever the boy said.

'All I'm saying is we could use a little something extra to assist us in exploring that energy. Cultures all over the world do it, or used to. Indians, aboriginals. Even,' he said, pointing out the window, 'the Celtic Gaels.'

'You see what I mean?' asked Lou, at her wit's end. 'You understand this is crazy, Paul? This is not what I had in mind when I agreed to some light genealogical research.'

'She would rather hang around in graveyards all day. So fucking *morbid*. At least I'm showing respect.'

I ground my knuckles into my jaw. 'I don't think it's a bad idea,' I said, enjoying the scandalised look on Lou's face, relishing the jubilant look on Brett's.

'That's settled then,' said Brett. 'Tonight. I have a print off of this amazing-sounding Hopi ritual. It's going to really be something.'

Lou pushed herself off the bunk and stormed into the toilets. I took her place.

'You shouldn't listen to her,' I told Brett. 'I think she's holding you back.'

He curled a hair around his finger. 'I sometimes think so too.'

I picked up the packet of grey powder and turned it over in my hand. Something was itching at me. I couldn't place it. An insistent worming-away at a certain area of my mind. It was like when you've left something at home, your wallet or your keys, and your brain's screaming at you to remember and you can hear the commotion even before you pat your pocket and realise – it's gone.

And then, I had it. I put the packet down and looked around. 'Brett,' I said. 'Have you seen Mikey?'

10

Brett explained the situation to me and I managed to stay calm. Just. To keep up appearances. Mikey had gone for a walk in the hills after tea, Brett told me, while I was out cleaning up the van. He'd wanted to stretch his legs.

'That's all?' I asked. 'Stretch his legs?'

Brett laughed. 'That's all.'

I said, 'Hm,' struggling to control my fingers as they writhed around themselves in my lap.

'I mentioned that we'd maybe be joining him,' Brett told me. 'The ritual, you see.'

I told myself over and over, as I got ready, that it was fine. It was all fine. I could trust Mikey. He'd just gone for a stroll. That was normal. It wasn't ideal that he hadn't let me know but I had been down on the path for a while. We'd go up into the hills and he'd be waiting for us.

Aye, well, he would want to be, wouldn't he?

As I pulled on some thick socks and a heavy jumper I heard Lou sneak in from the bathroom. There was a constricted quality to her breathing that told me she was upset.

'Everything OK?' I asked her, facing the wall.

She kept breathing. 'You know it isn't.'

'All right,' I said.

'This is incredibly irresponsible,' she said, and I turned to face her. Her eyes were pandaish with tear-diluted make up.

I shrugged.

'You don't give a shit, do you?' she cried. 'Are you trying to fuck him? Is that it? He won't do it, you know. He never does it.'

I zipped up my coat to the chin. 'Don't be disgusting,' I said. 'What's wrong with you?'

'You know he's been kicked out of two colleges for this shit? For getting high, for getting spaced out every day. Two separate colleges.'

'I'll get you outside,' I said, edging through the door and smiling at Lou.

I kicked around the back of the hostel for some time, chain smoking rollies, waiting for the Americans. I kept a close eye on the hills to the south, looking for Mikey to come stumbling down the gradient.

Eventually Brett came rushing from the hostel's exit, a thermos jammed under his arm. He was high with excitement. Lou followed on his heel.

'Let's go,' he said, pushing past me and leaping through the trees that ran around the car park.

We followed him in silence, into the clear night, where the fat, watery moon made the hills as light as early morning. He told us location was important, that he would know the spot when he found it. That there were mystical magnetic fields radiating unseen in the world around us, that all it took was tuning in to these forces to completely revitalise your worldview.

It was all bollocks of course, nearly as bad as Isaac's stuff about Egyptian and aliens in the sky.

We went across two hills and came to a stop on the crest of a third. Brett scurried around in the darkness, appearing to test the spot for various unknown qualities.

'This is it,' he said in the end. 'Perfect.'

Lou sniffed and dug her chin into the thick cowl of

her scarf. 'Just get it over with,' she ordered.

Brett asked us to sit around in a circle while he laid the thermos between us and pulled a stack of paper cups from his jacket pocket. The curvature of the hills around hid the dwindling lights of the village from us and it was easy to imagine away all of the far off structures of humanity. That you were a fresh species on a new earth, that the ground we kneeled on was being knelt on for the first time.

Brett explained what we would do, his lips trembling with nerves.

'You drink the tea,' he said, 'and then we all walk in our own direction. You keep walking and keep walking until you feel a tug. Apparently it feels a little like nausea, a little bit like homesickness. That's when you come back, walk back the way you've come, to here. Only it won't be here. It'll be like here and also not.'

He poured out three cupfuls of the mushroom tea. 'Everyone got it?' he asked.

'Aye,' I said.

Lou said nothing.

I watched as they raised their cups to their mouth, dark, dark hair glowing. I held mine to my mouth too and then let the tea pour out by my feet as I wiped my sleeve over my mouth. Lou and Brett screwed up their faces, saying how horrible the tea was, so I did the same. Then we hauled ourselves up.

'Now go,' said Brett, making legs of his fingers and walking them away.

'This is insane,' said Lou, backing off and down on the hill on the far side.

'Just try it,' said Brett, turning himself. 'Good luck,' he told me.

I walked down the hill and away from the Americans,

161

keeping Brett in the corner of my eye. He strode down the hill himself, arms swinging, head bobbing. Making sure he wasn't watching, I altered my course so that I was coming up behind him. I was stealthy, I was sleek. My hair was long and strong and I was hidden in the bushes and the trees.

I followed him for something like twenty minutes as he took a path into a plunging valley. A silver stream came tumbling down beside the way, the white noise it created masking the crunches beneath my feet. I followed him up the path and through the valley and it brought us out into higher, flatter ground. Brett's movements grew more erratic. He would stop for long moments and stare at the sky. He would become distracted and inspect the ground at his feet for minutes on end. I let myself be absorbed by the land on those occasions, wary of him spinning around in a flurry of paranoia and spotting me.

Off Brett went and I was on his tail. He traipsed through the marsh, through the bog. I skirted the edge of the damp land. His arms were going up and down at his sides, as if he was fighting off attacking birds. The drugs were kicking in. After another few minutes he ran into some trouble. The waterlogged land must have grown stickier because I found myself ahead of him and he wasn't moving forward any more.

My body shoogled as I stumbled downhill towards him, as Brett struggled to fight against the heavy mud. I shouted to try and get his attention. He was too far gone, in the marsh and the mushrooms. By treading lightly and being quick I was able to get by the worst of the mud, to pull Brett out by the oxters. I heaved him onto dryish grass and he lay gasping, eyes rolling, hands grasping. He was looking through me and past me and suddenly I felt silly for revealing myself. The mud wasn't so bad. He would have trudged his way out of it once his head had cleared. Nevertheless, I dragged him onto the dry land and he stumbled to his feet.

'This is it,' he slurred, dark-pupilled and sweaty. 'Through the outside and out into the inside. I'm here.'

'Come on,' I said. 'Let's get you back.'

'Everything's moving and I'm on the inside. What are you?'

I tried to pull him along but he stumbled over a clump of heather. He fell into me and I caught him on my chest. He gripped me on the arms. 'I need to go back,' he said with sudden urgency, pointing over my shoulder. 'It's pulling me back.'

I looked down at him and held him near to me and then I tried something on him I'd never tried before. You see, he was so close to me and his hair was so dark and I didn't feel I had any other option. I put my mouth on his mouth, to see what it was like. I could smell the tang of the earth that clung to him and his sour skin. I tried that out on him and he jerked his head away, as if I'd pressed a hot iron to his lips.

'No,' he managed to say, from the midst of his stupor.

'No?' I asked.

'Don't do that to me,' he slurred.

'All right,' I said, turning away from him. 'I'm sorry.'

I blinked once and felt my blood roaring in my chest, kicking in worse than ever before, humming like the ocean in a shell.

We came full circle, Mikey and I. After running and roaring in the woods we found we'd come back to the tree we'd hurled the bricks at earlier. We weren't lost exactly, but not trying to get anywhere. I remember that as Mikey had been throwing the brick parts he'd been calling the tree Mr MacPherson and telling it to do all kinds of terrible stuff. I just joined in, to try and make him feel better.

When we found ourselves back by the bricks... things are hazier there. One of us was up by the tree, the other by the bricks. One of us told the other to stand as still as they could and the other stood with their back connected to the tree with sheer terror. I was both of those boys. I was the one by the bricks, the one by the tree. I weighed the brick up in my hand, I felt the bark on the nape of my neck.

One of us threw and the other one braced. One of us winced and the other one swung. Neither was hurt. The brick glanced off a branch, as it was intended to. Both our hearts were racing and we did it again and again.

Eventually we got bored of even that.

Which one was which though?

I sauntered down to the hostel from the hills, kicking the mud from my boots on any boulders I passed. The night was full by then but I didn't care. I liked it. I was whistling a tune as I walked. Pop goes the weasel.

'Half a pound of tuppenny rice,' I murmured. 'Half a pound of...'

I stopped mumbling and I stopped walking. Lou had fallen into my path. She looked wild, hair all over the shop and her face dotted in scratches and daubs of filth. It had only been an hour, maybe two, since we'd parted ways. She had certainly had an experience.

I laughed. 'Woah!'

She looked at me like I was the first thing she'd seen in her entire life. 'Where's Brett?' she whispered.

'Eh?'

'You heard me.'

'How should I know?' I asked, pushing past her. 'He wandered off like the rest of us.'

'No,' she said, coming after me and holding the back of my jacket. 'I waited at the spot. He didn't come back.'

I twisted myself out of her grip and walked backwards away from her. 'I think you're still tripping.'

She growled in frustration. She actually stamped her foot.

I laughed at her. Right in her stupid face. 'You'd better go and make sure he's all right,' I said. 'People have accidents out here all the time.'

It was true. People did have accidents all of the time. People fell and hurt themselves. People didn't make the proper provisions, they didn't check the weather forecast before they set out, they didn't bring the proper footwear. These hills were a death-trap, I thought and slapped the biggest grin on my pus as I waved goodbye to Lou and made my way to the hostel. I would find Mikey waiting for me in our room, no doubt. We'd have a solid night's sleep and be off in the morning. If there was any justice in the world that Yank cow would be long gone herself.

I emerged from the trees into the hostel car park. 'Huh,' I said.

There was something wrong, but what was it? All the lights were off but that was normal. I took a second look at the car park and my brain fumbled. Where was the van? I ran through the evening in my mind. I'd cleared out the tat, I'd met the Americans and we'd gone up the hills. That was all. So where was the fucken van?

And then.

Mikey! That wee fucken snake.

I hurried around the building to check. The van had gone. I fumed and raged and burst into the hostel, hammering up the stairs to our room. Throwing everything on my bunk to the ground, I realised the keys were gone.

That wee fucken *snake*.

There was no one down on reception so I hopped the desk, landing cat-like and silent. I began to rifle through the drawers beneath, searching for a key, any key. I rifled through sheet after sheet of paper, of receipt, of map. The lights came on. The woman was stood in the doorway. My blood was kicking in so hard I nearly rushed her there and then.

'Do you mind explaining what you're doing?' she demanded, hands on nightie and hips.

'Oh,' I said, dragging myself along the desk towards her. 'Thank God. Thank God you're here. There's been an accident, up in the hills. One of my pals wandered off. He's gone.'

She pushed her two fat palms to her chops. 'You're joking.'

'I'm not. I'm really not.'

'Did you try calling mountain rescue?'

'No answer,' I moaned.

'No answer?'

'It was engaged.'

Her hands faltered. Her forehead creased. 'Engaged?'

I hurried forward, distracting her with my movement. 'There's no time. You need to lend me your car so I can raise the alarm. It's a matter of life and death.'

'Aye,' she said. 'Aye, of course.'

She opened the wardrobe at the back of reception, entering a combination into the safe inside. She fished out a clutch of keys and handed them to me with quivering fingers.

'Thank you,' I said, hopping back over the reception desk. 'I won't be long.'

I flew around the bends and swerves of the narrow road that ringed the island. I crunched gears coming

166

out of turns and my wheels whined as I floored it on the straights. The headlamps blasted out across the sea and the land, into the air as I flew over humps. Powered by pure indignation I drove relentlessly, scanning the car parks and the streets for any sign, any whisper of the van. The van he'd stolen from me.

That little fucken snake.

My mouth was full of saliva. My eyes were full of bile. I was shouting and growling and slamming my fist into the ceiling as I drove. I was rattling the steering wheel and lowing and grunting.

After everything I'd given him! After all the sacrifices I'd made! This was how he was going to repay me? By sneaking off and stealing from me? By taking what was mine. I did not know how I would react when I saw him. I was acting on instinct, like a shark. I had to keep driving, keep moving, or else the anger would consume me as sure as water consumes the shark.

In my mind I was running over the ferry timetable, trying to remember the final crossing. It was seven. I was so sure it was seven. But it might have been later. Could have been eight, nine, and if it was eight or nine and he had managed to get the van down to catch the final ferry then I was fucked. Absolutely royally fucked.

What would he do? Where would he go? Probably go crying back to our mother with his tail between his legs, telling her everything was his big, bad brother's fault. As per usual. He'd tried that before though, hadn't he? Tried to convince everyone that I was the bad guy, the sicko.

Look where that got him.

I hammered the car onwards, into and through the darkness. The water was on my left. No difference between the dark of the water, the dark of the land over the water, the dark of the sky. As I rounded an outcrop I

167

saw the main town ahead, streetlights seeping an orangey haze. I was counting on Mikey's lack of imagination. I was counting on him not considering hiding someplace clever.

I sped past the wooden lodges that marked the beginning of the main town, under the shadow of the hunting lodge. I was so close. I could see the white lights decorating the harbour. He would be there. I could feel it. He would be sitting there in the car park or something, maybe even asleep, maybe with his feet up on the dashboard. Laughing at me. Laughing at his big brother, his older brother, the one who gave him everything he had.

The car was moving then. No longer onwards. Sideways. Twisting. I tried to correct the skid. Was it into the movement or away?

I was calm again. I was at peace. The anger was missing. I'd stopped swimming and found I didn't need the water to breathe. All I needed was myself. Self-sufficient as an egg, I wandered through a golden dell. Lush mosses and broad leaves heavy with moisture drooped before me. The sun fell like honey from between high-up gaps in the canopy.

It was bliss.

I wandered here and there and for the first time... the first time in longer than I could think, I was happy. There was no tension in my jaw or in my arse. I wasn't holding energy anywhere. My heart was no longer fit to burst with hidden, red anxiety. All of my memories were ghosts. They couldn't touch me.

There was a disturbance somewhere behind me. I paused and turned to listen. It was the sound of a struggle, coming from a den covered by ferns and overhanging vines. Heavy breathing, skin frictioning on skin.

Just go, I told myself. This doesn't concern you. Keep on going. Keep on going.

I took a step towards where the ferns shook. I swallowed. The air was sweet. It was heavy. Wild garlic, rainwater, pine. The ferns shook and I swallowed and stepped forward.

Just go, I told myself. Don't look. It doesn't matter.

No, I said. It does.

The tensions were coming back to me. An ache was entering me by chest, a dull throbbing emptiness. I tried to move my arm to pull back the grassy veil but it was too heavy to raise. I tried my right arm instead and it worked. I moved the leaves away and saw what was beneath. My chest rung with pain.

Under the leaves was a mass. A mass of arms and hair moving against itself, dark and foul. Its hands were gripping itself, throwing itself around, wearing the grass away beneath it to bare earth. It had a face. The face was Mikey's face and it was my face. It looked at me as it twisted and writhed and seemed to be trying to destroy itself or a part of the mass. A smaller, weaker part of the mass.

I put the ferns back and ran. My left arm swung heavy at my side, the movement creating a needle to drive its way into my breastbone. A fluttering sound followed me. As I lurched forward I looked back. The mass was rolling through the undergrowth toward me, the ferns and low bushes shivering as it passed.

I picked up the pace, the dread spreading and bleeding into me, the land drying up, leaves turning tan. The rolling mass sped up too until it was thumping and crying with each thud, thud, thud it made against the earth.

I fell and the pain in my shoulder became very sharp and the mass was close to me.

Then, before it could catch me, I woke.

The motor was on its side in the ditch beside the road. I hung against my seat belt, my head suspended above the passenger seat, which was below me.

I hissed.

I managed to walk my legs out of the foot well, across the stereo and down onto the passenger door, unclipping myself so that I fell down onto it. I was upright then and saw the angle my left arm was at. It must have been dislocated or fractured in the crash. My palm faced outwards.

I turned it around and hissed again.

The passenger door was beneath my feet. The only way out was through the driver's, above my head. Somehow I managed it, climbing the seats, pulling myself up by the door handle and unrolling the window with my good arm. I hauled myself through the window and slithered down the windscreen to the wet grass below. Lying on my back, looking around, I got my breath back. The car was intact. I'd been expecting it to be like the ones on telly, all shattered glass and crumpled metal, but it wasn't. It was just resting in the ditch, on its side.

I sighed.

And then I realised it was morning. That it was a bright fresh morning and the grass was wet with dew. I crawled up the embankment to the road. Out on the water the ferry was plunging through sky reflections, toward the harbour.

I hobbled down the road to town clutching my bad arm against my chest. There was something up with my ankle too. I couldn't put much weight on it. It dragged behind me as I went along the central painted line of the road, hoping that no cars would come. My eyes were on the ferry as it pulled closer to the shore.

I would get him. My arm and my leg wouldn't stop me from getting him. I kept telling myself that as I entered the town proper and dragged myself along the promenade. Tourists were out already, milling around in their body warmers and bum bags. I walked straighter around them, leaving the arm by my side. The last thing I needed now was to draw attention to myself. As I neared the harbour I could just make out the tall, pale roof of the camper van, like a sail. It was in the queue waiting to board.

That snake.

I hobbled as quick as I could, a faltering jog, getting nearer and nearer. The ferry groaned. Black smoke was streaming from its chimney. I laughed, actually laughed aloud. 'Ha!' I said. He thought he was going to beat me. He really thought he was going to beat me. A couple of old wifeys turned their heads at my bark, but I ignored them, kept going.

I rounded the terminal and saw the first of the vehicles were beginning to board, trundling up towards the ferry's hull. I moved down the nearest line of traffic, tasting the engine's fumes, smelling the water, full of shells and gull bones. I was honked at as I stepped in front of car after car joining the queue. There was the van, only a few cars away. The engine was idling. All the curtains in the back were closed.

'What're you playing at?' someone shouted. 'Get off the road.'

I reached out and grabbed the handle. It was unlocked. I slid it towards me and slumped onto the floor of the van, pushing it closed again with my foot. I saw the roof of the van's sleeping zone – painted like a night sky. Deep blue background with all these little pinprickish dots of cream and yellow for stars and galaxies.

His eyes were wide. He was shaking his head, unable to believe it.

I kicked against the floor to push myself up against the sofa bed, coughing and laughing. 'Aye,' I wheezed.

We stared each other down for a good while.

Mikey licked his lips. He braced himself. 'What happened?'

'Car crash. Crashed the car.'

'What car?'

'Borrowed the hostel wifey's motor when I seen the van was gone,' I said, holding a hand against my ribs.

Out of the fresh air I realised how much I hurt. With the drive to catch the van gone, all that was left to fill me up was the ache. The cars behind us started to honk.

'You'd better get a move on,' I said.

There was this little pause, as if he was going to protest, as if he was going to do something, but then he shivered. 'Christ,' he said, turning back to the wheel.

I went down on my side and through my eyelashes watched him pull away.

I didn't even know he could drive.

A wet sob forced its way out of me. Not because of the pain but because I had missed him. When I'd been speeding down I thought I was angry. Maybe I had been, but I was scared too. Scared I'd have to be without him. Even when he was inside I had known there was a taut rope that trailed across the country, connecting us by the sternum. It told me when he was scared, when he was embarrassed.

I wiped my eye. You silly cunt, I told myself.

He drove us up the ramp and into the ferry's hull and parked us deep in the dark belly. All around us car doors were opening and closing. There was chatter and jackets being pulled on. The ship's thunderous rumblings. Mikey

172

faced the front until everything but the mechanics died down. Then he moved around to watch me out the corner of his eye.

'I'm not going to do anything,' I wheezed.

His mouth thinned. 'Your arm looks bad.'

'I think it's come out the socket.'

'Right. Do you want me to get a doctor?'

'Nah. Can't risk it. We'll do something on the mainland.'

'Right.'

I laughed but not with any joy. 'You're scared of me.'

'I'm not.'

'Aye you are,' I said. 'Come here. Over beside me.'

He opened his mouth but didn't answer. I ushered him over with my good arm. Eventually he gave in and scuttled into the back, perching on the far end of the sofa bed.

'How come you went?' I asked him.

He took a while to come up with the answer, playing with it in his mind. 'It was the parole thingmy,' he said. 'Mind how when I was back at home they were always saying how the meetings with the social worker and the police and that were like ultra-important? How I'd end up going back inside and doing the full term if I missed them? I got scared of that. I thought maybe if I went back and explained it to them in person, they would understand.'

'Oh,' I said. 'Right.'

'Aye.'

'You still wanting to do that?'

'Aye,' he said. 'I reckon so.'

'Well,' I said, pushing myself up against the sofa bed and patting myself down with my good hand. 'That's an OK idea. Not bad at all. But the thing is, is that whatever you tell them, you're going back inside. That's how parole works. That's how parole violation works. So as I said, it's an OK idea.'

Mikey's face crumpled.

'Now,' I went on, finding the item in my hip pocket. 'As to a better idea, how about that?'

I flicked the piece of paper towards Mikey. He caught it between two fingers and inspected it. I might have realised how much I'd miss the boy when he was gone, but I hadn't turned soft. I couldn't let him go wandering back home, blethering away to anyone that'd listen about this, that, and the next thing. Oh no. Too much at risk for me.

'You really think so?' he asked, turning Isaac's map over. 'What if it's bollocks?'

'If it's bollocks then we'll have had a nice drive.'

'Then we can go back?'

'Then we can go back.'

We passed the rest of the crossing in silence. Mikey sat in the driver's seat, looking at the crude map, and I put my head back on the sofa bed and closed my eyes. Isaac's group, the Church of the authentic fucken Jesus, whatever it was called, had sounded mental. Absolutely cuckoo if they let a cunt like him join anyway. But. If they were mental, if they were God-bothering losers, then there was a good chance they weren't up on criminal justice. They probably didn't read the papers for anything other than counting up all the letters in a headline to see if they made 666.

A black cloud was entering me by the eyes. I couldn't tell if it was exhaustion or concussion. What was it they said? Sleep was bad for a concussion? Or maybe it was good. Cleared the old synapses out. It didn't feel bad or sore, so I had to be safe. There was nothing I could do anyway. It was closing in fast.

11

We were outside Paisley when I woke, my body howling with pain. I stood up, struggling to walk along the moving van, and plonked myself into the front seat.

'I didn't know you could drive,' I croaked.

Mikey nodded. 'Aye. Got lessons inside. Never took the test though.'

'Shite, really?' I said. 'Go and pull over. I'll do it.'

He glanced at my arm, lying across my front like a dead fish, shook his head and laughed.

'I suppose,' I said, and winced from the pain speaking caused.

'What is it you do with one of them?' he asked. 'Is it dislocated, aye?'

'I dunno. Maybe.' I gave my shoulder a gentle prod with my good hand and a bolt ran through it.

'You'll need to get it seen to. It'll probably get poisoned or something if you leave it hanging.'

'Aye,' I said. 'Perhaps.'

'Or it might set like that.'

The road took us skirting the mouth of the Clyde. The water was greenish and a gang of riverboats was parked up by the road.

'Ha,' laughed Mikey, pointing. 'Like on that bairns' programme.'

'Rosie and Jim,' I said.

'Do you remember watching that?'

I did remember – Mikey sat on the arm of the couch beside me after school, even though we were too old for such rubbish.

'Not really,' I said.

We drove on, coming to a stop in a wee place nestled in the tail of Loch Lomond. We bought fish suppers for lunch and ate them in the van, parked by the water. It was good. I felt fond of my brother and I knew that if we kept on like this then we would be fine.

You could go two ways out of Balloch, west or east around the loch. Mikey studied Isaac's map, the tip of his tongue poking from the corner of his mouth.

'I mean,' he said. 'This doesn't really show you roads or anything.'

'No. That's true.'

'I think this is an... Is it an island?'

I took a look myself but couldn't make any sense in the messy renderings of mulls and sea lochs.

'I reckon we go this way,' Mikey pointed, 'around the top of the loch, then back down that side.'

'Aye,' I said. 'That looks about right.'

We drove on, taking the eastern road. The day was clear and apart from my shoulder and a few other nagging aches I was in good spirits. I remembered hearing that a bad shoulder would work its way back in, with time.

'Here,' laughed Mikey, tapping the steering wheel. 'What happened with those two? What did you tell them?'

I swallowed. 'What two?'

'Y'know? The American ones. That Louise, Lou-something, she was all right, eh?'

'She was OK,' I conceded.

'I reckon you had a bit of a thing for her,' he smiled. 'Picking them up from the train station and that.'

'I wouldn't say that.'

'No?'

'No.'

'All right, sorry. But so, what did you say to them?'

He glanced over a few times as I struggled to come up with a lie. What could I say? That I hadn't mentioned it? That I hadn't mentioned stealing a motor to come and find him? Or that I'd told them something else? But what?

'Eh...' I said. 'Just that I was going for some messages.'

'Messages,' he said and nodded, once, and just like that the good feeling in the van went. We drove on in silence, him not believing me, me hating him for not believing me. Neither of us able to say a word.

The road took us tight against the loch's east shore. I looked out over the water and tried to conjure up the king eel, but my heart just wasn't in it. All I saw was the loch's black surface and the low sky of brutish clouds, brilliant hazes of light shafting through.

We drove on until we ran out of road. Mikey turned and we went back the way we had come.

'Might have taken a wrong turn,' he said.

We came through a place called Drymen and went further east. We drove through lush fields, greener than you could imagine. So wet, so alive. Whichever way you looked the horizon was ringed by swollen mountains, closing in.

'You sure this is the way?' I asked, eventually.

'Aye, I am. Well, pretty sure. We go up this way.' He pointed at the oncoming road. 'Swing round the top of the loch and down.'

'All right,' I said.

Half an hour later we were approaching a suspiciously large town, the fields giving way to housing estates and roundabouts. A road sign confirmed it, welcoming us to Stirling.

'Fucken Christ,' I said.

'Aye, aye,' muttered Mikey. 'I know.'

Back we went. Back west. We were losing the day with all the fannying around. Back to Drymen and another try at going up and around the loch. Once again we ran out of road. It petered away in a land of rocky ochre hills and cold bodies of water.

'What are you playing at?' I said as the end of the road approached and the emptiness beyond opened up.

'It's a fucken hard map to follow,' he said.

'I know, but still!'

He pushed his fingertips into his eyes with frustration. 'This country,' he growled. 'How can it be so hard to get about in this fucken country?'

'Don't blame the country. It's not the country's fault.'

'No wonder it's such a shit hole when you can't even get from A to fucken B.'

He parked and went outside to blow off some steam. I opened up the back of the van and sat in the doorway, struggling to roll my fag. Once it was done I smoked it and watched him rampage up and down in impotent fury. I was too angry myself to laugh at the performance.

In the end we decided to camp where we were and try to get back to Balloch in the morning. Try going up the west side instead. There were some meagre rations in the van and we still had our gas stove. I did my best with setting up the stove but Mikey had to take over. He rooted out the supplies we'd taken from the old man's house and dispensed two tins of beans into the saucepan.

After dinner we went for a walk around the loch, turning back halfway because my arm was hurting too much. We went to bed early, out of boredom. Mikey pulled the sofa bed apart and we went down for the night. I slept on my right side to help with the pain.

I woke to a strange sound. It was like running water or bells. Light and tinkling. I pulled myself out of bed and opened the curtain. There was another van parked up beside us with a young man working away inside. A woman and a little girl were making their way across the grass to the loch, the little girl's laugh ringing out,

I opened the van door and stepped out. The man looked and I nodded. He nodded back. After some coughing, I rolled myself a fag and leaned on the bonnet of the van, looking out at the loch. That was the time to see nature, first thing. The water was full of lights and the sky and the land were fresh and empty. There was the slightest chill in the air that would soon disperse.

I watched the woman and the girl as they wandered down to the shore. The girl was about five or six, the woman maybe mid-thirties. They stood at the edge of the water and I could tell they were chatting to each other. Then the girl took off, into the water and the woman was trying to get her to come out, but also laughing.

I never understood the appeal in children. We had a couple of cousins growing up, Kevin and Darryl. Our mother's brother's bairns. I remembered them being hideous wee lumps, especially the younger one. He had them gummy eyes and a slimy mouth and he squinted at everyone. But his mother thought he was the best thing she'd ever seen, which is what I could never understand. They said that when you had a bairn your brain or your body pumped out a load of these chemicals that made you think it was great, the baby, despite being all weird and dirty.

There were a lot of things like that. Things I struggled

with understanding. The way that people sat and talked to each other about nothing at all, nothing important, nothing urgent. Just blethering. What was the point? What did that get you? Nothing, was the answer.

I watched the little girl play in the water and after a while the man came out of their camper and joined me, leaning on the bonnet of his own vehicle.

'She's some lassie,' he said, nodding to his daughter.

'Aye.'

'Whatever you say, she does the opposite.'

'I'm sure.'

'Here, how is this for a site? We saw your van and thought it must be allowed.'

I shook my head. 'We've only been here a night. Probably heading off later.'

'Ah,' he said. 'Right.'

I heard movement from inside our van, Mikey waking. I laughed, loudly, at the man's comment to let Mikey know I was talking to someone and to stay inside.

'You all right?' asked the man, confused.

'Aye, I'm fine.'

'That laugh,' he said.

'It was funny, what you said.'

'Was it?'

'Well,' I said. 'Best of luck.' I smiled at him and slipped back into our van.

Mikey was on the edge of the bed, bamboozled with sleep. His hair stuck out at the back from how closely I'd cut it.

'Who was that?' he whispered.

'Just some wankers. Tourists. A couple and a wee lassie.'

He nodded and then frowned. 'A wee lassie?'

'Aye.'

He ran his fingers through his hair and stubble and into

180

the cracks of his creased eyes. 'A wee lassie,' he whispered.

'What's the problem?'

'No problem.' He looked around the van, humming and hawing. He shoogled his knees. 'Shall we get going then?'

I sat down in the passenger seat, and twisted round to face him. 'What's the rush? Don't you want some breakfast or that before we head off?'

'Nah, I don't think so. I fancy heading off early. Hitting the road like soonish.'

I nodded. 'All right, if you say so.'

He jumped up with my permission and pulled his jeans on, hurrying to get the van started up. We turned it around and I could see the girl and her mother returning from the water, carrying a clear bag with water inside. The man waved at us as we took off and once we were away down the road Mikey let out a sigh.

'What're you sighing at?' I asked.

'I wasn't sighing. It was a yawn.'

'It sounded like a sigh,' I insisted. 'Like you were relieved.'

'Nope,' he said.

Our mother used to ask Mikey whether if I jumped off a bridge he would do the same. She was saying that he always copied me, that he looked up to me, that he did what I told him. As far as I could remember this was correct. When we played soldiers in the gardens I was always the sergeant and he was the private. I even remembered us playing trucks, on the living room floor. Mikey having the best truck, the shiny red one, and me holding out my hand for him to give me it, and he did. No words were exchanged, just the truck.

We drove straight through Balloch then up the west side of Loch Lomond. The water was still and calm, with the

181

hills on the far side reflected completely in the surface. At a point where the loch narrowed the road split in two and we took the left way, cutting across to the head of yet another body of water. I checked the napkin map. It looked like we were on the right track. We would go south and through Garelochhead and then we would be close to this *Very Heaven,* whatever it was.

Once we were through the town we started to see barbed wire fences springing up on either side of the road.

'What's all that?' Mikey wondered, nodding at the fencing.

'Not sure,' I admitted.

Grey hulking buildings began to form behind the fences. They looked like abattoirs or prisons. They made you feel cold.

'This is weird,' said Mikey. 'I wasn't expecting this.'

'No. Me neither.'

We crossed a roundabout and a sign read *HM Naval Base Clyde.*

'Oh,' said Mikey, pointing at the sign as he negotiated the roundabout. 'So it's the army or something. That makes sense, with the barbed wire and that.'

'The navy.'

'Aye. The navy.'

Something about the name stuck in my mind. There was something significant about it. Then I remembered. 'Christ,' I said. 'I know what this is. This is where they keep all the mad nuclear stuff. The nuclear subs and that.'

'Nuclear subs?'

'Like a submarine and it's got nuclear weapons in it. Like the A-bomb and that.'

'Oh,' said Mikey. 'Christ.'

I checked the map. Isaac was directing us south of there, so we kept going. The navy base was marked on the map with a skull and crossbones. The granite edifices died away and the road took us along by the water once more.

'That place gave me the willies,' Mikey said.

'I know,' I said, watching them vanish in the rear view mirror. 'There is something off about it.'

'Woah. Look at this.'

My attention snapped ahead. Hanging from the trees on the left side of the road was a large scarecrow or guy. It wore multi-coloured garments and had an afro wig on. The sign around its neck read *SHUN THE MEGATON*.

'What's that all about?' Mikey wondered.

I said that I didn't know. It looked like a protest of some sort, probably to do with the nuclear weapons housed behind us. I could only assume that someone had strung it up there as a warning. We kept on going and further down the road another sign appeared, nestled in the branches of trees: *HONEST INTENTIONS PEACE CAMP*.

'Peace camp,' Mikey read. 'Is this us?'

'I think it must be.'

'Here we go,' he said, turning left into the trees and onto a narrow path. There were signs and mad little figures dotted along either side of us. Mannequins dressed up in suits like politicians, holding plastic automatic rifles in their stiff arms. Bedsheets hanging between branches saying stuff like *BAIRNS NOT BOMBS* and *ATOMIC DEATH*. At the top of the path was an open area where we parked. A small wooden bridge led away from us, further into the woods.

'You sure this is a good idea?' he asked me.

I looked out into the trees with the hanging sheets. 'Aye,' I said.

Mikey gave me a woeful look and slunk out of the van.

I followed him and we wandered across the footbridge. There was bunting strung along the path to lead the way. The trees around were thick and old, green-barked with moss and lichen. The wind carried a soft tune that sounded like it was being played on a flute of some kind. I could smell a wood fire too.

We passed a clearing where the trees had been chopped away. There was a group of three men working, sawing wood and digging foundations. They stopped when they noticed us watching.

One of them held a hand up. 'Afternoon brothers,' he called.

'All right?' I shouted back.

'Here for a visit?' asked another.

'I suppose so.'

'Well, you're very welcome,' said the first.

'What're you building?' asked Mikey.

The second man laughed. 'Only the very first official church for the congregation.'

'Oh,' said Mikey. 'Right.'

'We can show you,' said the man. 'There's proper blueprints and everything.'

Mikey shook his head. 'You're all right.'

I gave them all a thumbs up and we kept going along the twisting path. The sound of human voices was growing louder and we were catching glimpses of people moving around ahead.

Mikey tucked his chin into the collar of his anorak.

A few heads turned when we entered the clearing but no one was concerned by our arrival. You would have struggled to notice two new faces amongst the hubbub we emerged into – a mass of moving people, a wild circle of tents enclosing them all. The sharp divide in the peoples

184

of the camp struck me immediately. Some were what we used to call crusties, meaning lots of dreadlocks and baggy pyjama bottoms and small beards and jewellery. The rest were dressed in what could only be described as robes. Identical magnolia robes. The camp was also split in two – one side a messy bazaar of tents, different sizes and colours, festooned in flags and banners and signs. The other side was cleaner and starker, an arc of canvas yurts.

The pair of us stood at the edge of the clearing and watched them. Most were busy at some kind of work, bustling between tents, holding papers, stopping to have intense conversations with their colleagues. Others sat around in chairs and on tree stumps in the clearing's middle, playing instruments and whittling.

'What now?' asked Mikey, quiet beside me.

'Just speak to one of them, I suppose. See what the story is.'

I looked around, trying to find a target – someone friendly or dumb looking. They were all intense in a very particular way. Every face I considered carried a stiff-jawed look of hard discomfort and I struggled to catch a likely eye. I was beginning to think Mikey might be right, that we should get out of there, when I saw him. Or rather I saw his hair, bouncing towards us among the crowd. Bright white, recently re-dyed.

It was Isaac.

'Lads, lads,' he was shouting, raising his hand above the heads, bounding and waving. We watched him approach till he stood in front of us, out of breath. 'Well,' he said. 'What're yous saying to it?'

'Not much,' I said.

'But yous came though, eh?'

'Aye. We did.'

'Grand,' he nodded. 'Grand. Well that's very good news. The Good News! How's it going wee Michael?'

'Fine.'

'I'm very glad. Ha!' he exclaimed, baring his teeth in a growl of delight. 'I cannae believe yous actually came!'

'Isaac,' I said. 'What's the story here man? What is this?'

He looked round at the clearing. 'What is this? It's only the bloody kingdom of heaven, present on this good earth.'

'Right. But what is it actually?'

'What is it actually? Well it's actually a peace camp, a protest camp, for the nukes down the loch. You've never heard of it? No? It's been here for ages man. Banning the bomb and all that.'

I nodded. 'I thought you said it was a church.'

'Oh! Right. See, there's two groups.' He held up a piece of his robes between two fingers. 'The ones in robes, that's my guys. The Church of the Real Presence of the Divine bloody Christ. The others, the hippies and that, they were here first.'

'Right. So why are yous all jammed into the same bit?'

'Ehm. Oh. I dunno actually. That's always how it's been. Anyway, never mind about all that,' he said, lunging at Mikey. 'Come here,' he said, pulling him in for a hug. He did the same to me and I cried out in pain. When he asked me what the matter was I pulled my collar down to show him.

'Holy hell,' he said. 'Your shoulder's knackered. What happened there?'

'Car crash,' I said. 'It's not that bad.'

'Is it fuck not that bad. Come on, let's get it sorted.'

He pulled the two of us along, through the clearing and towards the yurts. We passed by crusties painting

186

signs and skinning drums and we passed by churchies huddled in conversation and reading magazines. There was one yurt at the head of the clearing, slightly larger and grander than the rest. Isaac threw the door flap open to reveal a middle aged man, sitting crossed-legged on the floor. He had a vanity mirror set up and he was in the process of carefully combing his oiled hair into a sharp side parting.

His head shot up as the flap opened. 'Brother Isaac,' he said, throwing the comb and the mirror away. He had very large, hamsterish cheeks. 'How can I... Who are these two?'

'These are some friends I invited along, Michael and Paul. This is Brother Terry,' he told us. 'He's the boss of the church.'

'Now now Isaac,' said Brother Terry, standing and smiling. 'You know we don't believe in words like 'boss' or 'leader' here, do we?'

'No,' said Isaac. 'That's right. We're an organisation of brother and sisterhood, with power distributed equally and fairly,' he recited.

'That we are,' beamed Brother Terry, taking me and Mikey by the hand and greeting us like a salesman. 'Good to meet you boys.'

'Paul's had an accident,' said Isaac. 'Show Brother Terry.'

I pulled off my anorak with great difficulty and rolled up my T-shirt sleeve.

Brother Terry winced. 'My goodness,' he said. 'That's quite some sprain. Well, you've come to the right place. Did Isaac mention I was a doctor in the old world?'

'I thought you were a paramedic.'

Brother Terry's smile never faltered. 'There's not much difference between the two, not these days anyway. All

187

the exams are basically the same – it's just who you know. Come inside, let's have a look at you.'

I ducked into his yurt and kneeled in front of him. He looked me over, opening my mouth with his hand and peering inside, staring directly into my pupil. He got me to take my T-shirt off and he manoeuvred my arm around in his socket.

'Fuck,' I hissed.

'Bad pain,' he told me, 'comes from a bad mind.' Then with no warning at all he gripped me by the neck and upper arm and jerked my shoulder back into position.

It was lightning. It was an eclipse.

I fell backwards from the pain and lay on the floor of the yurt. I heard Mikey shout out.

'Clear your mind of badness,' advised Brother Terry. 'It'll help with the physical pain. Physical pain is an illusion, did you know that? The brain tells the shoulder to be sore but the shoulder itself isn't really sore.'

I wanted to tell Brother Terry that maybe I should break his nose and then see whether or not the pain felt like an illusion or not, but I couldn't. I sprawled on the ground and sighed and winced and felt my blood as it was forced through the screaming joint.

'Ach, come on. You're right as rain, son,' said Brother Terry, hauling me to my feet by my good arm. 'I'd want to watch out for those ligaments though. Once a shoulders been dislocated as bad as that for a few hours the ligaments are essentially knackered.'

Isaac and Mikey stood in the door of the yurt, watching me.

'All better?' asked Isaac.

'I wouldn't say that,' I told him.

'Are these two sticking around like long term?' asked

Brother Terry, flicking his index finger between Mikey and me.

'Well,' I sighed. 'Long termish, maybe.'

'You'll need to let my dad give them the once over if that's the case, Isaac,' said Brother Terry, shooing us away. 'You know the rules.'

Isaac led us back through the camp. We passed one woman, crouched on the ground, practising some kind of basic metalwork, hammering a sheet of steel into a flower shape. We passed a group of robed figures praying in a circle, on their knees. We passed a man laid back in a waxed beanbag, enjoying a gigantic joint. Everyone nodded at Isaac as we went and bongos were being played somewhere, unseen.

'Who are we going to meet?' asked Mikey, bamboozled by everything going on around him. 'Your boss's dad, was it?'

'Aye,' said Isaac. 'Brother Terry's dad set up the camp back in the 70s or something. He's dead old now, pretty scary actually. So he set it up 'cause he was totally cheesed off with all the war and nuclears and that and Brother Terry and his sister get brought up here. She's in charge of the protestors now. Well, no, I'm not supposed to say that about her either.'

I started to wonder what kind of soap opera this was, families and all that.

'So they don't get on?' I said.

'Brother Terry gets on with everyone,' said Isaac, solemnly. 'That's one of his prime attributes. But you can tell Beth's pissed off with the whole thing. You'll meet her, soon enough.'

We were nearing the side of the clearing cluttered with wacky tents. Again, one of the dwellings on this side was more elaborate than the rest. There was a muscular woman in a camp chair outside, a pile of papers on her crossed legs and a mobile between her ear and shoulder.

'Sister Beth,' said Isaac.

She glanced up. 'Don't call me that.'

'Sorry. Beth.'

'What can I do for you?' she asked.

'Brother Terry said I should introduce my friends to Brother Angus. They're sticking around for a bit.'

She took the phone away from her neck and rubbed her nose in frustration. 'He's not your brother, Isaac. He's our dad. You don't have to call him that, he's not part of your thing.'

'All right,' said Isaac. 'Sorry. Can we go in?'

'Probably not, actually. He's having a bad day today. Couldn't they come back tomorrow or something, when he's feeling better?'

'It's just...' said Isaac. 'I mean, Brother Terry did say for us to come.'

Beth sprang out of her camp chair, the papers spilling to the ground. 'I tell you what,' she said. 'You lot just do whatever it is you want to do, Isaac. How does that sound?'

Isaac watched her storm away, thin-lipped. 'That's a shame,' he said, ushering us inside. 'A proper shame.'

There was a vast pile of cushions and pillows piled on the floor of the tent, propping up a tiny, wizened man. He had a large oxygen tank under his arm, a tube connecting it up with the mask over his mouth and nose. There was a paperback in his spiderish hands, which he lowered as we entered.

'Afternoon Brother Angus,' said Isaac, bowing.

The old man frowned at Isaac for a long time, then he put the book down on his chest and fiddled with the mask. He was no larger than a ten-year-old boy. 'Eh?' he wheezed.

Isaac hesitated. 'I was just saying hello, Angus.'

'Aye. Hello,' said the old man, and then, 'Who're you?'

'I'm Brother Isaac. I'm part of your son's church,' said Isaac, his voice low.

'Terry? Terry's what? His purse?'

'No,' said Isaac. 'His church. You know?'

'It all goes over my head,' wheezed the old man, directing his words at Mikey and startling him.

'I just wanted to introduce you to a few mates of mine,' explained Isaac. 'See if they're OK to stay at the camp.'

'Aye,' said Angus. 'That's right. The camp. I invented it, did you know that?' he asked, again of Mikey. 'Something about... Christ, I don't know. It was a good cause though, you understand.'

'OK,' said Mikey.

The old man's eyes were milky but still full of crackling energy. 'Let me get you a bowl of stew,' he said, making moves to hoist himself out of his pillow pile.

Isaac rushed forward, calming the old man but also restraining him. 'That's all right, Brother Angus. You just rest yourself.'

'Aye. Rest. That's what I was saying. A good rest never did anyone any harm, did it Terry?' This was once again directed at Mikey.

'Nope,' said Mikey, shaking his head.

Isaac forced the mask onto the old man's face, waving for us to back out of the tent.

12

We set off into the hills, away from the camp. Isaac was excited about what he had to show us next – a small waterfall and plunge pool, hidden in the rocks far above the tents.

'This was where Brother Terry baptised me,' he said, pointing into the pool. 'A quick dunk under the water and I came out clean. Other folk get it done down in the loch. Doesn't matter though, eh? Water's water. Yous fancy going in?'

I declined but Mikey and Isaac stripped off and jumped from the overhanging boulder into the pool. I sat on the side and rolled myself a fag, watching them.

'Christ,' Mikey cried. 'It's freezing!'

'It's good for you,' said Isaac. 'Opens up the veins.'

I sat, smoking and enjoying the scenery. You could see across the treetops to the water of the vast loch beyond. Some kind of naval ship was coasting along, full of turrets and sticky out bits, an evil looking thing. I began to grow distracted, feeling myself shift around in time. I was in the woods, in the woods here and the woods before. The long ago day. Me and Mikey throwing bricks at a tree. Ticking off from the school and getting told off by the mums in the swing park. Someone else was there with us too. A little girl, one of the ones from the park before. I asked her why she wasn't at school and she told us she was ill. Why wasn't she at the swing park then? Because she'd fallen out with her mum. And then Mikey told her she should come with us. We had something to show her.

We walked with the little girl beside us. Mikey asking her what school she goes to, whether she likes it or not. She tells us it's fine. Mikey says he bets she's a little swot. A little brown-noser. No, she tells us. She's not.

I try to give him the eye, to tell him this is getting silly, we should take her back to the swing park. He ignores me. Keeps going, keeps asking her all these questions, mostly about the school. I can tell it's because of how he was embarrassed by Mr MacPherson, his teacher. He's taking all of it out on the wee lassie.

She asks us where we're going and he tells her not to be so nosy. That we've got something amazing to show her, haven't we Paul? Aye, I say. That's right. She trusts me, I think. Whatever Mikey ended up doing, what I did was as bad, or worse. Because she trusted me.

I don't know if he has a plan as he leads us forward, onwards, into the heart of the wood. It feels like his anger is the one in charge. This poor wee lassie. She only has moments of life left. She's so delicate that she flickers in my memory, somewhere between real and not. Mikey tells us to hurry up, that he wants to show us something. Something amazing.

And we follow him.

I shook my head and I noticed that Mikey and Isaac had swum over to the far side of the plunge pool and were treading water close together. They were talking but were too far off for me to hear. Their heads were turned away and all I could see was their arms moving and splashing in the water.

'Hey,' I shouted. 'Mikey. Time to get out now.'

193

He swum himself round to face me. 'Already?'

'Aye. That's enough swimming.'

Later on there was a big dinner. We had vegetarian sausages cooked in foil on the fire and oily mashed potatoes. Isaac wasn't around, having been taken away by Brother Terry on official business. We sat on a log among the munching crowd. There was a hippie girl on my right, wearing rainbow pyjamas, and a bald-headed church member on Mikey's left.

'Couldn't we have some proper bangers?' asked Baldy over the top of Mikey. 'This veggie nonsense is so dry.'

Rainbow Pants tutted. 'If you don't like it then don't eat it.'

'It's not like I've got much choice. Mind when that farmer dropped off a lovely side of lamb but yous lot said we had to throw it away.'

'It was disgusting,' moaned Rainbow Pants. 'All the blood and whatever in the plastic bag. Eugh.'

'That was good lamb, said Baldy, waving his fork at the fire. 'High quality.'

'I don't care what quality it was. If you want to murder animals, then do it on your side of the camp. This,' she said, gesturing to the middle of the camp, 'is meant to be a safe place. And that means safe for everyone.'

'What do you mean *safe*? It is safe, isn't it?'

'Safe means safe for everyone to express themselves without being stifled.'

'How is a nice bit of lamb stifling anyone?'

'I'm not going to discuss this with you.'

Baldy speared one of his sausages on his fork. He held it up and gave Mikey and me a *the-things-I-put-up-with* look before biting into it. Leaning over us, he said to Rainbow Pants. 'Who are this pair then?'

Rainbow Pants checked us out, scowling. 'How should I know?'

'What are you then?' Baldy asked us. 'Are you us or them?'

'We're mates of Isaac's,' said Mikey.

'Ah,' laughed Baldy. 'Nice one. Another few for the Church.'

'You're welcome to them,' muttered Rainbow Pants.

'I wouldn't say that,' I told Baldy. 'We're not paid-up members or anything. We're just here for a visit.'

'Oh,' said Baldy. 'Fine. Be like that.'

'A fine example of Churchly goodness there,' said Rainbow Pants.

'Are you coming along tonight at least?' asked Baldy.

'Aye,' I said, not knowing what he meant. 'We'll be there.'

'Oh Jesus,' said Rainbow Pants, rolling her eyes. 'Not another one.'

'We're perfectly entitled to perform our ceremonies are we not? Freedom of religion and all that. Brother Angus said so.'

Mikey pushed the chopped up sausages and mash around on his plate, uncomfortable with the argument going on over his head.

'Oh Brother Angus,' scoffed Rainbow Pants. 'He's so ancient he'd agree to anything. And it's only because Terry's his son.'

'I thought this was meant to be a safe place,' said Baldy, standing up and revealing his true height, which must have been pushing seven foot. He threw his paper plate into the fire and sulked off to the Church's side of camp.

'We're meant to recycle those,' Rainbow Pants sighed.

She introduced herself as Mairead and offered a many-ringed hand to shake.

'Pleased to meet you,' she said to each of us. 'Sorry about him. That lot are so fucking sensitive.'

'What're they all about?' I asked, leaning in, the fire's heat touching my cheek. 'Isaac's told us a bit about it but not what they actually do.'

'It's all bollocks mate,' Mairead said. 'It's just nonsense that Terry made up to make himself feel better. Angus kicked him out years ago – this is before my time mind – for being a waste of space. Then he comes back years later with these followers and his mumbo jumbo religion.'

All around the fire were similar clusters of people, sitting on logs, enjoying their food. Everything smelled of the spice of wood smoke, even the food in my mouth.

'I just ignore them when they go on about it but the best I can tell is that they think Jesus has been reincarnated. He's on earth somewhere. Hence why they're involved in our thing, in the nukes thing, cause they don't want governments blowing everything, including the Son of God, up.'

After tea was over and the night was drawing in Isaac reappeared, with Brother Terry in tow. He rushed over to tell us the Church was having a ceremony down on the beach and did we want to come?

'I dunno,' I said.

'I dunno,' Mikey echoed.

'Ach, come on. It'll be a laugh if nothing else,' said Isaac, giving us the old doe-eyes.

Not wanting to be disrespectful and harm our place in the camp, we agreed. Isaac punched the air then led us over to one of the yurts to be fitted for our robes. We walked in a large pack with the rest of the God-botherers through the camp and down the path through the woods, passing the footbridge and our van on the way to the main road. Beth, the muscular woman, was hanging around by the exit to camp. She caught her brother's eye as we passed. We crossed the main road away from camp and through the thin barrier of trees to the beach. I remembered the last time Mikey and I were on a beach. I remembered Duncan's muscles struggling under my grip like snakes. I remembered lowering him into the water. It was a good memory for me. A victory.

Brother Terry led the group to the water's edge. There were maybe fifteen or twenty robed figures standing there, facing the loch and the setting sun.

Brother Terry beamed. 'I can't tell you how happy I am to be here with you all on this fine evening the Lord has blessed us with.'

'Testify,' shouted someone from behind me.

Isaac whooped.

'I enjoy your enthusiasm,' said Brother Terry. 'You all know that we have difficult times ahead, yet here you are, dedicated and faithful. United in a common good. And does the good book not say, "Let those who would join in God's church be forever joined"?'

'Yes it does,' someone called.

He continued. 'It has been a long road and a hard one to boot, but here we are. Approaching our end goal. We all know about Revelation, do we not?'

'Aye,' said Baldy, 'we do.'

Isaac whooped.

'But think about it,' said Brother Terry. 'What else does that word mean. Go on, think about it. Take the time to consider it properly and carefully. Can anyone tell me?'

It was like being back at the school. No one wanted to answer for fear of being made to look stupid. I raised my hand a little. 'It means to find something out.'

'Exactly brother,' said Brother Terry, happy with me. 'Exactly right. A revelation. The stripping away of transient, corporeal material to reveal the true essence of a thing. He is out there you know. He walks among us, unseen. Jesus Christ. He might be an Inuit fisherman or a toddler, sick with diarrhoea, in an Amahara tribe. We do not know. All we know is that we can feel him out there, waiting for us, patient, waiting for the great revelation of his true identity.'

Brother Terry paused for a moment with a look of great sincerity on his face. The crowd waited, tense. Then he smiled and everyone began to cheer and Isaac was whooping loudest of all.

Brother Terry struggled to speak above the noise. 'It is a good feeling, isn't it? To know that salvation is so close at hand, within the lifetime of a man? This is an old story but I feel compelled to share it with the newer members.' Hands reached out and stroked my back. I could tell it was happening to Mikey as well. 'I was in an exodus of my own making, was I not brothers and sisters? Cast out of my father's house, wandering in the desert. Aye, I had the base pleasures of alcohol, of money, of fornication, but was I happy?'

A low rumble went through the group – displeasure at the base pleasures Brother Terry had mentioned. Something told me he had only really been troubled by the first of those three vices.

'No. No, I was not happy. But then I dreamed. It was a glorious dream, was it not? In my dream He came to me. God, the son, the ghost. He came to me as a little girl, clad in grave clothes. A murdered child. He spoke to me in the little girl's voice, saying, I am with you. I am within you. I am beside you.'

The group was well-versed in brother Terry's sermon, clapping each time he said *you*.

'But you all know me. I am not a crazy person, am I?

198

Oh no. Am I to think that a dream of a murdered child speaking with the voice of God is enough? No. Goodness no. But what happens next my brothers and sisters? I wake up, in my den of filth, of fornication and booze fumes, and turn on the television. What do I see but that same girl, murdered in this world, in our world.'

Several people hissed, the rest stood in silence, their eyes open and mournful, accepting each of Brother Terry's words. I looked at Mikey and he looked back. It was just a coincidence. Nothing more.

'I will be honest with you brother and sisters,' said Brother Terry, his eyes filling with moisture. 'It floored me. I packed my things at once and headed north. I severed all ties, just as you have done. I burned all bridges, just as you have done. I let myself become reborn, just as you have done.'

Brother Terry had his hands in the air and he was moving through the crowd, gripping people by their own airborne hands.

'And now. And now. He is coming, is he not? Have we not felt his presence drawing closer? Have we not read the signs? Have we not studied closely the forecasts? He is coming to save us and all he needs is a signal. A signal that we will provide.'

He roared that last sentence and the crowd went wild, stamping their feet and clapping and screeching. The sun was coming down low above the hills across the water, dying and bleeding and scorching the horizon. The blood was in the water too.

'Get in there,' laughed brother Terry, gesturing to the water, 'you filthy heathens and wash yourselves clean.'

The crowd streamed around us and splashed into the water, wading out to waist height. Only Mikey and me and Brother Terry still stood on the shore. We watched as the robed figures knelt and drew up handfuls of loch water, pouring it over their heads and smiling. Some of them submerged themselves completely, bobbing along beneath the water. I had never seen such concentrated joy in a group of people.

Brother Terry sidled over to us. 'Can't I tempt you?'

I shook my head. 'I don't think so.'

'That's a pity,' he smiled, 'and you?'

Mikey grimaced. 'I don't think so,' he said.

'That sounds like a firm yes. Lads,' he shouted to the people in the water, 'another one for the dook.'

They all cheered and two of them, including Baldy, stomped up the beach and proceeded to scoop Mikey up, carrying and throwing him headfirst into the loch.

'You're sure?' asked Brother Terry.

'Sure,' I said.

'That's a pity,' he said again. 'I had thought the two of you showing up out of nowhere, the significance of that, was something of a sign, but never mind. One of you is better than none.'

'What do you mean?' I asked. 'What significance?'

He ignored me, looking instead at the nuclear base across the water. 'They can smell it,' he said. 'Smell something on the wind. Something changing, and they don't like it one bit.'

And with that he waded out himself, patting his brothers and sisters on the shoulder, helping Mikey to stand and embracing him. I noticed that he didn't deign to wet his own head. His oiled, sharply parted haircut remained in perfect order.

13

I woke with my nose pressed against the thin fabric of our tent and in that moment of time, barely out of dreaming, I thought we were back in the field again. To my surprise I experienced a surge of pleasure in this idea. I thought, I'm free. But then I turned onto my back and saw shadows moving on the canvas and I remembered. Mikey and I emerged blinking into the morning air to see the whole place alive with moving bodies, making themselves ready. So much excitement in the camp that you could feel it all up and down your arms. We dressed and followed the crowd as it made its way out of camp. We walked in a sea of dreadlocks and braids and misshapen hats.

Mairead had joined Beth near the front and we walked beside the huge bald guy. I was surprised to see him as I had pinned him down as one of the Godheads. We followed the same route as the night before, down the bridge and past the van. I noticed the builders were out working on the church again. They stopped their work to watch us as we passed. We walked up the road, back towards the roundabout Mikey and I had passed on the way there. Every so often a car would come along behind or in front of us and we would all have to step into the grassy ditch that ran beside the road. The cars would pass and the people inside would ogle us.

'Michael,' Mairead shouting down the group. 'Are you needing a sign?'

I looked to Mikey and then realised she was addressing me – in the confusion of the march she'd mixed us up. I explained and she laughed, saying how similar we looked. We were given a large banner to hold between us that read *NUCLEAR BOMBS MEANS NO CLEAR FUTURE*. Making our way up to the roundabout and the embankment beside the entrance to the naval base, I saw there was a steady stream of traffic turning in.

'What happens now?' I asked Baldy.

He pointed at the embankment. 'We stand there and give them a load of grief.'

He was right. We crowded on the embankment across the roundabout from the base's entrance and held our signs up and shouted at the workers as they drove in.

'It's a bit daft this,' I whispered to Mikey.

'I feel daft. Everyone's looking at us.'

Mairead was at the front, creating energy. 'What do we want?' she would shout and then we would tell her what we wanted. No bombs, or whatever.

There was a pile of rubble down the back of the embankment. When no one was looking I stooped down and picked up a small pebble. I threw it towards the queue of cars, disguising the motion as a lavish handclap above my head. The pebble swan dived through the air and for a moment I lost it in the brightness. Then a sound went *ching* and one of the motors braked. Out of it climbed a man, his sleeves rolled back to reveal blueish arm tattoos. He looked at his motor for a moment before turning to the protest.

I got a worm of excitement in my belly from his visible anger.

'Excuse me,' he shouted, gesturing to the tiny crack that shone on his windscreen.

Mairead turned, confused. 'Sir,' she called. 'Please keep driving. This is a peaceful protest.'

The man shivered. 'Tell that to my fucken window,' he said, pointing to his motor.

Mairead peered over the road to the man's motor and the line of cars piled up behind it. All their windows were rolled down so their drivers could ogle the confrontation.

'That wasn't us,' she told him.

'It fucken was,' he said. 'I seen the rock. It came off of you lot.'

'Piss off,' I shouted, from deep within the crowd.

The man marched right over to us, blocking the traffic coming the other way too. 'One of yous is going to pay up,' he said. 'Now.'

'We're not paying anything,' said Mairead. 'This is a peaceful protest.'

'If I wasn't a law abiding soul then I would take a great measure of joy in murdering every one of you lot,' he told us.

Mairead stared at the man for a while. You could see the cogs turning and inside I urged her to be rash. Instead, she faced us, leaving the man out in the cold.

'What do we want?' she asked and we told her, some more reluctantly than others.

The man stood in the road, watching us chant. 'I want a new windshield,' he shouted after a few runs through of the ditty. 'Does nobody care about that?'

'Piss off,' I shouted again.

That one made him cock his head. He nodded, smiling, and waddled backwards to his motor. I could see him in his car, urging the waiting vehicles to go around, his hand flapping from the open window. When they were past he drove into the base behind them.

We went back to banner waving and I soon grew

bored. I left them to it and sat beyond the embankment at the edge of the woods, rolling myself a fag. I lay back against the grass and watched the sun shining through the leaping flags and boards and banners.

I thought back to those long years when Mikey was inside. What had I done? I'd finished school, I'd had odd jobs, signed on a wee bit. I had kept my head down. There was still a lot of what was called the stigma. Everyone knew I'd been with Mikey on the day he'd done it and I was never trusted again, not really. People would look at me funny or even be hostile, on the bus for example. Not that I'd been close with many folk in the first place. I'd had one good friend in primary school who had stuck by me.

Pungo Henderson was his name, the one good friend. Me and Pungo had fought viciously when we were in the primary school over something now lost to history. He ended up with a chip in his incisor and then after that we were mates. I couldn't remember me and Pungo ever really talking to each other in the way you saw other lads do. We would do stuff together and go places together and we would comment on the things we saw but it was all very, look at that, and, aye, I know, it's mental.

That's not to say there wasn't a connection between Pungo and me. There was, but it was unspoken. We didn't need to discuss where we would wander to after school because our feet would take us there. One time we finished ourselves off together, facing over a steep hill, the wind blowing cold against the ends of our cocks.

When I told Pungo about the whole Mikey thing he gawked at me though his thick spectacles. Not out of horror, that was just how Pungo looked. He asked me what would happen to Mikey and I told him he'd probably get the jail. His top lip had curled back and he'd gurgled. That was how Pungo laughed. He wasn't laughing at me, just at the madness of the situation.

I couldn't remember what happened to Pungo. For a long time after we'd finished at the school he had worked nights at the supermarket, pushing cages of frozen food in the early hours under fluorescents. There were times when I couldn't sleep and I would go out for one my night walks, popping in to say hello. His glasses would be completely white from the lights and the cold mist from the freezers. He would ask me if there was any info on Mikey and I'd tell him about the latest parole news, all that kind of stuff.

A little while after that Pungo went away. There was a hassle about him walking into the woman's toilets when a customer was in there and I never really got the full story because I never spoke to him again. He moved away because of the backlash. I didn't remember if I ever missed Pungo once he was gone. In fact it was a relief, of sorts, because looking at Pungo made me remember the silly childish stuff we used to get up to, like the finishing ourselves off over the steep hill thing, and other stuff too.

Once, before Mikey did what he did, Pungo and I were messing about at the school in the evening. We must have been fourteen, maybe younger. We were sitting on the stairs leading to the school entrance, in near silence. Pungo was probably doing his deep breathing and I was probably looking at this and that, thinking about things. Maybe complaining about my stepdad. I had a hard time with him.

See, the thing about my stepdad was that he was Mikey's actual dad, which made us half-brothers or stepbrothers maybe. That distinction was always made clear even though it had all happened when I was wee, back before I could remember. My own dad had been a trucker who had trucked away before I came along. Our stepdad had long hair and he wore the T-shirts of the heavy metal bands he liked. That was where Mikey and I picked up the habit, the long hair thing.

So I was probably complaining to Pungo about my stepdad favouring Mikey in some way. Maybe how Mikey had got a bigger portion at tea the night before or he was getting to go to SeaWorld and I wasn't. I probably told Pungo about a lot of that stuff while he breathed deeply.

And then this wee kid shows up in the playground. Just a normal wee kid and me and Pungo spy him and go, Aha, here's a likely target. We ask the wee boy what he's up to and he tells us he's just messing about. Ooh, we go, like he's in trouble. You're not allowed up here, Pungo Henderson tells the wee boy and the wee boy gets all defensive. I'm allowed wherever I like, he tells us.

Pungo doesn't take kindly to wee the boy's cheek. He tells the wee boy if he's not careful he'll end up getting his head kicked in. We go down the stairs and stand up close to the wee boy, not letting him get past when he wants to leave. We box him into a corner, between the school itself and a wall. He's struggling and trying to get away from us and he seems especially creeped out by Pungo but we won't let him get away and we're saying he's going to be in so much trouble. So much trouble.

Eventually he got away by slipping between Pungo's clasping hands. He took off like a rocket, dodging across the playground away from us. We shouted after him. I noticed that Pungo's face was shining and his top lip was curling back and he was gurgling, enjoying himself.

206

But that was just boys being boys. That wasn't anything like what Mikey did.

I finished my fag and threw it into the trees behind me. The protest was still ongoing. Mikey looked over his shoulder, giving me a pleading look.

'Paul,' he shouted over the din they were making. Again, 'Paul!'

I heaved myself up. I shrugged.

'Come and see,' he said.

I hopped up the back of the embankment and peered over Baldy's twisting shoulder. There was a line of white cars pulling up in front of the protest. Their doors opened and men in suits clambered out, all of them paunchy and many of them moustached. One of them pulled a notebook from the chest pocket of his mackintosh. He held it in front of him as he approached the front of the group.

'I was wonderin if I could ask a coupla questions,' he said.

He watched the front row of the protest with a dry smirk, waiting for someone to talk. Was he police? Was he CID or whatever?

One of the hippies down the front said, 'Well...' but was immediately silenced by the man in the mac. He plunged his fist through his upheld notebook and into the face of the hippie who had spoken. Quick glances flew around the roadside like gunfire. Had he really just done that? Where were these fuckers from?

Then the scuffle broke out.

The paunchy men laid into us with gusto. They had the sleeves of their mackintoshes and suits and donkey jackets rolled up as they cuffed us and knocked us and pushed us. I dodged through the melee, doing my best to avoid any violence directed at me while maintaining a presence in the group. I saw Baldy being rolled down the embankment. I saw Mairead batter away a man wearing Cuban heels and a handlebar moustache with the stick of her sign.

Where was Mikey?

The men in suits were shouting orders to each other, telling their colleagues to restrain us. They weren't having much luck. Like me, the protestors were slippery, resisting but never assaulting their attackers.

Then I saw him.

He was cowering behind the tallest policeman. As the copper ran and hustled and tried to pin down the hippies, Mikey shadowed him, ducking and dodging to remain unseen.

'Mikey, you clown,' I shouted over the noise.

He stopped and looked up. The tall policeman's elbow went back and caught Mikey on the cheekbone. My blood started kicking in from the noise and from Mikey getting hit. I pranced through the bodies and kicked the tall policeman in the back of the knee. He went down on the ground. I got Mikey and off we went into the trees behind the road. The rest of them could deal with the palaver they'd started. The land above the road was steep. We scrambled up it on our hands, away from the shouts and roars behind us. We hoisted ourselves up by the bare roots spilling from the hillside and managed to hide in a dense copse, halfway up.

'Shite,' I whispered, over and over again, peering out, seeing nothing.

Mikey continuing to gulp and to shiver.

They've found us, I thought. They've fucken tracked us down. The police were probably holding down the protestors, showing them a photograph, saying, Have you seen this man? We've had reports that he's in the area.

See, he was put away for doing in a bairn years and years ago and now he's gone missing, not been present for his parole meeting. Yes indeed, a very suspicious figure. Not only that but we've got two missing persons on our hands now and we're *very* concerned that they may be linked. I put my arm around my brother, feeling his ribs jitter. His hand went up to clear off the gore from his face.

'Leave it,' I said. 'They won't recognise you all fucked up like that.'

'But it feels horrible,' he whispered.

'Just leave it,' I whispered back. 'It's better.'

His voice was bloated with frustration. He said, 'I want to take it off.'

I held him closer than ever. I gripped his bones. I said, 'Listen to me. Just leave it, all right?'

He wriggled himself free a little and made a noise of protest.

My blood was moving through me like music. 'I swear to fucken God...' I spat.

'Fine,' he said.

We waited up there, in the wet vegetation, until the bodies below thinned away, until we stopped seeing the blue lights sift through trunks. Then we slid down the hillside on our arses, back to the road. It was empty.

'Oh,' I shouted, the air rushing from me. My blood coming back down again was like emerging from beneath water. 'Oh thank fuck!'

Mikey was less enthusiastic than I was. He lurked at the roadside, nursing his injuries and keeping his eye trained on me.

I laughed. 'We were this close,' I said, showing him the space between my fingertips. 'Who knows what you might have told them.'

He nodded.

209

'Come on,' I said. 'I'm starving.'

I went off down the road but didn't get far before I realised he wasn't following. I turned back. 'Well?'

'It was you that chucked the stone at the bloke's motor, wasn't it?' he asked. His face was squeezed with anger.

'Was it fuck. It was probably one of them hippies. They were dying for it all to kick off.'

'I seen you, man,' he said, a tiny crack in his voice. 'I seen you throw it. Why've you got to be like that?'

'You've lost it,' I told him. 'You've only been here a day and already you've gone loopy. You're going to be easy pickings.'

'I haven't lost it. You chucked the stone. I saw it. Why've you got to be like that when...' He couldn't go on and his chin was dimpling with emotion.

'You fucken baby,' I called him.

'Why do you keep doing this to me?' he asked. 'I'm supposed to be your brother.'

'Keep doing what?'

'Keep getting me into... into...' he looked around himself.

I nodded, getting what he was going for. 'You get yourself into trouble, mate.'

'Do I?'

'Aye. You do,' I said.

'I don't think I do get myself in trouble. I think it's you,' he pointed towards me, his arm straight as a rod, 'that gets *me* in trouble.'

14

We wandered into camp and stood by the fire in our torn clothes and the blood crusting on Mikey's face.

'*Hello*?' I shouted, after too long being ignored.

Faces turned to us like satellite dishes shifting towards their signal, none of them I recognised, until Beth emerged from her father's tent.

'You pair,' she said, marching towards us.

'Aye?' I said.

Beth said, 'Hold on,' and then turned, facing the camp at large. 'All right,' she said, her voice raised. 'Just so everyone knows, I'm making an executive decision. These two here,' she said, her finger moving between me and Mikey, 'these two are hereby banished from the camp. Got that?'

I took a step closer to her. 'We're banished?'

'You heard me,' she said. 'A pair of fucking liabilities you two.'

I couldn't think of anything to say. I looked at Mikey and he shrugged. What I would've given to show her how powerful I was, how easily I could beat her. Just a moment alone together and I would show her.

'Just a second, Sister Beth,' said a voice from behind me.

Beth screwed her eyes up. 'What now?'

'You're being hasty,' said Brother Terry, emerging from behind the far side of the campfire.

'Honestly,' said Beth, holding her hands up. 'I do not have time for all this. I've put up with you for so long Tel but please, just get on with whatever you want to get on with in peace and quiet.'

Brother Terry nodded. 'I'm happy to do so.'

'Good.'

'Unless it interferes with our freedom of religion.'

Beth moaned.

'You don't agree, Sister Beth?'

The entire place silent.

'No, no, I agree. Whatever Tel, I agree.'

'Then these two stay,' he said, nodding at us.

I was expecting a gasp from somewhere but none came. Everyone stared at us

'No,' said Beth. 'They don't. They caused trouble at the protest, meaning these goons start showing up – these plainclothes or private security or whatever they are – and then best of all they come straight back here. Do I have to go on?'

'You can go on if you like. They stay.'

'They go.'

'They're very brave parishioners, standing up to the authorities like that. Did you know that our very own Jesus Christ was seen as something of a terrorist in his time? A Jewish fundamentalist. Yes, there is a rich tradition of non-compliance in the Church.'

Beth made a face.

Brother Terry smiled. 'Do we need to get Father involved?'

'Oh Jesus. Fine, fine. Tell me why they stay?'

'Because,' Brother Terry said, circling the campfire and grasping hold of Mikey's robed shoulder, 'of this one. He's who we've been waiting for.'

Beth laughed. 'You don't mean to say...'

'I do.'

I'd had enough of their carry on by then. Either we were in or we were out. I put my hand up. 'What's the story here?' I asked.

Brother Terry put a gentle finger against his own bottom lip. 'How do I put this best?' he wondered. 'Hm. Well, your brother is the Christ reborn. In the flesh. How's that for starters?'

Then the gasp came, from the robed side of camp. Beth started to laugh though her face was untroubled by any genuine amusement.

'Laugh all you like Sister, it's true. I've read the signs, I have divined the portents. I just never expected he would walk into our laps so easily.'

Mikey shrugged himself free of Brother Terry's grip. 'I don't know what you're on about mate.'

'I'm on about you. You're it. You're him. You probably don't know it yet but you are.'

Even under all the blood I could tell that Mikey was rattled. He was tense in the arms and was keeping his back to the fire. 'Nah,' he said. 'You've got it wrong.'

'Can I politely disagree? You are. Isaac has told me a lot about you, of the sacrifices you've made, of your long years in the desert. I mean, look at today even. You've shed blood in order to assist the greater good. What is more Christ-like than that?'

I watched Terry as he spoke, his bulging cheeks working away, his slippery hair blazing. I watched his eyes as he mentioned Mikey's long years in the desert and then I realised.

He knew.

'It may not be clear to you just this second,' he continued, 'but momentous events are close at hand. Your revelation is coming.'

And then Beth exploded. 'This is what I mean,' she was saying, pushing folk out the way and getting her brother by the front of his robe. 'You are the problem here. Things were fine until you showed up.'

Brother Terry wasn't looking at her but rather over her shoulder. I followed his gaze and was surprised to see a miniscule, weathered man in the opening of the largest tent. It was their father.

'What's going on?' he breathed, his hand flapping up and down the front of his leather vest.

Beth and Terry fell apart, standing to attention. The old man glowered at them.

'Well?' he said.

'Nothing,' said Beth.

'Nothing,' agreed Terry.

'Good,' he said, shuffling back into his tent, pulling the waist of his cords back up his skinny arse.

The camp held its breath, waiting for the next thing to happen. Terry took the lead, sweeping through them all, dragging Mikey along by the sleeve of his robe with me following behind.

'We can discuss this later,' he told Beth as he brushed past her.

He deposited Mikey and me inside the largest yurt, closing us in with him. He turned on the electric light that hung from the pointed ceiling and stood in front of us, beaming.

'You slimy bastard,' I said. 'You know.'

'Of course I know,' said Brother Terry. 'Do you think I'm daft? You heard my sermon the other day. Your brother's case was always very important to me. To the church, I mean.'

Mikey looked baffled. He gave me one of his looks.

'This one,' I said, letting my finger stray very close

214

to Brother Terry's face, 'knows all about you, Mikey. All about you getting the jail and the wee lassie and everything. It's all part of this sick thing he's got going on here.'

'Fuck,' exclaimed Mikey.

'What is it you want?' I asked. 'If it's cash then you're out of luck.'

Brother Terry nodded. He put his hands together. 'I do not believe that an evil man cannot also be a good man. Some evil is necessary. Consider Judas, one of history's most reviled traitors. He is hated, is he not, for the wrongs he committed against the Christ? But why?'

I sighed.

'Exactly. The whole thing rests on Judas. Without Judas's betrayal then the rest does not happen. We don't have the crucifixion, we don't have the ascension, we do not have our sins being washed away by the Lord's sacrifice. So why should we hate a man that commits evil if the evil leads to good?'

I knew what he was getting at. He was saying that Mikey doing what he did was a good thing, because it brought him here, to the camp, where Brother Terry and his cult thought he could be Jesus and reveal him. It was bollocks – that much was clear.

'Do you see what I'm saying, Michael?' he asked.

Mikey sucked his lip. 'You think I'm Jesus but only not yet. Something else happens and then I am.'

Brother Terry laughed. 'That's a fair summary.'

'So what do you want from us?' I asked again.

'I just want you to stay and be with us so that we can learn from your brother.'

'And then what?'

Brother Terry looked at me and I was struck by the peace in his face. His eyelids were so heavy they appeared

215

slick, oiled in some way. 'And then something happens and everything changes.'

I walked headfirst into Isaac as I left Terry's yurt. He'd been kneeling by the door flap, listening in, and I nearly toppled over him.

He looked up at me, forehead furrowed.

I told him to come with me and I dragged him up, stumbling and lurching, out of the camp and higher on the slope. We didn't speak until we made the waterfall. The tumbling foam hissed in falling white bundles. I made Isaac sit down on a rock, jutting like a molar from the earth, dark from the fall's spray.

'You said you wouldn't talk about it,' I said.

He gathered his robes up in twisting hands. 'I know I did. I'm sorry. It wasn't the right thing to do but Terry…' He looked at the water, at the grey lather formed by the colliding streams.

'What about Terry?'

'It's just… He knows stuff. He can tell stuff about you, sometimes without you even knowing it yourself. After I left you guys at the ferry and I hitched up north he could smell it on me. He was like, Isaac, tell me about your travels. And I was all like, Oh naw, nothing much happened Brother Terry. But he knew something was up.'

He finished talking and looked at the falls.

'So you sold us out, just like that?'

'Aye.'

'And what did you tell him – exactly, I mean to say?'

'What did I tell him?'

'Aye.'

'Well you know how he's, like, obsessed with… Y'know, the wee lassie? Whatever her name was. And obviously…'

I cut him off. 'Gail Shaw.'

'Eh?'

'That was her name,' I said.

The blood was kicking in. New veins were blooming in my neck, my arms, raised like worms.

'Gail Shaw?'

'Aye.'

'Right,' he said. 'I think I kent that.'

He could sense something coming off me, some odour, some pheromone. It was animal, the caution he wore. His head was low as he considered me, watching my stillness.

'You all right?' he asked.

'Me?' I laughed. 'I'm fine.'

He swallowed. 'Are you... Are you going to do something to me?'

We were quiet for a time, him low on the rock, me standing, swaying. He held his hands together.

'No. I don't think so,' I said.

'Right,' he said, and then, 'I'm sorry.'

I found myself smiling from nowhere. 'It's fine.'

He smiled too. 'You look like your brother when you're happy. I never noticed before.'

'Folk say that,' I said.

I wasn't going to do anything to him, I knew that. My blood was going down and I was growing calmer.

I was getting better.

But though.

But there was the frothing, churning water below us. There were the rocks, jutting over the edge like green fingers.

I wasn't going to do anything to him. I was going to put my hand out and help him up because, aye, maybe he'd let us down, and maybe he was a snake, but I sensed it would be good for me not to act.

217

I put my hand out. He looked at it and then took it. I swung him up and there was a moment, mid-swing, where something moved in me, like a snake uncoiling in my belly, like a scorpion's claws rattling in my throat. He was upright and we were touching and I could do whatever I wanted to.

The evening meal was in full swing when we got back. There was a great cast iron cauldron over the fire, held up by poles, and the clearing was heavy with the old smell of soup boiling. Mikey was sat on his own by the fire, hunched over with elbows on knees. He'd cleaned himself up and his mouth was free of blood.

We went down either side of him.

'What the fuck,' he whispered to me, 'is going on?'

'Tell me about it.'

'They think I'm God or Jesus fucken Christ, man. No offence, Isaac.'

'None taken.'

'And that Terry knows everything about everything.'

'Aye,' I nodded.

I sat beside him for a while and we watched the people preparing food. My instincts were telling me to move, to pack up and go, to drive the van until we reached a place where no lives moved in the vicinity but our own. But there was also the possibility that out there in the winding roads were unmarked vehicles, coasting corners, keeping many eyes peeled for young men matching our descriptions. At least here in camp we had the element of disguise on our side.

'I say we ride it out,' I told Mikey. 'See what happens.'

'You reckon?' asked Mikey, locking eyes with the fire's movements, his pupils flickering from its light – orange on his chin, his jaw.

'Aye, I reckon.'

'Maybe,' said Mikey, and we ate together and were quiet.

I couldn't shake the comment he had made earlier. What had he meant by me getting him into trouble? I mean, aye, all right, maybe I'd had to make a few tough decisions so far. Maybe I hadn't always chosen wisely either, I could hold my hands up to that. I wasn't perfect. Who was? Maybe we should have just run off when all the stuff happened with the archaeologists. Maybe he'd have been happier if we just sat in a cold tent getting probably the police called on us by that nosy bastard whose house we took. Maybe we shouldn't have picked up the Americans and maybe whatever happened with me and the lad, whatever his name was, maybe that shouldn't have happened. Mikey's problem was that he didn't realise how hard all this was on me.

I squinted at him through the fire's heat as he spooned up the lumpy paste. Aye, I'd be watching him all right because of course I cared about him and of course I wanted him safe, but he had another thing coming if he thought he was going to beat me.

'You all right?' he asked.

'Aye,' I said. 'Fine. You?'

'Fine.'

Did he ever think of all the sacrifices I had made? Did he think of the stares I felt creeping hot on my spine as I walked in public after he went?

Did he ever think of that?

Did he fuck.

Everyone assumed that I was fine. My mother was more concerned about Mikey's appeals and then her man, Mikey's dad, running off, to ever give me a second thought. He left with no warning in the months after

Mikey went and then it was just me and Mum, alone at home, ignoring each other, sending sharp wee comments under doors and around corners.

I thought I'd try and find a phone to call our mother, let her know how well I was doing without her help, without her pushing her beak in where it wasn't needed. Perhaps I would take a stroll down to the village, see what she thought about that.

When they spoke to me in court, the lawyers, they wanted to know exactly what happened that day in the woods. That was easy for me, I could tell them precisely. I went though it scene by scene for them, as if it was playing on a screen before me. I told them about how he'd come home livid from school after his telling off from Mr MacPherson, about how I, acting as the responsible older brother, had suggested we tick school to blow off some steam.

Did I think that was a responsible thing to suggest? they asked me.

No, looking back, I didn't. But I also didn't realise what it would mean, in the long run.

I told them how we'd escaped the school and been chased off of the grounds by the jannie, chased from the swing park by the mums, hurled brick pieces at the tree.

They asked if all this was relevant.

Maybe not, I told them, but they had asked me to tell it as I remembered.

My story seemed too exact, they said.

Well, they could hardly blame me for having a good memory, could they?

They pricked up their ears when I mentioned the wee lassie. That got their attention right enough. I told them how she'd shown up and how Mikey had made her follow

220

us, telling her he had something to show her, deeper in the woods.

Did I remember what she was wearing?

A dark blue school blazer, gym socks, hair in a smooth pony. This wee pin of a bird perched on her lapel.

I could remember that in so much detail?

I could.

And what had happened next Paul? Young Master Buchanan?

What had happened next, those years and years ago when my brother's face was fresh, hairless, round? When we were young together and knew close to nothing? What happened was that we marched through the trees, through the twisted and shaded trees, Mikey ordering, sometimes carrying, the little girl on with us.

Her name was Gail Shaw. She was nine years old. Her mummy and daddy loved her very much. All this I learned later.

I had stopped and touched my fingertips on my brow, waiting, in court.

Is the witness unable to continue?

Drew the fingers away, pushed my head back, breathed sharply through my nostrils. I'll struggle on.

They understood it was difficult for me but enough of the theatricals, if I didn't mind.

Aye, course.

They wanted to know where we went, so I told them, exactly. This place in the woods, it's a place famous as a place you could go shagging or drinking and there's this great big treehouse up in the highest, thickest, oldest tree. Famous. Everyone knows that bit. We take her there and Mikey asks her what she thinks, of the treehouse like. The wee lassie says that aye, it's nice enough but that she'll have to be getting back to her mum, back to the swing park.

Do something, Mikey had said.

Do something? she asked.

Aye, do something.

Like what?

Like anything.

And then she looked at me, and when I described how she looked at me I laid it on thick for the courtroom. That look, my God. So sweet a child, so gentle a look.

All right, Mr Buchanan. Just the facts, if you don't mind.

Mikey had said it again. Do something.

Her voice small, damp, soiled. What d'you mean?

If she didn't know then Mikey wasn't going to tell her.

All right, he'd spat, pacing around her in a slow circle.

She had looked up, through the cracks in the treetops, to the dreaming freeness of outer sky. She was so far away from all of that.

And, and, and.

I didn't intervene. That's the guilt I'll have to carry around for the rest of my living days, I told the courtroom. Maybe my brother is guilty of whatever you accuse him of, but I too am guilty, of the crime of allowing a precious candle to be snuffed out.

I saw one woman in the back row's eye bulge from the shining bloat of a tear.

Perfect.

All right Master Buchanan. Again, just the basics if you please.

Sorry sir. It's just a difficult thing to discuss.

The court understands. What happened next?

He spoke to her. He said she would never amount to anything, that she was stupid and useless and weak. He was shouting at her, close to her face and all her face was closed up from the terror of it.

The tearful woman put her hand against her nostrils, closed her eyes, sniffed. I didn't know who she was.

And what happened next?

What happened next?

I stood and watched and I didn't know what to do or say to turn it around and save the little girl, the wee lassie, and then it all gets difficult to remember and I'm by the fire in the camp, eating soup, remembering being stood in the court, my back sweating in my cheap supermarket suit, remembering all the days and nights in between, in bed, alone, remembering remembering remembering.

In the dream I had pulled back the ferns and found the fleshy mass in undergrowth with its ridges of jutting muscle and odd scratchy tufts of hair, wrestling with itself, grinding into itself in the dew. Hands gripping and squeezing and rinsing life from human sponge.

And that was what had happened next.

Except that's not how I told it, in court. I wasn't as daft as that, was I? If I was guilty of anything it was the white lie of when I left the scene. You see, your honour, I didn't realise how far it would go, could not anticipate the depth of my brother's sickness, and so I fled. Before the deed itself, that is.

And does Master Buchanan not feel that this version of events is a little convenient for he himself?

Aye, perhaps, but something being convenient doesn't stop it being true.

Come clean, Master Buchanan. Come clean. You were present at the scene and you know it. Your version of events has been curated to extricate yourself as far as possible from what happened. Frankly, the court isn't buying any of it.

I fled. I was absent. I was no more present than you

were, than any of us were.

No further questions, no further anything, because once again I had won. I was on top. I remembered sitting in the hard court chair and looking across the room and feeling my blood kick in so hard that I had to fight myself not to laugh or scream.

I breathed in and the smell was vegetables – stinking lentils and earth. Tang of wood smoke in wet rubber tree scent.

Mikey was eyeing me across the shimmering hot air the fire released.

'I was miles away there,' I said.

I waited until midnight and then set out. I walked into town by myself, in the dark, with the moon and her reflected blades floating out on the loch to guide my path. There was a wee country pub there, much like any other – warm, musty and small. They had a pay phone in the back that I fed silver coins to. I knew our number off by heart.

She picked up on the third purr.

'Deirdre Buchanan,' she said.

'It's Paul.'

'Oh,' she said, the word escaping from her like gas.

'How's it going, Mum?'

'Oh, you know,' she said. 'I'm getting by.'

'That's positive.'

'Is Michael there? Any chance I could have a word?'

'He's not with me. He's somewhere else.'

'Ah,' like something small and sharp being twisted into her.

'I'm here though. Aren't you interested in talking to me? Hear about all the things I've done?'

'Absolutely.'

'Aye?'

'Uh. How's your health?'

I sighed. 'All right then.' I took the phone away from my ear.

'No,' said the little metal voice escaping the receiver. 'Don't go.'

I held it to my face and it was still warm. I imagined her panicked breath spilling out the holes, tickling the miniscule hairs of my ear.

'Well,' I said. 'What's the situation back there? Are the press still sniffing around?'

'The press?' she asked.

'Aye.'

'Well, no. I don't know what…'

'Good,' I interrupted. 'That's great news. How about the police, the social services?'

'They've been going crazy ever since you took him. He's on parole, Paul. He needs to see them once a week at the very least. They'll take him away again when he comes back home,' this last part spluttered with fear or maybe anger.

'We'll see about that,' I said. 'Here, have they mentioned the psychiatrist or whatever it was?'

'No,' she said. 'I don't think so.'

'Mikey's insistent,' I explained. 'He doesn't want to see a psychologist or a psychiatrist or anyone like that. He just wants to forget everything that happened and move on.'

'Fine. If that's what he wants.'

'He doesn't ever want to talk about that day ever again. It's too much for him.'

'That sounds reasonable,' she said. 'You need to bring him home and then we can explain it to them.'

I snorted. 'Hm.'

225

'Is that a good noise or a bad noise, Paul?'

'It's a wait and see noise,' I said, replacing the receiver.

I used the pub's bogs and then set out across the carpet for the door. I was nearly away when a shape caught my eye.

It was a dark loudness, it was sharp briars.

It was a woman's hair – curly, familiar. She was at the far end of the bar looking grim, a group of people around her. She was sipping from the head of a Guinness.

My brain laughed.

No way, it said. Can't be!

'It is,' I said to myself.

Sam, from the dig, in a pub within walking distance of us. Just sitting there.

My brain laughed again.

She was deep in conversation with some hill-walker type – the anorak, the boots, all the usual gear. He was nodding along to her words. I couldn't take it, so I went outside. Across the water the moon was wobbling over black hills. I didn't know what that land was. Some kind of munro or beinn or mull. These places, these fucken names.

15

Next day I found Mikey sitting on a pile of bean bags in the middle of camp, watching performances by the congregation. Some of them played instruments, others sang. A small acting troupe had formed overnight. They performed a series of short vignettes, including Elisha and the bears, and the drunkenness of Noah. Baldy made a decent job of playing Noah, stumbling and falling, revealing skin-coloured tights beneath his robes.

After the play, a woman came forward on her knees, hands gripped together. Her hair was grey, wet with grease. She pleaded with Mikey to take her into a yurt and lie with her so that she may carry his light onwards. Mikey looked at me and I put my hand over my mouth.

One of her brothers led her away. They kept their eyes to the floor, they talked in hushed whispers. I caught them watching Mikey when his back was turned, as if he was the first thing they'd ever laid their eyes on, the world's first object, moving before them.

I could see Isaac and Brother Terry were having a conversation, over by the yurts. They were deep into it, heads close together, using their hands and fingers to make their points. I decided that I'd had enough of their secrecy, so I strolled over to Isaac once he was alone and walked him over to a quieter area of the camp. I asked him what was going on and he explained a plan was afoot to cause some damage to the base's perimeter. His skin looked waxy and he was dark beneath the eyes.

'Is everything all right?' I asked.

He nodded. 'Fine.'

'I don't need to be worried about you?'

'No,' he told me, his eyes closing for a moment.

It was to happen that very night. They would sneak along to the darkened base and they would cut away a section of the fencing that encircled it. This would cause the alarm to be triggered inside the base, wasting a whole day's work and other associated hassle for the employees.

I let him go about his business and that evening I watched them leave. There was something wrong with Isaac, I could tell. His head was hanging as he left the camp with the others and the last I saw of him was his rounded shoulders slinking into the woods, a pair of bolt cutters hanging by his side. The fire smouldered and the faintest tinkles came from the breeze moving bells hidden high up in the trees. I went into our tent and undressed. Mikey's snores were gentle – very far off trucks – and the smell was nothing like our old tent, it was clean canvas and air-dried laundry.

'I'm sorry,' I said to the dark.

Mikey mumbled in his sleep.

I had done the right thing in taking him, there was no question about that. If we'd stayed then the press would've got even worse, the social workers would have driven him crazy. There was no need for him to see that psychologist, just to go over old ground. Let sleeping dogs lie.

I mean, aye, maybe I had exaggerated the press's interest.

Perhaps.

They had been there though, a wee gang of three or

four of them that I saw from the bathroom window. And they took that photo of Mikey and put it in the paper, didn't they?

I growled to myself, frustrated by the hardness of thinking about it.

Next day the rain came. We'd been lucky to go so long without it. They spread a massive tarp across the camp, tying it to the trees all around, but the water still got in. It leaked through tears in the fabric and ran in silly brown trickles from higher land. Everyone stuck to their tents, the odd person wandering through the clearing to check the fire or have a word with someone else. I suppose they were waiting for a sign that the efforts down at the base had paid off.

We killed the afternoon in the yurt, waiting for the rain to finish. It was quite peaceful. You could hear the irregular drumbeat of raindrops falling on the trees' canopy, other louder plops from the camp's tarpaulin.

I was lying back on my bed when I decided to tell Mikey my idea. 'I was thinking,' I said. 'We should think about heading back.'

He sat up. 'Oh aye?'

'Aye. Once we're finished here, head back down the road. I think we've given it long enough.'

'Hm,' he said, trying to contain his excitement.

'What d'you reckon?'

'I think that sounds all right.'

'Grand.'

After that we were in fine spirits for the evening meal. One of the hippies had made this huge volume of bean chilli and the clearing was heady with spice and tomato. Everyone sat together under the tarpaulin, blowing on chilli and chattering away.

I looked across the fire at everyone as they ate. I had some of my food. I looked across the camp and began to feel anxious.

I thought, where the fuck was Isaac?

I put my bowl down in the dirt and pushed myself up by the knees and paced around the camp. There was no sign of him in any of the tents or tepees or wagons or yurts that I peered into. He wasn't down at the latrines or the field or even out by the building site for the Church's first official building. As I wandered back to the camp proper I speculated that perhaps he'd done a runner, sick of the oddness of the camp or the Church.

Brother Terry was lying on his back, ankle of his right leg resting on the knee of his left, the robe falling back to reveal an udderish swinging calf. Some of his hair had fallen onto his forehead and his eyes were giddy. I stepped inside and the rain noises closed us off.

'You again,' he said, with no contempt.

'Me again.'

'You know,' he said, working a pin into his teeth, dislodging some trapped morsel, 'if it wasn't for your brother, I'd have done something about you already.'

He laughed, making sure I knew I was not allowed to take this seriously.

'I bet you would've,' I said.

'Be a safe bet.'

'I just wanted to let you know. Isaac never came back from the fence thing last night.'

He threw his little pin onto the floor of the yurt. 'You seem like a very angry person, Mr Buchanan,' he said.

'What does that have to do with Isaac?'

'Something, maybe nothing. Just an observation. Why is that?'

'I just seem to find myself in frustrating circumstances.'

230

'You know, maybe you remember, you yourself were featured heavily at the time. The murder, I mean.'

'Is that right?'

'Yes it is. Well, maybe heavily is the wrong word to use. But you were certainly a person of interest to those of us following the case closely.'

'Huh,' I said.

'Very interesting. But as we all know, your brother was the guilty party, wasn't he?'

'It was a long time ago. He was young.'

'No one's blaming either of you, not here. This is a safe place, Mr Buchanan.' He was rubbing the odd, smooth skin of his calf as he spoke. From the angle I was at, his face was all melting chins and nostrils. 'I've shown my hand. I consider the actions that were taken, when you were young, to be immensely useful.'

'Some folk would call that sick.'

'A genius is a person who refuses to see things in the prescribed fashion. The world changes for the unreasonable man, and all that.'

'Hm,' I said.

'Why are you here?'

'I came to tell you about Isaac.'

Terry ran a small hand over his potbelly. 'Ah. Isaac. He's gone I'm afraid. Concern yourself no longer with Brother Isaac.'

'Gone? Gone where?'

'He has moved on, in service of the Lord.'

I crouched down beside Brother Terry. He smiled. 'You'll have to be more specific,' I said.

'Oh, you lot. You lot and your dreary obsession with the black and whiteness, with the ins and outs, with the technicalities. Isaac has gone on a mission.'

'All right,' I said, letting the silence hang. Brother Terry

231

sniffed, so I sniffed too. It was the fruity dampness of wet nature.

I spoke to him, in my head. I said to him, I could do anything I want to you, now, and there is nothing you can do. I told him he didn't realise, didn't understand, the power that I had swelling and vibrating in every joint of my body.

Eventually he broke. He spluttered out a giggle. 'Aw, I'm no good with secrets,' he sighed. 'But what does it matter, I suppose? I may as well say. I've sent him off into the base.'

Brother Terry waited for my reaction but it didn't come. I just crouched and noticed my power.

'He's going to blow the fucker up.'

'Wow,' I said.

'I know,' he smiled.

I could do it now. Lunge for him and take him out of this world with just my fingertips.

Instead I said, 'Right,' and I crouched there under the dim canvas, the only light coming from the lamp that hung over Terry. 'What if I wanted to stop you?' I asked.

'Well, you know you can't?'

'What if I called them up? Those plainclothes police that jumped us before.'

Brother Terry winked at me. 'Oh, those men are not police. Not by a long shot.'

'So,' I said.

'Yes.'

'I'll just go,' I said.

'Probably for the best.'

I paused by the door. I could hear everyone outside moving around, the fleshiness of their bodies flapping and smacking and wobbling.

'What's it for?' I asked, looking out into camp.

232

'Jesus,' he said. 'What a lack of imagination. It's the revelation of your brother. I realised I needed something big to force the Lord's hand, something monumental to really clear out the cobwebs.'

He said the whole thing matter-of-factly. There was no fervour in his voice, no zeal in his eyes. It was as if he was describing his plan to repaint the front room in time for Christmas. Then he produced a flannel from somewhere and laid it out over his eyes.

I stood outside of his yurt. I could see everyone's skin, soft and fragile, and their eyes and hair. Nothing to protect them. I thought about Isaac and how scared he'd been the day before, dark-eyed and distracted. I imagined him lurking in the base, huddled in silos and lying panting behind walls. Surely they would fill him full of bullets before he could cause any mischief. Surely they would. Surely he would die leaping a fence or barricade, metal flying around him, his hair nimbusing torchlight.

I had been born too late to ever be really frightened of the bomb. Our mother told stories about being at school and getting a lesson specifically about how to drop their skinny wee arses under their old fashioned school desks if they heard the bomb alarm going off, as if a few layers of mucky wood was enough to protect them against a cloud of pure energy ripping through the school house. That was never a worry for me, certainly not for Mikey. We'd grown up as scared of nuclear blasts as we were of pirates or Jack the Ripper. I tried to think back to anything I knew about atomic explosions. I remembered a documentary I'd seen about Japan in the war, about the shadows of Nagasaki's population blasted onto walls.

I went back to Mikey and tapped him on the shoulder. 'Come with me,' I said.

'What's up?' he asked as we stood together in the dripping woods away from camp.

'I was just having a word with Terry.'

'Oh aye?'

'Aye. He was saying he's asked Isaac to blow up the base.'

'Right,' Mikey said. 'Wow. That's not good.'

I shook my head. 'Nope.'

'What'll we do then? Would we die if he did?'

I gave the question a few laps around my mind. 'I think the whole country would. Maybe the whole world.'

'Fuck.'

'I know.'

'What if we did the old... you-know-what, on that Terry chap.'

He mimed strangling.

'Wouldn't stop Isaac from doing whatever he's going to do,' I said.

'That's true,' said Mikey, squatting down and stretching his arms. 'One of those classic catch 22s.'

'I mean, I wouldn't call it a catch 22 exactly.'

Mikey nodded, sagely. 'Good call,' he said. 'So...'

'So,' I sighed, letting my lungs empty of breath until they pinched. 'We play it by ear, I suppose.'

'I suppose so.'

'Give it another day or two.'

'It might all blow over by itself.'

As night bloomed and ink seeped into the sky, the rain continued to fall. It was a constant thrumming battering on the tarp, in the trees, in the dirt. Some of the hippies laid out sandbags at the east end of the camp to stop runoff spilling from the hills. There was a growing tension coming from the Church, particularly in relation to my brother, a mounting intensity to the way they considered him. A young man had thrown himself across Mikey's path as we'd returned from our discussion, begging Mikey to trample him. Another started crying over their tea that evening. When someone else asked what the matter was, the upset party sobbed and told us he couldn't cope with how absolutely beautiful Mikey was.

Brother Terry commandeered the central area of the clearing after the plates were tidied away. He kicked a few camp chairs away and stood with his arms out at ninety degrees.

'Brothers,' he said, cocking his head. 'Sisters.'

A polite ripple of applause spun around the clearing from the religious constituency.

'How glad it makes me to be here before you as the Lord blesses us with his gift of rain. Let the flowers and bumblebees be happy, and drink.'

Baldy punched the air in delight.

'What a significant day this has been. Perhaps the most important of the Church's history, not including my return from the world outside.' He shuddered theatrically, then extended his hand towards Mikey. 'Can we all just take a moment to consider that every single thing I told you turned out to be true? That our Lord would return to us, dumb and unaware of his significance. That for his true nature to be revealed a great sacrifice would have to be made?'

'It's true,' said a voice from behind me, 'he did say that.'

'Thank you Brother Slank. Most kind. The sacrifice I spoke of –' He bent over slightly at the hips, his hands at his sides now. '– is in the post. It is imminent. The hour of our reckoning is upon us.'

A murmuring swooped around the camp like a low

flying bird, a soft gust of sound passed through heads like wings.

'Some things are going to happen soon that might seem quite confusing or a little bit unfair. To those of you startled by those soon to be happening occurrences, I say only this – change is often uncomfortable, but it is always necessary.'

And then he clapped.

And then the lights came on.

All around the circumference of the clearing torches shone inwards, together. Confusion and hysteria broke out instantly, Brother Terry moving through the darkness and the light beams, hands behind his back like a friar. I held Mikey by the arm and we did our best to stay out of the way.

'Keep your head down,' I said, without looking at him. I was concentrating on the figures moving inwards like a tightening knot, casting their torches around, slicing the night.

'Remain at ease brothers and sisters,' roared Brother Terry. 'These men are not here for you.'

It was those strange plainclothes police. A band of them moved into the clearing from all sides, the rain on their suits and raincoats glittering in torch and firelight. They began to round up the protestors, grabbing them by their arms, knees in the smalls of backs. The noise was ghastly. All I could smell was wet clothes. The Church's members watched on as the police moved among them, passing them over to visit violence on their neighbours.

Over the top of the yells and roars, Brother Terry's voice, rising. 'Stay calm. This is not really happening. Any negative emotions you are feeling are simply discomfort at rapid and unusual change.'

I spied a gap, over by the back of the yurts. Perhaps we

236

could sneak through, make our way to the van, and fuck off out of it forever. I pulled Mikey and we fell into the dark trees, heads full of the richness of sodden leaves and decaying earth.

'Stay down,' I whispered. 'We'll go around.'

'No,' said one of the men, hidden in the darkness, 'you won't.'

He brought us back by our scruffs and heaved us onto the ground before the fire.

'What'll we do with this pair?' asked the man of Brother Terry.

The two of them loomed over us, Godlike in the fire's nightmare glow, sparkling and cracking behind us along with the moans of beaten humans.

'Contain them,' said brother Terry.

Our hands were tied behind our backs by the man and we faced the ramshackle row of tents that had once housed the camp's protestors. One of the police emerged from the largest tent, carrying Terry and Beth's father in his arms, an ancient infant. He tossed the old man onto the earth like a bag of sugar.

A woman in crowd screamed. The old man lay on the ground, very still, as all around him the people he had gathered in that place were rounded up and marched away.

16

There followed a long night.

Mikey and I, in the dirt, on our fronts. The faces of the Church ringing us like flames on a burner. Our ribs and collarbones aching and singing.

'He is like us yet, brothers and sisters,' spoke Brother Terry of Mikey. 'He knows how to suffer as us.' He was enjoying himself, striding and smiling and tasting the air with his cracked tongue.

'Pain is an illusion,' he boomed, later on. 'The mind creates sensations as ways of coping. If you are scared or are in pain or are angry you are running from God's word.'

We had not spoken for the entire night but we'd been thrown down with our heads close. I could see the skin around Mikey's mouth stained dark where the spittle mixed with dirt, brushing his cheeks when he moved his head. As the parishioners mooned around us, nervous and quiet, we listened to the whining trees and rasping wood sounds, straining for any other far off noise.

We were anticipating bombs.

Mikey fish-flopped over to me in a quiet moment. He opened his mouth and I shushed him before he could speak, wriggling sideways on my belly to get closer.

I mouthed, *What*?

'They're going to kill us,' he hissed.

I shook my head. No. 'It'll be the bomb gets us.'

'Well, anyway!' he whispered, voice tight with fury.

'What's your rope like?'

He stretched himself upwards at the head and feet like a seal. 'Tight,' he wheezed.

'Mine too,' I said.

I'd been working against my ties the whole night. They had not budged.

And then I saw this wave of hopelessness crash over my brother's face. He closed his eyes and his mouth and his nostrils flared from heavy exhalation and he looked so young. He looked like the boy he was, tied up on the ground, scared, friendless, in a different part of the world. For the first time in our journey I felt a worm working its way into my breast and it was guilt. It was churning and writhing itself into my flesh, coming from the outside, and I was looking at Mikey and seeing everything the world had taken from him. His adolescence, his pride, his future, his past. And I had been complicit, because I had tried to protect him. That had been my intention and look how it turned out.

Everything you touch, I thought to myself, turns to shit.

I suppose I must have slept because one moment it was dark and the next it was light. My spit had trailed down my top lip and were pooling in my nostrils. I woke up snorting and gasping for breath, my first thought that I was being choked or smothered in my sleep.

'Christ,' I gagged, spitting and blowing my nose into the dirt before my face. I swivelled round as best I could to get away from the mess. My hair was so long it trailed in the wetness and clung to my jaw.

All I could see of Mikey was the crown of his head, the

little wonky spiral of stubble with a heart of white scalp. I rolled over and bumped him. He didn't rouse.

'Mikey,' I hissed.

No response. I rammed my shoulder down on his stuck out elbow and he sprang up with so much force that he slipped onto his back.

'What's going on?' he shouted, his voice ringing out among the birdsong and insect hums of early morning.

'You were asleep,' I said.

'No way.'

'Aye.'

'Has anything happened yet? Any explosions or that?'

'Nothing yet.'

'I hate this, this waiting.'

He was right. The woods ached with potential. All air was welcoming a blast.

'We need to do something,' I said. 'I'm not going to sit here and wait to get fried.'

'What then?'

I rolled myself onto my back and then over to my front, grunting. The ties were still strong, especially around the ankles. 'Fuck knows.'

We lay together for a while, struggling to face the sky, the branches and leaves like spilled ink against the pure white morning. A jet flew over, unzipping the clouds, while I thought.

It wasn't until late in the day that I started to lose it. I'd been on the ground, my limbs tied, for maybe half a day and I started to lose my mind. I couldn't stop picturing Isaac, over in the base. What was taking him so long? Was that part of the plan, that he would lie low to let suspicions disappear and then...

I kept gasping, thinking I'd heard an oncoming

explosion but it only being wind rifling leaves or my own breath, moving in my chest.

It'll all be over before you know it, I told myself. You won't even be around to hear the sound. Everything you've ever known will be gone, like *that*, take some comfort from the suddenness of it.

'Mikey,' I said.

'What?'

I couldn't think of what I meant to say, so I said nothing, and then some time passed, which might have been another half day or a solitary heartbeat.

The camp was melting away, only the steaming fire remaining. I was nowhere. I was within fear. One of the robed figures, smaller than the rest, was coming towards me. I strained my neck to face forward, spine aching. She was getting close, but why was she so blurry? Was it the fire's smoke or were my eyes giving out from stress?

'What's going on?' I asked and no one answered me.

She squatted in front of me and then I could see her face. She cocked her head at me, her eyes round, wide.

'Tell me what's happening,' I said.

'You're losing it, Paul,' she said.

'I can't be.'

'You are,' she said, pushing her hair behind her ears as she inspected me. The look she had, it wasn't pity, it was something else.

'What's going to happen to me?'

'The fire's going to rip through you. The atoms are going to pierce a million holes in your skin and everything about you's going to drip out. You're going to float away.'

'No,' I pleaded.

'It's true.'

I nodded and let my face drop, into the dirt made damp

241

by my mouth's leakings. 'Where have you been all this time?'

'By myself,' said the wee lassie.

'I'm so sorry.'

'Why did you let it happen to me, Paul? Why didn't you stop it?'

'I… I couldn't,' I choked. I was crying. I hadn't cried since I was a baby.

'I think you could have. I think you didn't want to.'

'No,' I said, shaking my head, burrowing my lips into the rank earth. I couldn't face her.

'I think you liked watching.'

I said nothing. Dirt clung to my teeth like rich cake.

'I think you got off on it. Are you crying, Paul?'

'Yes.'

'Do you remember how I cried? Do you remember how I bawled and pleaded for my mummy?'

'Yes.'

'Do you want to go home? Do you want to go home, where it's warm?' She didn't wait for me to answer. There was no malice or anger in her voice. 'Do you know how long I was out in the cold for before a dog sniffed me up?'

'A long time,' I said, finally bringing my face up again.

'A long time,' she said. 'Come with me.'

There was her face, just like in the papers. Straight, thin hair, a placid look. A school photograph, I think.

'I don't want to,' I sobbed. My lungs burned, from the pressure and from the fear. I could feel my cheeks and eyes fill with hot blood. 'Just tell me what's going to happen. Please?'

'I already did.'

'But, no,' I said, jerking myself towards her on my belly. 'Be honest, tell me the truth. It can't be the truth. I'm not going to die.'

242

'You are. You're going to die and then it'll just be me and you, together, forever.'

My mouth was open and my eyes were closed.

'Do you remember what you said to me?'

I shook my head, eyes full of the blackness of lids.

'You asked me what I was crying for. You told me it would all be over soon enough.'

'That was Mikey, not me.'

'It was both of you.'

I shook my head. No.

'Well guess what?' she said and I opened my eyes. She was inches from my face, peering into me like a curious bird. 'It'll all be over soon enough.'

I gasped and blinked and she was gone and I was on my back and my hands were crippled from the weight of me. My brother was over me. He was beautiful and real. I saw for the first time that he had heavy eyelashes like a girl's.

'Paul? You all right man?'

'I was dreaming,' I said.

'You were shouting.'

'It was horrible. Mikey, it was *her*. She was here.'

'Who was?'

'The wee lassie. It was the wee lassie Mikey. She told me we were all going to burn.'

His face fell. 'There's all dirt on you.'

'She was here Mikey. I seen her.'

'I don't want to talk about that,' he said, shuffling away and lying down.

A sound appeared in my throat that was both amusement and horror. My blood had been roaring away for hours and I was exhausted.

'She was here,' I repeated. 'She's all right.'

My brother ignored me.

243

In the time I'd been out a few more police had arrived. They stood around by the opening of the path, conversing with Brother Terry who was now fully robed. He was wearing an elaborate feathered headdress also.

'Hey,' I shouted, twisting my back. 'What're yous lot saying?'

They cast annoyed glances in my direction but did not address me.

'Hoi! Hoi! Look at me. What's going on? When's the boom?'

One of the coppers gave me the fingers and I laughed, loud and mad. I no longer feared what they would do to me.

'Fuck off,' I shouted. 'Fucken pigs. They're going to kill us. Listen, listen! They're going to blow us the fuck up.'

A few of the campers, loitering by the fire and in the doors of tents, started to show an interest. Their faces went from me to Brother Terry.

'It's true,' I screamed.

Brother Terry pinched the bridge of his nose and nodded, before ambling over to address the camp at large.

'There may be,' he said, 'a *small* explosion or two. It's nothing to worry about. It's all part of the grand plan. Don't listen to this lunatic, who I would remind you is only present because of his brother's status.'

I saw the big bald guy scowl.

'That seems sort of maybe dangerous,' he said, stepping forward.

Brother Terry muttered something beneath his breath before smiling and nodding. 'It won't be,' he confirmed. 'Now, can we do something about this one?'

The police then proceeded to attack me. I did my best to curl into a ball so as to protect my body but inside I couldn't even feel them. I was flying above the treetops, the land wide open for miles around. Silver lochs cradled the feet of mountains in their bends, carnivorous birds arced curves of perfect still re-entry, the ice-blue universe pressed against the sky's dome. I flew until I felt radiation burn my belly and I saw the sprawling base below me.

I could pick out Isaac by the colour of his hair. He looked up at me and waved. I waved back and then he pulled a strap on his rucksack. I was buoyed upwards by the force of the blast, a bowl of hot cloud forcing me to the edge of the sky. All my clothes had been burned away and my dick flapped like a dog's tail in the rippling wind.

Once the men were done they left me alone to recover. I asked Mikey when it was going to happen and he told me that he didn't know. He wouldn't look at me when I sobbed.

Then the next night came too and it was obvious even to me that things were starting to unravel. The Church lit the lamps around the camp and had a go at rustling up dinner. They did not do a good job.

People were dishevelled. It was too quiet.

Brother Terry approached us as his followers were hunched over bowls of something foul smelling. Or rather, he approached Mikey. He kneeled in the dirt beside him, the headdress wonky on his slick hair. He sighed.

Mikey gave me a look.

Brother Terry sighed again and blinked and there was moisture in his crow's feet.

'Am I doing the right thing?' he whispered.

Mikey opened his mouth and then closed it again.

'You're not,' I said. 'Definitely.'

'I wasn't asking you, you mad bastard,' he snapped, and then to Mikey, 'Well?'

'It feels a bit much,' said Mikey.

'But didn't you say you were the resurrection, that anyone who believed in you would live after death?' There was a hint of desperation in his voice, a pleading quality.

'Maybe,' said Mikey.

'So what does it matter if it goes wrong, if my plan doesn't work? We'll all be all right, won't we?'

Mikey looked up at the sky. 'It's hard to say exactly.'

Brother Terry nodded, apparently satisfied. As he walked away he checked his watch and muttered, 'What the fuck's taking him so long?'

Then the first explosion came.

A noise, one slow roll of thunder and everyone stood up, apart from Mikey and me.

I lost it again.

My body convulsed against my will. I screwed my eyes so tight shut that my brain was sore and auras of colour vibrated in the dark. I waited for the end to come, but it didn't.

Everyone – the Church, the men, Brother Terry – stood at the far end of camp, watching the far off base through the trees. They were whole, their bodies unvaporised.

'What the fuck?' I whispered, my mouth gummed with lack of water. I could smell my own breath.

Mikey struggled to his knees and then hopped to his feet. I looked up and his head blocked out the moon. He squatted and helped me to my own feet. It was difficult. My head was full of static and my joints trembled from my weight. We worked in silence, the backs of the group to us, before starting to hop across the camp.

My breath skipped and my nose ran and overhead was

the sound of jets roaring, clouds rubbing. We hopped out of the clearing and onto the path. We managed to cut our hands free on sharp branches and then were able to untie our own knees and ankles. I felt weightless, free for the first time. My blood was kicking in harder than ever before. If I'd stumbled upon Brother Terry I could have executed him with even the softest parts of my hands.

On we went, sprinting down the path, over the foot-bridge, towards the van. There were lights in the trees, lamps left by the protestors, but also torch beams knifing into black spaces. There were shouts following us.

I think I was shouting but all sound was so far away. I might have been screaming but the words were like gentle whispers in the recess of my mouth.

'Oh fuck,' I whispered. 'Oh God. Oh Jesus Christ,' I screamed.

And then the van loomed out of the trees, huge and pale, and we were in it and Mikey was trying to drive but in my hysteria I fought him off.

'No,' I whispered. 'It has to be me.'

There were hands slapping on the windows of the van, curled fists thumping on the glass, I couldn't see their faces, just the hands, skin paling against the glass.

'What are you laughing at?' asked Mikey.

I didn't answer him. I wasn't laughing.

I lurched the van forward and turned out onto the road. The loch was wild with moonlight and I had my foot on the floor and the engine was squealing.

'Change the fucken gear,' said Mikey, shaking my arm.

I did as he said and we zoomed away, the dark houses and dark greenery smearing by us while the water and the moon stood solid.

'We're going to do it,' I whispered.

'Stop shouting,' pleaded Mikey.

I stole a look at his face. It was horrible.

'Sorry,' I whispered.

Bright light shone on the side of Mikey's face. I checked the rear view. Headlight, full beam. They were after us. Mikey flipped himself off his seat and stumbled into the back.

'I think it's them coppers,' he shouted through.

'We'll see about that,' I whispered, forcing my big toe as hard against the accelerator as I could.

We were approaching the base, its huge concrete structures were manifesting in the black sky. A column of smoke was rising from the inside – the fruit of Isaac's labour.

Keep going. There was a tankful of petrol. Keep going.

Eighty miles an hour.

'They're flooring it,' shouted Mikey.

I gritted my teeth and kept going. The road was veering beside the base and I was only a few feet away from the wall of nearest building. We'd clear it soon enough and be in open country.

'C'mon you bastard,' I whispered to the van, pressed back against my seat from the onwards, onwards, onwards thrust.

'They're right behind us,' said Mikey, and I knew he was right because the van was bathed in white light, and in that white light I saw figures emerging from the woods on the right like angels. I really thought they were ghosts or angels, I believed it. I saw them hold hands to their faces to shield themselves from the brightness of the cars. One of them wore an elaborate feathered headdress.

We were nearly beyond the base when I felt the wheels go out from under me. The van spun.

An eruption of matter blasting across the road.

I think I was smiling. I think my eyes were half-closed. The world was ringing, roaring.

Well, I thought. Here it is at last. Now we'll see what's next.

The van spun around and came to a stop and we were facing back the way we'd come. The base's fence and the wall we'd passed were littered across the road and the coppers' car was on its back, burning. Smoke was rising from the van's bonnet, hypnotising me. Fingers forced their way around my neck muscles, forced their way into my mind.

Leave me alone, I said, I'm watching the fire.

'Paul.'

Just let me be. Let me go.

'Paul. Fucking move.'

The smell that hit me as the van's door opened. . . electric smoke and broken rock and something else, something irony. The road was smeared with a glistening substance. It was blood, coming from the coppers' car.

'Wow,' I said.

I looked at the coppers' car and I looked at the hole blown in the side of the base and then Mikey came into focus, right in front of me. His mouth was moving but my hearing was gone, blown. He was pleading with me, tugging at my clothes, throwing his head back in the direction of the woods.

'It's blood,' I said, as I checked my own body.

I let Mikey drag me across the road, past the upside-down car and the fire warmed my face. The car's interior looked like a jar of jam – glass and red jelly. I let myself be pulled over the ditch and into the woods and away from the carnage on the road.

We ran through the trees and the smell of smoke was still heavy in my lungs.

It doesn't matter, I tried to tell Mikey, I'm going to die

anyway. The wee lassie said.

He didn't turn back so I kept pace with him, running doubled over, dodging the trees that threw themselves in my path. Where were we going? I didn't know anymore. This whole time I'd known exactly where we were going and I'd been in charge and no one ever beat me, not once, and now I was following my brother into nothingness and I did not care. I would follow him and I would do what he told me and I would be glad.

There were ghosts in the forest. At first I thought the Church had caught up with us but then I ran through one of them.

I said for Mikey to look at them. There was Duncan and there was the American boy and there was the man whose house we'd taken and there was the cat that I'd locked in an abandoned cellar out by the old Sinclair tile factory. They were watching me from behind trees but I wasn't scared of them because I knew they wouldn't do anything until the wee lassie was close.

When we reached higher ground we looked down through the trees and we could see the smoke rising from the base and out on the loch there was a tiny fire. A tiny fire, in the water. You could just make out its flailing limbs and the water reflecting fire around it.

'Is that Isaac?' I asked.

Mikey didn't answer me, so I mustn't have said it out loud.

17

I sat on the hillside and looked down at the reservoir below. Mikey was at the bottom of the hill, bathing in the water. Every part of me held pain, from my brains to my legs. We'd run through the night and slept in the open.

I pushed myself up and crawled. The hillside was steep and I had to lean right back to shuffle down. It took me a long time.

'All right?' Mikey asked, when I was close.

'Aye,' I said.

His tattered robes were hung over a big rock and he stood naked in the reservoir water up to his arse.

'Some night,' he said.

I nodded.

'You OK then?'

'Aye,' I said. 'A few cuts and bruises. You?'

He shook his head. 'Fine.'

It was a warm morning. The sky was open and the hills light. I had never felt so dislocated from the world.

'Where are we?' I asked.

'Not sure. We went for about an hour, maybe three miles or so?'

I nodded and looked at my own tatty clothes. I'd need a wash too. My hair was clinging to my neck with its lankness and I could feel the sweat and dirt in my beard.

'You reckon they're coming after us?' I asked.

Mikey scooped up a handful of water and let it fall onto his face, then he shrugged. 'Dunno. Maybe. Probably not.'

'God,' I said. 'The inside of that motor. Jesus.'

'I know.'

We both thought about that for a moment and then I stripped off and joined him in the water. I shuffled forward, doing my best not to hurt my feet on the stones. I submerged myself and let the cold water cling to my skin, sat with my arse on the rocks. I re-emerged, breaking the surface, and bobbed around with just my head above the water like a crocodile.

'What now?' I asked.

'I suppose we just keep going,' said Mikey. 'Stay off the roads, maybe try and catch a train someplace. We could hide in a train toilet or something.'

'That's a good idea,' I said.

Once we were clean we let ourselves dry in the air and got dressed again. We set off on foot around the reservoir and headed into the hills. I had a recurring fantasy that we were being followed. I would glimpse figures in the corner of my eye but when I turned to look they were gone, only the blank land staring back at me.

We talked little as we walked, breaking the silence only to consult each other on matters of direction. Which path we should take, whether we should go over or around the oncoming hill. Mikey was different, I could feel that. At some point in the previous few days he had changed or maybe he had been changing slowly and only now was I catching up to him. He seemed solid in a way he never had before. He took the lead as we walked, and I followed in his footsteps.

In the afternoon we took a break on the east side of a hill we were descending. We had no food or water of course but we took a break anyway, sitting on our arses, hugging our knees, looking out over the country.

I had a flash of the explosion. My vision went black. I touched my eyes.

'You all right?' he asked.

'Aye, fine. Just remembering.'

'You were off your head last night.'

'I know,' I said.

'There's something wrong with you.'

I couldn't argue. 'Aye,' I said.

He swallowed. 'I think if we make it back in one piece you need to get yourself seen to.'

'Maybe.'

'I mean, fuck,' he said and his voice broke and he put his forehead on his arms. 'We've *done* things Paul. The things we've done, I never thought that would be us. I thought that once I was on the outside it would be normal. Like it would be the life folk have on the telly or in films or that.'

'I'm sorry. I thought I was doing my best.'

'That Duncan bloke. We put him in the fucken *water*.'

'What do you want me to say?'

'I just want you to say fucken something about it. I've been going out my mind about the whole fucken thing and I don't know how you can just sit there as if it never happened to you. How can you do that?'

He tilted his head and looked at me from under his brow, his face soured with disgust.

'I'm not going to argue with you,' I said.

'C'mon,' he said. 'Let's get a move on.'

And so off we went.

My feelings of paranoia did not abate through the afternoon. I had the constant strong impression that enemies

253

were on our tail, hiding just out of my eye line, concealing themselves behind whatever cover the land provided. I felt there were camouflaged soldiers lying on their fronts in the grass and that any moment I would hear an insectish whining and a bullet would ripple out of my chest.

We kept going on and on and in the early evening we crested a hill and found a large body of water below us. I recognised it from our irregular drives of a few days ago – it was Loch Lomond. At least we were on track.

We walked down the hill towards the loch as the day was dying. The place was thick with insects, midges and flies. My soles ached and my stomach had gone past hunger. My insides felt cavernous, full of air and echoes.

'We'll need to see about some food,' I said to Mikey, who was ahead of me on the downward slope.

'How'll we do that?' he asked without turning.

I didn't have an answer so I kept going.

At the bottom of the hill we crouched in the trees to observe the road that clung to the loch's west shore. Nothing was coming so we skipped over it and into the band of trees on the other side. Past them was the shore. The day had become overcast and dark and the islands out in the water were black whales breaking the surface.

'Shall we head down to Balloch again? We can try and get a train in the morning,' said Mikey.

I thought about the little I knew of the geography. It would be about the same amount of walking again to reach the town.

'I can't face it,' I admitted. 'Why don't we hole up here for the night, try the walk in the morning?'

'Hm,' he said, looking around. 'Just sleep on the beach like?'

'Well, no, we could find a spot.'

Mikey looked away from me.

'Please?' I asked.

He sighed and said, 'All right.'

We walked down the shore for a bit. The breeze coming off the water was mild but it went right through me, chilling me to the bowel. I hunched my shoulders as we went, burrowing my hands deep into my pockets. Mikey strode on in only his tattered robes, appearing not to notice the cold.

In time we came to cluster of lodges a few feet from the water. There was a rack for canoes and a couple of motors parked outside.

'Here we go,' I said, hopefully.

'What?'

'Looks like one of them's empty. That'd do for the night.'

'You're joking.'

'We're desperate. No one's going to get hurt.'

'I think we should keep going.'

'Let's just see, eh?' I said.

We crept up from the beach and went low past the windows of the inhabited cabins so as not to be seen. I peered into the window of the dark cabin, seeing furniture covered with sheets through the blinds.

'It's deserted,' I said. 'Everything's put away.'

I looked back. Mikey was shaking his head.

'It's too risky. We can't be drawing attention to ourselves.'

I was already running with the idea though. A warm bed for the night, maybe a bit of food lying about. Oh aye. That'd do. I waddled over to the nearest cabin and grabbed the shovel that was leaning against it. Up close I could hear a television running inside. We'd need to be quiet.

Our cabin had a second door around the back. I

checked no one was watching and jammed the blade of the shovel into the jamb, twisting and leaning. It opened with a small cracking sound.

'There we go,' I said.

We went inside, checking each room for occupants. Nothing. Empty.

'I'm going to see if there's food,' I said, leaving Mikey standing in the living room.

The kitchen cupboards were close to bare but I found a few tins of beans and soup and things and a half-full bottle of whisky. It wasn't much but it would keep us going. I set myself to work straight away, opening tins and firing up a few saucepans on the hob, selecting us a tin each of ravioli, chicken chunks in cream and Heinz tomato soup. Helping myself to a tumbler of whisky, I leaned on the bunker. The first few sips went to my head without warning.

Mikey was stood in the doorway.

'We've done this before,' he said.

'Have a whisky,' I said.

'This is just like the last place, all over again.'

I held my hands up. 'We're not hurting anyone. One night and we'll be gone. What's a few tins of fucken pasta to the rich bastards that own these places?'

Mikey shook his head.

We had our whiskies and bowls of food through in the living room, on our laps. I had never enjoyed a meal more. Mikey downed his whisky but only picked at his food, pushing the lumps of ravioli around the bowl.

After tea we kept up with the drinking. I dug out a second bottle from a cabinet in the corner of the living room. As I inspected the bottle I realised someone was looking in the window.

'Mikey,' I said. 'There's a man.'

He got up from the couch and looked out too. The man waved. He was an older guy, a hillwalkery look about him, all proper and put-together. I'd seen his type before. I felt like maybe I'd seen *him* before.

'Well,' Mikey said, 'here we go.'

He ducked out into the hall and opened our front door. I followed, lingering at his shoulder.

'Evening,' said the man, squinting at us, like he was looking into the sun.

'Evening,' we said.

'Just thought I'd pop over and introduce myself. We're staying in the Duke of Argyll lodge, just over there.' He held his arm out to the furthest cabin.

'Oh,' said Mikey. 'Right.'

'Me and the wife and kids,' squinted the man.

'Well,' said Mikey.

The man shook his head. 'Sorry. Where are my manners? John Bun,' he said, shaking Mikey's hand.

'Hiya John,' said Mikey.

John Bun went on squinting for a few moments before realising the introduction wouldn't be returned.

'It's a fine spot,' he said.

'Aye.'

'We didn't realise this cabin was booked. The agent said it was empty.'

'We only just arrived.'

'Oh. Very good.'

John Bun looked at the sky. We looked at him.

'Well,' he said. 'I'm just off to Luss with the family, let me know if you need anything picked up.'

'Should be fine,' said Mikey.

'Righto,' said John Bun, backing away from the cabin, holding his palm aloft. 'See you later.'

'What a goon,' I said as Mikey swung the door shut. I scoffed. 'John Bun.'

'Mm,' said Mikey.

I poured us each a whisky from the new bottle and we settled down. We drank mostly in silence until we'd made a dent in that second bottle. The night dragged on and midnight took a long time coming. I knew Mikey would be as drunk as me, if not worse. He was lying on the opposite couch, his arms tightly crossed, brooding. The windows were full of night.

'What'll you do?' I asked. 'When we get back.'

He shrugged.

'It'll be fine,' I said.

'What makes you think that?'

'I just know it'll be fine. I've arranged something.'

He shuffled himself higher up on the couch. 'What d'you mean?'

'Well – and now don't get pissed off about this – but I spoke to Mum the other day. I called her up from the village.'

He opened his mouth and looked at the roof. 'You phoned Mum?'

'I spoke to Mum. I made some arrangements for us, for when we get back.'

He put his glass down on the carpet, pushed himself fully upright. 'You spoke to Mum. Our mum?'

'Aye.'

'You said when we left that we couldn't contact anyone while we were gone. You said they'd be tapping us and monitoring us and if we contacted anyone that'd be the end of it.'

'Did I?'

'Aye, you did.'

'Right.'

'I can't fucken believe you,' he said, licking his lips. I could see he was pushing his tongue against his bottom teeth in anger.

'Don't worry mate. I've got it all sorted. I said that I would arrange everything with them social workers, that I'd tell them it was all my idea and it was just a wee holiday and it was nothing to get so excited about.'

Mikey's face was black. He did not respond.

'So it's all sorted,' I confirmed, sipping my whisky.

He nodded and then bent forward to pick up his glass. He weighed it in his palm and then hurled it against the wall of the cabin where it exploded into a firework of shards.

'Christ!' I shouted but he was already on his feet, across the floor towards me. He held me down by the chest and shook me and growled, baring his teeth.

'You do not fucken speak to my mum about me, all right?'

'Aye,' I whimpered. 'Aye of course.'

'You do not speak to anyone about me. You know nothing about me.'

The front of my shirt was balled up in his fists and he was pressing his knuckles into my ribs and weighing down on me and I forgot how much taller he was.

'Nothing gives you the right to talk about me,' he spat.

'I'm sorry,' I said, my hands up, surrendering. 'I was just trying to do my be...'

He stood up quickly, throwing me away from him. 'Don't give me that doing-your-best shite. You don't care about me. You don't give two fucks about me, Paul. All you care about is your own fucken skin.'

I didn't like that. I would take the abuse if it made him feel better but I wouldn't just sit there while he questioned my intentions.

I stood up to meet him. The cabin was silent, just two brothers and their loud breathing.

'All I care about's my own skin?' I asked.

'Aye. Your own skin,' he sneered.

'How fucken dare you? How fucken *dare* you,' I said. 'You don't know the things I've gone through for you. Fair enough you got the jail, but I was out here, alone. I had to deal with Mum's shite, I had to deal with your dad fucking off. I had to deal with the looks on the faces of folk who knew I was related to something like you.'

'Is that so?'

'Aye.'

'Poor wee thing,' he said, moving around me. We were circling each other, kicking furniture out of the way. The broken glass shone in the carpet. 'So some folk looked at you funny? Boo fucken hoo. I got the fucken jail,' he said, holding the chest of his robes in his fist.

'Aye all right,' I said. 'D'you want a fucken medal for it? I didn't have a single friend. I was on my own.'

'That was your doing. It's not anyone else's fault that you're a creep,' he said, his nose wrinkling at that final word.

'Nobody wants to be pals with a beast's brother,' I said.

Mikey stared at me. He looked right into and through me and his eyelashes were thick and dark and he stared at me and then put his palm against his cheek. He laughed.

'You fucken believe it, don't you?' he asked.

'What?'

'All these years I thought you were lying. I don't know if that's better or worse.'

'What're you on about?'

He took a step forward, cocked his head. He rubbed his lips with a finger. 'I didn't kill anybody, Paul.'

260

'Fuck off Mikey,' I snorted. 'You're not in court anymore.'

He laughed again. 'I just can't believe you believe it. I did not kill that lassie.'

I felt myself heating up, I felt my blood kicking in. Heat flowed through me, alcohol and rage pumping up and down my body. I couldn't speak.

'It was you,' he said. 'You killed her.'

A black spot appeared in front of me, obscuring Mikey. 'I didn't,' I heard myself say.

'You did. You fucken strangled her with your own hands. You made her go with us into the woods and you wouldn't let her get away and you put her on the floor and put your hands on her neck. You told me it was just a game and I knew it was wrong but you were my big fucken brother.'

His voice cracked. I couldn't see him from the pulsating black orb in the middle of my vision.

He coughed. 'I didn't know what was happening. You said it was a game and then the police came round the house and you said that was a game too and you told me everything to say cause you were my big fucken brother and I trusted you and all I ever wanted was for you to be my pal.'

There was my voice. 'I don't know what you're talking about,' it said.

'You were my big brother,' said Mikey, behind the spot.

'I still am,' said my voice.

'No,' he said. 'You're not.'

And then I rushed him, shouldering him in the gut and pushing him backwards over the couch to the floor behind. I was on him like a dog and I couldn't see a fucken thing.

261

He was a liar. He was trying to save his own neck and I was going to show him what happened to liars.

Something connected hard with my temple and I toppled off him. Mikey's fist. I fell sideways and he shook me loose and I was crawling up the carpet to him. I took a boot to the nose but I kept going.

'Fuck off,' he screamed.

'You're a liar,' I said.

We had each other by the head, we were rolling around, trying to jab digs into the soft parts of each other's faces. We were tense and jabbing, digging, punching, but too close to one another to get any sort of purchase on our hits.

Mikey got his knee under my chest and flicked me off him and I sprawled across the floor of the cabin. The black spot that hung in my eyes vibrated and grew and I grunted and got myself over him again. My fingers wrapped themselves around his throat.

'You're a fucken liar,' I heard myself say.

I felt the heat coming from his neck, felt the tubes and long muscles squirm beneath my fingers. He was scratching my arms, clawing for my face, but I was too quick for him, too strong. I squeezed with all my might, I pressed down with all my weight.

He was making sounds like a frightened bird, squawking and clucking.

'This is what happens,' I grunted, 'when you try and beat me.'

And then the black spot removed itself with a blink and Mikey was gone and the wee lassie was peering back at me. The heat in her neck was suddenly scalding and I released my fingers as if burned. She didn't move. She looked at me.

'I'm sorry,' I said. 'I thought you were my brother.'

262

'No,' she said, coughing a little. 'I'm not.'

I scrambled over to her and touched her very gently on the neck. I asked her if it hurt, if I had hurt her.

She shook her head.

'Thank God,' I said.

Eyes like plates, hair splayed across the carpet. 'Why would you want to do that to your brother?'

'He was saying… he was saying it was me that killed you.'

She smiled. 'It was though, wasn't it Paul?'

'No,' I said. 'I didn't. It wasn't me.'

'But it was, Paul. Try to remember. Try to remember what you did to me.'

I pushed her away and crabbed myself across the floor from her. She rolled onto her front and crawled towards me.

'Remember? Remember how your teacher made you feel? Remember the little worm of anger that burrowed through your insides, telling you to pass that on?'

She was getting closer to me and I had my back against the wall.

'No,' I said. 'It wasn't like that. It was an accident. I didn't know what to do.'

'It wasn't an accident. You enjoyed it. You were teaching me a lesson.'

I could remember it. I could remember my hands around her neck. My chest was heaving and dry, unable to produce words.

'It's going to be me and you,' she told me. 'Forever.'

I closed my eyes and said, 'I'm sorry,' over and over again. I wanted her to know how sorry I was, for everything. How I would take it all back if I had the chance.

When I opened my eyes she was gone. The room was dark. Mikey was standing over me, rubbing his neck. There was nothing in his face, nothing at all.

'She was here,' I choked.

'Who was?'

'The wee lassie. She spoke to me again.' I crawled over to him and held him by the bottom of his robes, pulling myself up. 'Mikey, it was me. I remember.'

'I know it was.'

'What am I going to do?' I asked.

'I don't know.'

I slumped down, letting go of him. 'Jesus.'

The feeling was something crawling beneath my skin, flies hatching in my hair. I wanted to scratch myself all over. The others, Duncan and that, they were a different story. They were people that tried to get in our way, asking for it, I could deal with them.

But the wee lassie.

I knew she'd be waiting for me the rest of my life. I knew I would see her in crowds, I knew she would slip into my bed at night, shivering beside me. What could I do? Where could I go, when she would always be there?

'I'm losing it, man,' I told Mikey. 'You have to help me. We need to stick together. If I don't have you I don't know what I'll do.'

He poured us a glass of whisky each and mine rattled against my teeth as I tried to drink.

'Maybe we should go to bed,' said Mikey.

'I won't sleep.'

'I don't know then,' he said.

I rolled the glass around in my hand and then put my head against the wall. 'You were in there for ten years.'

'Aye.'

'Was it bad?'

'It was pretty bad.'

'Oh God,' I said. 'Oh Jesus Christ.'

We sat like that for a while, me on the floor by the

wall, Mikey leaning on the back of the couch. We didn't look at each other. We drank our drinks and sat and in my head I was doing somersaults, just to keep from losing my mind.

Maybe, I thought, just maybe, I could make it all right. We would go home in the morning, I would settle everything out with the social workers, with the police, tell them it was my idea to take Mikey away and not tell them exactly the reason why I didn't want him speaking to anyone, especially a psychologist, but tell them it was because I was worried about him.

Aye, they'd have to understand that, wouldn't they?

And then once all that was sorted I would change myself. I would become dedicated to goodness, volunteering, being kind to our mum, helping old ladies with their shopping. All the good stuff – I would do it all. Maybe if the wee lassie could see that, how much goodness I could conjure in myself, maybe then she would leave me alone.

I would be quiet, I would be like a monk, I would cause no trouble and I would turn the other cheek. Forever. Every day. I would show my penance to the world and I would die alone as an act of contrition. I would do anything Mikey asked of me.

Maybe if I did all those things I could make it right again.

Aye, I thought. Maybe.

And then through our window came the brick.

18

All caution gone from us, we crowded against the fangs of glass at the broken window. Standing on the grass outside was a band of people, gripping torches like stubby swords in their fists, men and women alike, jeering at the sight of us.

'There they are,' someone screamed.

The leader of the pack was a smallish, curly haired woman, frothing and yelling, using the butt of her torch to chink the remaining glass into us. John Bun was there too, his bawling head one among many. Now I remembered where I'd seen him – in that pub, with Sam.

We went out through the cabin's back door and into the woods. We flew across the ground like jungle cats, like bulls.

A voice from the lochside shouted, 'Get them,' before the trees blocked it out.

Over and under bough we went, panting, skipping over noose-like roots in the darkness. Screams pursued us, the odd flicker of torch's light on wet leaves above our heads.

'What's going on?' heaved Mikey when we had some distance on them. 'Was that the police?'

'Did you not see the woman?' I asked, my jogging making my voice staccato.

'No. What woman?'

'Sam,' I said.

He glanced over his shoulder, not losing pace. 'From Duncan?'

'I think so. I saw her in this pub near the camp.'

'What pub?'

I didn't want to bring up speaking to our mother again, so I said, 'Just this pub', and as I recalled that evening I remembered the prim-looking gentleman she'd been speaking to. John Bun.

'Let's stop,' he said, and we paused, leaned on trees, let our eyes adjust to the darkness, sent our ears crawling over branches.

'We've lost them, I think.'

Mikey leaned over, palms on quivering knees, and spat a yellow chunk of phlegm. He winced up at me. 'What did they want?'

I squeezed my eyeballs with fingertips. 'I think she's rounded up a mob, for Duncan.'

We were quiet for a long time. We were by ourselves. We shivered, alone.

A few crashing sounds off in the distance, muted to a rustle.

'Fuck,' we hissed, taking off again.

I had to get Mikey to safety, to the road.

I was so tired. I was beat, but I kept on, kept jogging through the trees. Every so often we would come to rest, hoping we had lost them, every so often they would track us down. We were not alone any more though. The ghosts had come back and they were trailing along beside us, watching. I felt no animosity from them, just a cold interest in their watchful eyes.

Up ahead the trees began to thin – the road forming.

'Here it is,' said Mikey, pulling me up.

We had a breather by the roadside, looking back across

267

the treetops to the dark water. No moon shone in the sky, everything held the same shades of navy and grey.

'I think we should split up,' I breathed.

Mikey squinted. 'How come?'

'Confuse them.'

Mikey shook his head. 'That's not a good idea.'

'I think we'll have to,' I said, pointing back into the woods. 'I'll head back the way we came. You try and take the road.'

Mikey looked into the trees, he looked at the road. 'Paul,' he said.

'It's the best way to do it,' I confirmed. 'You'll be fine. We'll meet up in town. OK?'

He shook his head. 'It's not a good idea. We can both go along the road.'

I put my hands in my armpits. 'You'll be fine,' I repeated. 'But, just in case...'

'What?'

'Tell Mum I said sorry?'

He choked then, putting his hand out for me. I stepped back.

'Will you?'

He nodded. 'Aye.'

'Because I am, you know that?'

He nodded again.

'Right. Well. See you in a bit, Mikey.'

'See you, Paul,' he said.

I walked backwards, down the hill, into the trees, allowing them to reabsorb me. He watched me going, his pointed elbows jutting from the hem of the robes. I waved, once, and he waved back.

I had company along the way. Each of them had joined me, in time, as I fought back through the trees. Every single one of them, except for the wee lassie. They moved in line with me along the path, stopping when I stopped, changing course when I changed course. Coming close to me when I felt brave, putting these rushing judders of fear up me when our skins touched. The air around me was thick with dead men.

I found the mob eventually. They had holed up in an overgrown area of pathway, branches intertwining overhead. The beams of their torches flickered through the spaces between trees to my hiding place a few feet from them.

'...keep going...' I heard one voice say.

'...lost them...' said another.

'...kill the fucker...'

Wedging myself between two ancient trees, I did my best to concentrate, to try and overhear what their plans were. I didn't let myself think about what I was doing because if I thought about it I would try to talk myself around. We could not afford that, not after how far we'd come, the things we'd had to do.

There were more mumbling voices but nothing I could pick out. So I had no choice – I let myself go. I was alone in the world and because I was alone I was free. Pushing out of my hiding place I fell onto the path, revealing myself to the mob. I caught a rapid glance of them all before torches swung to my face and I was blinded by light. Hands grabbed me and hurled me against a trunk and then to the floor.

'Which one is it?' someone asked.

'Is that him?' asked another. 'Is it?'

'Let me past, let me past,' screeched a female voice, and a break in the light formed and a face came to me. The hands on my shoulders dug in and pulled me up to face her.

It was Sam. She wore an expression I'd never seen before on any human.

'Do you remember me?' she asked.

I told her yes.

'Did you know I was looking for you?'

I shook my head. What good would it do to explain?

'You killed Duncan, didn't you? You and your brother?'

I looked at her for a moment, at the creases and wrinkles that rage made upon her. All I hoped was that I could take some of that from her. I told her yes.

'We found him,' she said to me. 'He was down river. I had to identify the body.'

'I didn't know that,' I said.

'You sick fuck,' she said and she spat, right in my face, her warm liquid trickling down my nose. 'Get him up.'

The hands pulled me to my feet and the torches shone in my face.

'Take him into town,' she told the men on my side, the faces I couldn't see. 'He's going away for a long time.'

'Wait though,' one of the gruff voices said. 'Which one is he?'

'What does it matter?' asked Sam. 'We'll get the other one soon enough.'

'Are you Michael Buchanan?' someone shouted.

'Yes,' I said.

All around me a groan rumbled through the mob. Lips manifested by my ear and someone screeched, 'Fucken beast!' directly into my brain.

'That poor wee bairn,' I heard a woman mutter.

And with that they were on me, spitting into my face, pulling me back to the ground. The torches were being discarded and the mob was revealing itself. I was surprised by how normal it was. Your plain, average blokes and wifeys, maybe a dozen of them in total. They set about me, laying punch after punch into my waiting face. I felt my teeth move in the bone and the fragments of my nose come away.

Not a single blow hurt me. I could barely see them in fact. I was watching someone else, the short figure beyond.

The wee lassie was waiting for me.

'Stop it,' screeched Sam. 'We need to take him to the police.'

She was ignored, pushed back. They kept up the beating for a good while, concentrating on my face and torso. I was slick with blood. I was slick with their saliva.

I lay on the ground once that part was over. I could hear Sam screaming away, telling them it was going too far, pleading with them to stop.

'Look at his pretty hair,' said a man's voice. 'Just like in the photo.'

I was pushed forward to my knees, the mob milling around me, arranging themselves. A hand on the nape of my neck, forcing it forward. At the other end of the path one of them was holding Sam by the waist as she fought to try and get to me. She'd underestimated my brother's reputation.

Something cold scraped over the back of my skull, something that stung. My neck tickled and big fingers grasped at the ticklish area, then the same fingers forced my mouth open and pushed the ticklish stuff inside. It was my hair. They were shaving me.

They kept going until my mouth was filled with bloodied bundles of hair, lodged tight, deep into my throat. I struggled to breathe, so mashed was my nose. I couldn't tell how much they cut but I knew they were taking the skin with it.

I looked past them all, past the busy mob, past the writhing Sam, to the wee lassie. Waiting for me.

'Here it comes,' she whispered and her voice was as loud as an avalanche in my head.

'Will it be all right?' I asked. 'After?'

'You'll have to wait and see,' she said.

A kick in the back. I hit the dirt.

'What's he fucken saying?' someone shouted. 'He fucken talking, is he?'

'Must be enjoying himself,' spat another.

'See how much he enjoys this.'

They were quiet then as they prepared the next stage of my punishment. I let myself lie on the earth and feel the muck push itself against my ruined face. Sam kept on with her howling. 'No. Not like this. You can't.'

A hand lifted my head, rather tenderly, and slipped something over my face and onto my neck. I slumped forward and the rope around my neck tightened.

Ah, I thought. So this is it.

It tightened further and its pressure lifted me up. I was on my knees and then I was standing, pirouetting around. The path was busy with people, watching. My body did the rest for me, automatic, my toes scrabbling to stay connected with the ground, my fingers struggling against the rope on my neck. My skull was filling with the last of my blood, growing heavy and tight.

And then they gave a great heave on the rope and I had to give up, because I was airborne.

They hoisted me further and further until my crotch was level with their heads.

Just a matter of time.

And there she was.

Waiting for me.

19

The man gets up very early in the morning, because of the commute. He switches off his alarm before it even goes off, to keep his wife from waking with him. She sleeps in complete surrender, her palms facing the ceiling at either side of her head. A kiss stolen from her forehead is the only interaction he permits.

He makes himself a quiet breakfast in the pre-dawn. His children are light sleepers and don't need to wake until he's well on the road, so he has to make do with a piece of fruit at the kitchen table.

He showers downstairs in the smaller bathroom and keeps a cache of toiletries in the cabinet here so that he can complete his morning ablutions. He maintains a working wardrobe in the hallway cupboard and selects an outfit from there once he has dried himself.

The house is silent.

Even the family dog does not know he is awake. It snoozes in its basket, through the glass of the living room door. Once he's ready for work the man lets himself out and the morning chill nips his freshly washed skin. He doesn't mind any of it – the early rises, the need for quiet, the poor breakfast.

His car is nice, newish. It starts first time, every time and he relishes that consistency. The man had a difficult upbringing. He was prone to being drunk or high often, right up until he met his wife. People knew him as the life and soul and for a long time that was enough, to be known as a hard drinker and wild man. His heroes had been the likes of Oliver Reed, Richard Burton. He slept in frequently, struggled to hold down jobs, his doctor mentioned that he should watch out for his liver enzymes but the man shrugged it off.

And now look at him.

Look at him rising early out of a delicious sense of commitment. Owning a car that starts with a gentle purr. He truly enjoys it. There are some men at his workplace who complain about being tied down, about the restrictions of family life. He chuckles at their desperation but inside he cannot relate.

He drives his newish motor through the countryside, towards the city. This is one of his favourite times of the day. The land is so special. Every day he sees the same mountains, the same lochs, the same dark bunches of trees, and every day they look different. When his wife came to him to explain that she'd fallen pregnant he knew exactly what to do. He found a rural estate agent and he negotiated a promotion from his employers.

He chooses to leave the stereo off, feeling it too early to enjoy even music.

His second favourite part of the day is coming in the door in the evening when his children give him their hugs and they have a meal together. He is able to wrangle their day's stories out of them in a way that no one else can. When their mother asks them how school was they say merely, 'Fine.'

He's thinking of the day ahead, already planning his schedule to the minute, when he sees a person by the side of the road. The person, a young man, is dressed in a garment that looks more like a towel than any piece of apparel the man's ever come across. The young man's standing in the ditch, not hitching exactly, but looking lost and desperate in a way that tugs on the man's heartstrings.

Ever since his own difficult upbringing and wild years afterwards the man has a soft spot for wayward young men. He is able to see through the stubbornness and the sarcasm to the soft boy inside. At his workplace he has taken more than one difficult apprentice under his wing.

There's a passing place further down the road that the man pulls into. He rolls down his window and waits. He can see the young man watching the car in his rear view mirror. He's not going to pressurise the young man, just wait and let him come if he wants to.

The young man looks back up the road and then to the man's car. He shakes his head and approaches.

'Needing a lift?' the man asks, when the face moons into his window.

'Maybe,' says the young man, tugging at the neck of his garment. 'Where you going?'

'Glasgow,' says the man. 'But we can go a bit out the way if you need.'

The young man scowls. 'No. Glasgow's fine.'

'So?'

'Aye,' agrees the young man. 'Fine.'

He jogs around the back of the car and settles into the passenger seat.

Off they go.

The man won't speak to his passenger too soon, doesn't want to startle him or put him on the back foot. He sneaks glances at him though. The young man's clearly been in the wars. His hair and beard have been inexpertly trimmed and there's a rank smell coming from him. That's not to mention the bizarre robe he's wearing. Aye, cause that's what it is, a robe.

When enough time's passed and the man can feel his passenger relax he attempts some conversation.

'So,' he says. 'Can I ask?'

'What's that?'

'About the getup.'

'Oh,' says the passenger, looking down at what he's wearing, noticing it for the first time, 'that.'

'It's certainly unusual. What was it, fancy dress or something?'

'Aye,' says the young man. 'Something.'

'I hope you don't mind me saying but you don't look too well. You eating all right?'

'I'm tired,' admits the passenger. 'I've been on the road for a while.'

'Aye. I bet. When I was your age I was always tired. Burning the candle at both ends.'

'Hm.'

The man thinks that this person he's picked up is perhaps one of the most lost-seeming young men he's ever encountered. He wishes there was something else he could do for him, something more concrete and long-lasting than a lift to town. But also he thinks of Leonard Cohen singing about fallen robins and supposes that maybe a lift to town, maybe the phone numbers and addresses for hostels and halfway houses, will suffice.

'If you want to talk about anything,' says the man, 'we could do that. You don't know me and I don't know you.'

The young man shakes his head. 'Nothing to talk about.'

'All right. I understand. Will you tell me your name at least?'

'My name?'

'Aye. What's the harm?'

The road comes towards them and under them. The sky is casting off the gunmetal shades of night and pinkening with morning. The young man chews his lip and faces the road.

'My name,' he says again.

'Not if you don't want to.'

'No. It's fine. My name's Paul.'

'Paul?'

'Aye.'

'That's a fine name. Well Paul, I'm just going to keep driving and I'll drop you off wherever you need me to and I'm not going to say anything else but if anything does come to mind, you just say it, all right?'

He looks at the young man calling himself Paul.

Paul nods. He understands.

ACKNOWLEDGEMENTS

Thank you to the Arts & Humanities Research Council and the University of Edinburgh School of Literatures, Languages & Cultures – for financial support during the writing of this book.

Thank you to Alan, Allyson, Bennett, Dani, Jenni, Maria, Rebecca, Ross, and Sabrina – who all read early chapters and versions of this book.

Thank you to Alex E, Dan P, Luke, Phil, Tom, and all other Marchmont Pilgrims – who were not afraid to keep the madness alive.

Thank you to Alex D, Alison, Holly, Ian, James, and Lesley – for a home away from home.

Thank you to my mother and the rest of my family, as well as Andy and Maureen – for all kinds of support.

Thank you to Janey – for absolutely everything else.

www.sandstonepress.com

f facebook.com/SandstonePress/

y @SandstonePress